Signs of His Love

Brides of Silver Creek Book 1

Lilian Roemy

Old Crow Press

First edition 2025

To my family for their never ending support.

Contents

Prologue

DENVER, COLORADO TERRITORY, 1874

The eviction notice lay crumpled on the floor beside Sarah's worn boots, its harsh black letters stark against the faded boarding house carpet. Seven days to vacate the premises. She had read it three times, each word cutting deeper than the last.

Sarah Elizabeth Williams sat on the narrow bed she'd shared with her dying mother just two weeks ago, staring at the single trunk that now held everything she owned in the world. The room felt impossibly empty without Mama's gentle breathing, without her soft voice reading Scripture by candlelight, without the hope that somehow Papa would return in time to say goodbye.

She couldn't blame Mr. Hensen for the notice. It had been weeks since any rent payment had been made, and he had a business to run, other tenants to consider. He'd been more than patient during Mama's final illness, allowing them grace when Sarah's teaching wages barely covered medicine and food. But patience had its limits, and those limits had been reached.

Papa had been traveling to the mines for work more and more frequently, sending money when he could. But two years ago, the letters and the money had stopped coming. Not when the doctor's bills mounted beyond their meager savings. Not when Mama grew too weak to take in sewing. Not when her last breath whispered his name into the Denver winter night.

Sarah's eyes filled with tears as a vivid memory washed over her.

Mama lay on the bed, her once vibrant face pale and drawn, her breaths coming in shallow gasps. Sarah held her thin hand, fighting back sobs.

"He's not coming, is he?" Mama whispered, her eyes filled with a deep, resigned sadness.

"No, Mama," Sarah managed through her tears. "I'm so sorry."

A faint smile touched Mama's lips. "I forgive him, Sarah. Your papa is a good man, but even good men can be weak. Promise me you'll forgive him too."

"I promise," Sarah choked out, though anger and betrayal burned in her heart.

"God has a plan," Mama breathed. "Trust in Him, even when you can't see the way. He'll guide your path."

The memory faded, leaving Sarah alone with her grief. She faced a truth as cold as the Colorado mountains: she was utterly alone.

"Miss Williams?" Mrs. O'Grady's Irish accent carried through the thin door, accompanied by her hesitant knock. "There's a gentleman here to see you. Says he's from the territorial school board."

Sarah's heart lurched. The teaching position in Silver Creek—she'd almost forgotten they were due to arrive today. In the chaos of her mother's illness and death, the letter offering her work in a remote mining town had seemed like a distant possibility, not a lifeline.

"I'll be right there," Sarah called, her voice steadier than she felt.

She smoothed her black mourning dress, the only decent gown she had left, and reached for her mother's Bible on the bedside table. The leather was worn smooth from countless readings, and the ribbon bookmark still marked Mama's favorite passage in Jeremiah. "For I know the plans I have for you," declares the Lord, "plans to prosper you and not to harm you, to give you hope and a future."

Hope and a future. Sarah clutched the Bible against her chest, feeling the weight of her mother's faith pressing against her doubts. How could God's plans include such overwhelming loss? How could there be hope when everything familiar had been stripped away?

But what choice did she have except to trust?

Downstairs, a middle-aged man in a rumpled suit waited in Mrs. O'Grady's parlor, his pocket watch in hand. "Miss Williams? I'm Samuel Johnson from the

Silver Creek School Board. I apologize for the short notice, but the train leaves in two hours, and the board is most eager to have our new teacher in place."

"Two hours?" Sarah's carefully maintained composure wavered. "I thought I had more time to prepare—"

"The previous teacher departed rather suddenly," Mr. Johnson interrupted, his tone suggesting there was more to that story. "The children have been without proper instruction for weeks. Can you be ready?"

Sarah glanced around the boarding house that had been her refuge since Papa left. Mrs. O'Grady stood in the doorway, her kind eyes bright with unshed tears and something that looked like pride.

"You go on, dear girl," the older woman said. "Your mother always said you were meant for something special. This might be it."

Plans to give you hope and a future.

Sarah straightened her shoulders, feeling her mother's faith kindle something brave within her chest. "Yes, Mr. Johnson. I can be ready."

As she climbed the stairs to collect her trunk, Sarah whispered a prayer that felt both like surrender and defiance. She didn't know what awaited her in Silver Creek—whether she would find the new beginning she desperately needed or simply a different loneliness. But she would face it with the faith her mother had died believing in, carrying her mother's Bible and the flickering hope that God's plans might truly be bigger than her understanding.

Behind her, Denver bustled on, indifferent to one young woman's leap into an uncertain future. Ahead lay Silver Creek and whatever destiny God had written in its mountain shadows.

The train whistle echoed across the city like a call to adventure, and Sarah Williams stepped forward to answer it.

ONE

S arah's legs ached as she stepped off the train onto the wooden platform of Silver Creek Station. The journey from Denver had taken nearly two days, and she'd barely slept, her mind too full of worries about what lay ahead. Mr. Johnson had read a newspaper or dozed for most of the trip, leaving her alone with her thoughts.

The late afternoon sun cast long shadows across the platform as Sarah took in her first glimpse of Silver Creek. The town was smaller than Denver but seemed bustling with activity. The main street stretched before her, lined with wooden buildings—a general store, a saloon, what appeared to be a bank, and various other establishments whose purposes she couldn't immediately determine. In the distance, the silhouette of mountains provided a majestic backdrop, their peaks still capped with snow despite it being late spring.

"Come along, Miss Williams," Mr. Johnson said, his voice brusque as he motioned for her to follow. "We need to see Mr. Montgomery about your accommodations."

"Mr. Montgomery?" Sarah asked, hurrying to keep up with his long strides while managing her heavy trunk. "I thought I was to live in the school?"

Mr. Johnson frowned, not slowing his pace. "There's been a change of plans." He glanced at her with what seemed like annoyance. "The schoolhouse was damaged in the last storm. The roof partially collapsed, and it will take time to repair."

"Oh," Sarah said, her heart sinking. "Where will I stay until then?"

"That's why we're going to see Mr. Montgomery. His family has agreed to host you temporarily. They have the largest house in town and plenty of room." Mr. Johnson adjusted his hat. "It's most generous of them, considering the circumstances."

Sarah tried to hide her dismay. She'd been counting on the quiet independence of the teacher's quarters attached to the schoolhouse. The prospect of imposing on strangers, and it seemed wealthy ones at that, filled her with dread.

"And where will I teach until the schoolhouse is repaired?" she asked, struggling to keep the worry from her voice.

"We're working to complete repairs as quickly as possible," he continued briskly. "If they take longer than expected, Reverend Wilson has graciously offered the church meeting hall as a backup option, but we're hoping it won't come to that."

They turned onto what appeared to be the main street of Silver Creek. Despite her anxiety, Sarah couldn't help but observe the town with interest. It was clearly a mining town. She could see men in work clothes moving about, their faces bearing the grime of a day spent below ground. The distant clang of metal on metal and the occasional rumble of carts suggested the mines operated well into the evening.

"Is that the church?" Sarah asked, nodding toward a white clapboard building with a simple steeple.

"Yes." Mr. Johnson pointed to a building further down the street. "And that's the schoolhouse there, or what's left of it."

Sarah could see workers on the roof, removing damaged shingles. The sight made her stomach tighten. How was she supposed to establish herself as the town's teacher when she didn't even have a proper classroom?

"Mr. Montgomery's home is up on the hill," Mr. Johnson said, gesturing toward the north end of town where a large house stood apart from the others, overlooking Silver Creek. "His family founded this town when they discovered silver here thirty-five years ago. They own the largest mine in the area."

Sarah nodded, taking in this information. She'd heard of the Montgomery Silver Mine, even in Denver. It was said to be one of the richest strikes in the territory.

As they walked, Mr. Johnson pointed out other buildings—the doctor's office, the post office that also housed the telegraph, and the weathered sheriff's office. Sarah tried to commit them all to memory, knowing she'd need to find her way around town on her own soon enough.

By the time they began the climb up the hill to the Montgomery house, Sarah's arms ached from dragging her trunk, and her legs felt like lead. Mr. Johnson had offered no help, seemingly oblivious to her struggle.

"Mr. Montgomery is a busy man," Mr. Johnson said as they approached the house. "He runs the mine and handles most of the town's affairs. His father built this town from nothing, and Jack, that is, Mr. Montgomery, has continued that legacy since his father's passing six years ago."

Sarah barely registered his words, too overwhelmed by the sight of the Montgomery home. It was a grand two-story house with wide verandas and tall windows. Flower beds lined the walkway, filled with blooms she couldn't name. It was the finest house she'd ever seen outside of Denver's wealthy neighborhoods.

Mr. Johnson rapped on the front door with his knuckles. A moment later, the door swung open to reveal a young woman with dark hair and bright blue eyes.

"Mr. Johnson," she said, her expression brightening. "And you must be Miss Williams, our new teacher!"

"Miss Montgomery," Mr. Johnson said, with a slight bow. "This is indeed Miss Sarah Williams."

"Please, come in," she said, stepping back to allow them entry. "I'm Charlotte. Mother and I have been looking forward to meeting you."

Sarah followed Charlotte into a spacious foyer, trying not to gape at the polished wood floors and elegant furnishings. The house was as impressive inside as it was outside, with high ceilings and fine furniture that spoke of wealth and taste.

"Mother is in the parlor," Charlotte said, leading them through the foyer. "I'll have someone fetch your trunk, Miss Williams."

"Thank you," Sarah said, grateful to set down her burden.

The parlor was a large, airy room with tall windows that looked out over the town. A woman sat in a high-backed chair near the fireplace, her silver-streaked dark hair pulled back in a severe bun. She rose as they entered, her posture impeccable.

"Mother, this is Miss Williams, our new teacher," Charlotte said.

"Miss Williams," Mrs. Montgomery said, extending her hand. "Welcome to Silver Creek. I am Eleanor Montgomery."

"Thank you for your hospitality, Mrs. Montgomery," Sarah said, taking the woman's hand. "I'm sorry for the imposition."

"Nonsense," Eleanor said, though her smile didn't quite reach her eyes. "We're happy to help in the town's time of need. Please, sit down."

Sarah perched on the edge of a settee, acutely aware of her travel-worn appearance. Eleanor Montgomery was elegantly dressed in a fine blue dress that emphasized her still-trim figure. Charlotte, too, wore a fashionable day dress that made Sarah's simple brown traveling outfit seem even plainer by comparison.

"Mr. Johnson, will you stay for tea?" Eleanor asked.

"I'm afraid I cannot, Mrs. Montgomery," he replied. "I have matters to attend to before I leave this evening. But I'll leave Miss Williams in your capable hands."

After Mr. Johnson departed, Charlotte rang for tea, and Sarah found herself alone with the Montgomery women.

"You must be exhausted from your journey," Charlotte said kindly.

"It was rather long," Sarah admitted. "But I'm grateful to have arrived safely."

"I understand you're from Denver?" Eleanor asked, her tone was polite but reserved.

"Yes, ma'am. I've lived there all my life."

"And what brings you to Silver Creek? It's quite a change from city life."

Sarah hesitated, unsure how much to share. "My mother passed away recently. I needed to find work, and when I saw the advertisement for a teacher in Silver Creek, it seemed like an opportunity."

"I'm sorry for your loss," Eleanor said, her expression softening slightly.

"Thank you."

Charlotte leaned forward, her eyes alight with interest. "Have you taught before, Miss Williams?"

"I've tutored children in Denver," Sarah replied. "And I assisted at the school there for a time. My mother was ill for several years, so I couldn't take a formal teaching position, but I've always loved working with children."

A maid entered with a tea tray, momentarily pausing the conversation. As Charlotte poured, Sarah noticed the fine china and silver service. It was further evidence of the Montgomerys' wealth.

"How many students will I have?" Sarah asked, accepting a cup of tea from Charlotte.

"About twenty," Charlotte replied. "Ages six to sixteen. Most of the older boys only attend in winter when they're not needed in the mines or on the ranches."

Sarah nodded, sipping her tea. She'd expected as much. In frontier towns, education often took a backseat to the practical needs of survival.

"The council was quite pleased with your credentials," Eleanor said. "Though I must say, we were surprised a young woman would travel so far alone for a teaching position."

There was a question in her statement, and Sarah felt herself tensing. "As I said, my mother passed away, and I have no other family in Denver. I needed to support myself."

"No other family at all?" Eleanor pressed.

Sarah hesitated. "My father had been traveling to work the silver mines for several years, but two years ago he left for the mines south of here and we haven't heard from him since."

Understanding dawned in Eleanor's eyes. "I see. I'm sorry, my dear. That must be very difficult."

Before Sarah could respond, the parlor door opened, and a man strode in. He was tall and broad-shouldered, with dark hair that curled slightly at the ends.

His blue eyes, the same shade as Charlotte's, surveyed the room before landing on Sarah.

"Jack," Eleanor said, rising. "This is Miss Williams, our new schoolteacher."

Jack Montgomery's expression remained impassive as he crossed the room, but Sarah caught the slight tightening around his eyes when Eleanor introduced her.

"Miss Williams," he said, his voice deep and measured. "I wasn't aware Mr. Johnson had finalized the hiring."

The comment hung in the air like an accusation. Sarah felt her cheeks warm.

"Jack," Eleanor said with a warning tone.

"It's all right," Sarah said, lifting her chin slightly. "Mr. Johnson did mention there had been some... discussion about the position."

"Discussion," Jack repeated, his gaze steady on hers. "That's one way to put it."

An uncomfortable silence stretched between them. Sarah felt heat creep up her neck, but she forced herself to meet his gaze. Whatever reservations he'd had about her hiring, she was here now, and she needed his cooperation.

"Well," she said, rising with as much dignity as she could muster, "I hope my work will prove satisfactory." She extended her hand. "Thank you for opening your home to me, Mr. Montgomery. Whatever the circumstances, it's very kind."

He took her hand briefly, his grip firm. "It's a temporary arrangement until the schoolhouse is repaired."

His tone made it clear that he wasn't entirely pleased with the situation. Sarah withdrew her hand, feeling her cheeks warm.

"Of course," she said. "Mr. Johnson said it will take some time to repair?"

"Yes," Jack replied. "The damage was extensive. I've assigned my best men to the repairs. I'm estimating two weeks, at least."

An uncomfortable silence fell over the room. Charlotte broke it with a bright smile.

"Jack, Miss Williams has traveled all the way from Denver to teach our children. Isn't that admirable?"

Jack's expression didn't change. "Indeed. Though I wonder why anyone would leave Denver for Silver Creek."

"As I was just explaining to your mother and sister, I needed to find work after my mother's passing," Sarah said, lifting her chin slightly.

Something flickered in Jack's eyes—surprise, perhaps, or a fleeting sympathy quickly masked. "I see. My condolences."

"Thank you."

"I'll be dining late this evening," Jack said. "We've had some equipment go missing from the north claim, and I need to investigate."

"Missing?" Charlotte asked, alarmed.

"Probably nothing," Jack said, but his expression suggested otherwise. "Just need to make sure our operations are secure."

And with that, he was gone, leaving Sarah with the distinct impression that Jack Montgomery was not at all pleased to have her staying in his home.

Charlotte sighed. "Please forgive my brother, Miss Williams. He's not usually so abrupt."

"It's all right," Sarah said, though she felt unsettled by the encounter. "He must be very busy with the mine."

"He works too hard," Eleanor said, a note of worry in her voice. "Ever since his father died... well, he's taken on too much responsibility, I fear."

Charlotte changed the subject, asking Sarah about the latest fashions in Denver, and the conversation turned to lighter topics. Sarah still felt uneasy, as her stay at the Montgomery house seemed more challenging than she expected.

Later, as Charlotte showed her to her room, a spacious chamber with a four-poster bed and its own washstand, Sarah wondered about Jack Montgomery. There was something in his eyes, a sadness or perhaps a hardness, that had caught her attention despite his cool demeanor.

"I hope you'll be comfortable here," Charlotte said, opening a wardrobe. "The view is lovely in the morning."

"It's a beautiful room," Sarah said honestly. "Thank you for your kindness, Miss Montgomery."

Charlotte smiled, her eyes warm. "Please, call me Charlotte and I shall call you Sarah. I suspect you and I will be good friends. I'm glad you've come to Silver Creek. We've needed a teacher for some time, and I have a feeling you're exactly what this town needs."

After Charlotte left, Sarah crossed to the window and looked out over Silver Creek. The sun was setting, painting the town and the distant mountains in hues of gold and pink. It was beautiful, but Sarah felt a pang of homesickness for Denver, for the familiar streets and the grave where her mother lay.

She unpacked her mother's Bible and placed it on the bedside table, drawing comfort from its presence. Then she knelt beside the bed, closed her eyes, and prayed for strength, for guidance, and for the wisdom to navigate her new life in Silver Creek.

"Lord," she whispered, "I don't know why You've brought me here, but I trust in Your plan. Please help me be the teacher these children need, and to find my place in this town."

As she rose and prepared for bed, Sarah wondered what challenges awaited her in Silver Creek, and why Jack Montgomery had looked at her with such cool assessment, as if she were a problem to be solved rather than a person to be welcomed.

Whatever the reason, she would face it with the same determination that had brought her this far. After all, she had nowhere else to go. Silver Creek was her home now, at least for the foreseeable future, and she was determined to make the best of it.

With that resolution firmly in mind, Sarah climbed into the unfamiliar bed and drifted into an exhausted sleep, dreaming of silver mines, stern-faced men with sad blue eyes, and the twenty unknown children she would soon meet.

TWO

J ack Montgomery stood at the window of his office, watching as the last of the day's light faded behind the western mountains. The lamp on his desk cast long shadows across the room, illuminating the stacks of ledgers and mining reports that demanded his attention. He should return to them, but his mind kept wandering to the unexpected guest now living in his home.

Miss Sarah Williams. The new schoolteacher.

She wasn't what he had expected. When the town council had informed him they'd found a teacher from Denver, he'd imagined someone older, more severe, like Miss Penn who had taught him as a boy. Instead, Miss Williams was young, probably only twenty-two or twenty-three, with thoughtful hazel eyes and a quiet dignity despite her obvious exhaustion from the journey.

Jack turned from the window with a sigh. What did it matter what she was like? She would stay at their house until the schoolhouse was repaired, teach the town's children, and that would be that. Her presence in his home was a temporary inconvenience, nothing more.

Jack returned to his desk where Blackwood's latest offer lay beside a troubling report from his foreman. Three separate incidents of sabotage in two weeks—support beams weakened, equipment damaged, workers reporting strange sounds in the tunnels at night.

Coincidence? Or was Blackwood playing a more dangerous game than simple business rivalry?

A soft knock at the door interrupted his thoughts.

"Come in," he called, expecting his foreman with the day's production reports.

Instead, his mother entered, her expression determined in a way that immediately put Jack on alert.

"Mother," he said, rising. "Is something wrong?"

Eleanor closed the door behind her and crossed to the chair facing his desk. "I thought we might discuss our guest."

Jack suppressed a groan as he sat back down. "What about her?"

"She seems like a respectable young woman," Eleanor said carefully. "But I can't help but wonder about her circumstances. A young woman traveling alone, with no family or connections... it's not right."

"She said her mother died recently," Jack pointed out. "And her father went south to the mines."

"Yes, quite convenient, isn't it?" Eleanor raised an eyebrow. "No one to verify her background or credentials."

Jack frowned. "The town council checked her references. Mr. Johnson traveled to Denver specifically to interview her."

"Mr. Johnson is not the most discerning of men," Eleanor said dismissively. "I simply think we should be cautious. After all, she'll be teaching the town's children."

"Including none of ours," Jack reminded her. "What's your concern, Mother? That she's not qualified to teach reading and arithmetic to miners' children?"

Eleanor's lips thinned at his tone. "My concern is that we know very little about her, yet we've opened our home to her. Your sister seems quite taken with her already."

"Charlotte is taken with anyone new," Jack said, a hint of fondness softening his voice. "She's been bored since returning from visiting our cousins in Baltimore."

"That's precisely my point. Charlotte is impressionable. Miss Williams may seem refined, but we know nothing of her background or her... moral character."

Jack set down Blackwood's letter with more force than necessary. "She's a schoolteacher, Mother, not a dance hall girl. And she'll only be here until the schoolhouse is repaired."

"Nevertheless—"

"I have more pressing matters to attend to than speculating about Miss Williams' character," Jack interrupted, gesturing to the papers piled on his desk. "Blackwood is making another play for the north claim."

Eleanor's expression shifted to one of concern. "What does he want now?"

"The same as always. Access to the vein we discovered last winter." Jack handed her the letter. "He's offering a partnership this time. Claims it would be 'mutually beneficial' to work together rather than compete."

Eleanor scanned the letter, her brow furrowing. "You're not considering it, are you?"

"Of course not. I don't trust Blackwood any further than I could throw him." Jack took the letter back. "But he's persistent, I'll give him that."

Eleanor stood, smoothing her skirts. "Your father never would have entertained such an offer."

"I know that, Mother," Jack said, an edge creeping into his voice.

"I didn't mean—" Eleanor sighed. "I only meant that your father was an excellent judge of character. He would have seen through Blackwood's schemes immediately."

"As do I," Jack replied. "That's why I've rejected his offers three times now."

Eleanor nodded, satisfied. "Very well. I'll leave you to your work." She paused at the door. "Will you join us for breakfast tomorrow? It would be polite to make our guest feel welcome, at least."

Jack resisted the urge to point out that his mother hardly seemed concerned with making Miss Williams feel welcome a moment ago. "I'll be there," he promised instead.

After his mother left, Jack returned to the window, gazing out at the darkened town below. Silver Creek had changed so much since he was a boy. What had once been little more than a mining camp was now a proper town with a church, a school, several businesses, and nearly five hundred residents. His father had built that, transforming a silver strike into a community.

And now it was Jack's responsibility to maintain it—the mine, the town, his family's legacy. The weight of that responsibility pressed down on him daily, especially since the accident five years ago.

He closed his eyes, but that only made the memories more vivid. The sound of splintering timber, the men's shouts, the clouds of dust and debris. And Matthew, his best friend since childhood, crushed beneath the fallen supports. Three men had died that day, but it was Matthew's face that haunted Jack's dreams.

Jack opened his eyes and turned resolutely from the window. There was no use dwelling on the past. He had a mine to run and a town that depended on him. Whatever his personal demons, he couldn't afford to let them interfere with his duties.

He sat back at his desk and pulled the production reports toward him, forcing himself to focus on the columns of figures. But as the night deepened, his thoughts kept returning to the young woman now sleeping under his roof, and the strange disruption her presence seemed to promise.

***

The small graveyard behind Silver Creek's church was peaceful in the early morning light. Dew sparkled on the grass, and birds sang in the nearby trees. Jack stood in front of a simple stone marker, his hat in his hands.

MATTHEW CARTER BELOVED SON AND FRIEND 1844 - 1869 "GOD WORKS ALL THINGS FOR GOOD"

Jack had never understood why Henry Carter had chosen that verse for his son's tombstone. What possible good could come from a young man's death? What Divine purpose could justify the loss of a life so full of promise?

"You let him die," Jack muttered. "And for what?" He stared at the stone. "I prayed that night. First time in years. Maybe you thought it was a joke."

He turned to leave but paused. His hand lingered on the brim of his hat. "I won't ask again."

But he didn't walk away as fast as he meant to. Something held him there, if only for a moment.

"It's been a while since you visited."

Jack turned to find Henry Carter standing a few feet away. The older man had aged considerably in the five years since Matthew's death, his hair now completely gray, deep lines etched around his eyes and mouth. But his gaze was kind as he regarded Jack.

"I've been busy," Jack said, the excuse sounding hollow even to his own ears.

"Too busy for old friends?" Henry asked, but there was no accusation in his tone.

"The mine—"

"I know all about the mine, Jack. I still work there, remember?" Henry moved to stand beside him, looking down at his son's grave. "Though not for much longer, I suspect. These old bones aren't what they used to be."

Jack frowned. "You know you'll always have a place at Montgomery Mining, Henry. Even if you can't work the tunnels anymore."

Henry smiled slightly. He was quiet for a moment, then asked, "How are you, really? And don't tell me 'fine' or 'busy.' I've known you since you were knee-high to a grasshopper."

Jack stared at Matthew's name carved in stone. "I'm managing."

"Still not going to church, I take it?"

"You know I'm not."

Henry sighed. "Matthew wouldn't have wanted that, Jack. He wouldn't have wanted you to turn away from God because of what happened."

"It wasn't my choice," Jack said, his voice tight. "God turned away from me first."

"That's not how it works, son."

"Isn't it?" Jack turned to face the older man. "Three men died that day, Henry. Good men with families. Where was God then? Where was His protection when those supports gave way?"

Henry didn't flinch from Jack's anger. "I don't know. I don't understand God's ways. But I know that blaming Him hasn't brought you any peace."

Jack looked away, unable to deny the truth of Henry's words. "I should go. Mother's expecting me for breakfast."

"Is that so?" Henry's eyes crinkled. "I heard you've got the new schoolteacher staying with you until the schoolhouse is fixed."

"News travels fast," Jack muttered.

"It's a small town," Henry replied with a shrug. "What's she like, this teacher from Denver?"

"I hardly know. We only met briefly yesterday."

Henry gave a thoughtful nod. "We've had a hard time keeping teachers here, one way or another. I hope she stays."

Jack nodded. "So do I."

Henry smiled faintly. "Then make sure she feels welcome. First impressions go a long way in a place like this."

Jack acknowledged the advice with a slight tilt of his head. "I'll do my best."

Henry placed a weathered hand on Jack's shoulder. "Don't be a stranger, Jack. The living need you more than the dead do."

With a last nod toward Matthew's grave, Henry turned and walked back toward town, leaving Jack alone with his thoughts.

Jack remained for a few more minutes, staring at the verse on Matthew's tombstone. "God works all things for good." What a cruel promise that seemed, standing in a graveyard filled with lives cut short.

As he turned to leave, he noticed a small bird building a nest in the eaves of the church. It was meticulously placing twigs and bits of grass, preparing a home for its young. Such a small, inconsequential thing, yet the sight of it made Jack pause.

Matthew had loved birds. He'd known all their names and calls, could identify them by the smallest glimpse of color or sound. Once, years ago, he'd shown Jack a nest built in almost the exact same spot, pointing out the mother bird feeding her chicks.

"It's like a sign," Matthew had said. "Every spring, new life begins. No matter what happened before, God gives us another chance."

Jack shook his head, dispelling the memory. It was just a bird, nothing more. No sign, no message from beyond. Just a coincidence that meant nothing.

He set his hat back on his head and started toward home, quickening his pace. His mother would expect him for breakfast, and he didn't want to be rude, not today, not with the new teacher under their roof.

But even as he walked away from the grave, the weight in his chest didn't ease. He kept telling himself he was done with faith, but the ache had never really left. Maybe that was the hardest part. Not that God had stopped listening, but that he'd forgotten how to ask.

***

When Jack entered the dining room, he found his mother, Charlotte, and Miss Williams already seated. He murmured an apology for his tardiness as he took his place at the head of the table.

"You've been out riding already this morning?" Eleanor asked.

"I had some business to tend to," Jack said, offering no further detail. His boots were still damp from the dew-soaked grass behind the church.

"Miss Williams and I were just discussing her plans for the school," Charlotte said. "She'll be preparing lessons while we wait for the repairs to be finished."

Jack nodded. "I'm sure the children are eager for classes to resume."

He turned his attention to Sarah, noticing more now in the morning light than he had in the rush of the previous evening. Her chestnut hair was neatly coiled, and her blue dress, simple but well-made, brought out the green in her hazel eyes. She looked composed, but not quite settled, as if still finding her place in the household.

"I hope your accommodations have been comfortable," he said.

"Very much so," she replied politely. "Your family has been most welcoming."

"I was thinking I might take her around town after breakfast," Charlotte offered. "She should meet a few families, maybe stop by the general store or the post office."

Eleanor nodded. "A good idea. And I imagine Reverend Wilson would be glad to say hello as well."

"I'd like that," Sarah said. "And if there's time, I'd like to see the schoolhouse. I'd like to get a sense of what's needed."

"It's in rough shape," Jack said. "But the repairs are underway. I'd say two, maybe three weeks before it's ready."

"In the meantime, we'll make sure you're comfortable," Charlotte added with a smile.

"You're all very kind," Sarah said, glancing at Jack as she spoke. He wasn't sure he deserved the gratitude, but he gave a small nod in return.

"It's nice having someone new at the table," Charlotte said. "Silver Creek doesn't get many visitors."

"Or many who stay," Eleanor added, her gaze flicking briefly toward Jack.

He ignored the jab and turned back to Sarah. "How long have you been teaching?"

"This will be my first official teaching position."

Jack lifted a brow. "So, no classroom experience?"

"Jack," Charlotte warned under her breath.

"It's a fair question," he said, keeping his tone even. "The town is trusting her with its children."

"I understand your concern," Sarah said calmly. "I assisted regularly at a school in Denver, so I'm familiar with the structure and curriculum. I just wasn't able to commit full-time while caring for my mother."

Her voice wavered slightly, but she steadied it. "After she passed, I needed a new beginning."

Jack felt the edge of his skepticism soften. "I see. I didn't mean to doubt your intentions."

"I appreciate that, Mr. Montgomery. I care deeply about giving these children a firm foundation."

There was quiet conviction in her tone that Jack couldn't dismiss.

"Well, I'm glad you're here," Charlotte said. "We need someone who understands children need more than facts. They need someone who believes in them."

Sarah smiled. "That's exactly how I feel. Education shapes more than minds. It shapes character."

"And will you be including religious instruction?" Eleanor asked.

"The Bible will be among our readers," Sarah said. "And I believe teaching morality is important. But I'd never try to replace the role of a child's family or church."

A tactful answer, Jack thought, and probably the smartest one she could have given.

"Speaking of the church," Charlotte said, "we should attend services together on Sunday. Reverend Wilson gives the most thought-provoking sermons."

Jack noticed a slight tensing in Sarah's expression at the mention of church attendance. Was she not as devout as she appeared? But her next words dispelled that notion.

"I'd like that," she said. "I've found great comfort in my faith, especially since my mother's passing."

Charlotte beamed. "Excellent! We'll make sure you meet everyone. The whole town attends services... well, almost everyone." She cast a meaningful glance at Jack.

"Charlotte," Eleanor warned quietly.

"It's all right, Mother," Jack said. "Miss Williams may as well know I don't attend church. I'm sure the town gossips will inform her soon enough if we don't."

Sarah looked slightly taken aback by his bluntness. "I didn't mean to cause any discomfort, Mr. Montgomery."

"You didn't," he said. "My spiritual practices, or lack thereof, are my business. I don't impose them on others, nor do I expect others to impose theirs on me."

An uncomfortable silence fell over the table. Jack knew he'd spoken too harshly, but something about the mention of church always put him on edge. It reminded him too much of his father's unwavering faith. A faith Jack had once shared before the accident shattered his beliefs.

"I understand the schoolhouse needs new books and supplies," Charlotte said, clearly trying to change the subject. "Perhaps we could look into ordering some from Denver?"

"That would be wonderful," Sarah said, seeming relieved at the shift in conversation. "I brought some materials with me, but not nearly enough for twenty students."

As the women discussed books and teaching supplies, Jack observed Sarah. There was something about her that intrigued him, despite his initial reservations. A quiet strength, perhaps, or a depth of character hinted at in her thoughtful responses and the dignity with which she carried herself despite her reduced circumstances.

Jack had encountered many women since his return from college, most of them the daughters of wealthy mine owners or Denver businessmen whom his mother hoped he might marry. They were accomplished and beautiful, but few had impressed him with their character or intellect. Miss Williams, despite her lack of wealth or social standing, seemed different somehow.

It was an unsettling realization, and one Jack quickly pushed aside. His focus needed to remain on the mine, on protecting his family's legacy and ensuring Silver Creek's prosperity. The new schoolteacher's character, however admirable, was irrelevant to those concerns.

Yet as they finished breakfast, and Charlotte prepared to show Sarah around town, Jack offered to accompany them, surprising not only his mother and sister but himself as well.

"Are you sure you can spare the time?" Eleanor asked, clearly puzzled by his unexpected offer.

"The mine will survive without me for a few hours," Jack said. "And Miss Williams should know who's who in Silver Creek if she's to teach here. Some of our residents can be challenging."

"That's very thoughtful of you, Jack," Charlotte said, giving him a curious look.

"It's nothing," he said gruffly. "Just being practical."

But as they set out into the bright morning sunshine, Jack couldn't quite explain, even to himself, why he'd chosen to join them. Perhaps it was Henry's words about the living needing him more than the dead. Or perhaps it was simply that, for the first time in a long while, he was curious about someone new in Silver Creek.

Whatever the reason, Jack walked beside Sarah Williams down the main street of town, pointing out buildings and introducing her to townspeople, his usual reserve temporarily set aside as he fulfilled his duty as host. And if he occasionally found his gaze lingering on her profile as she smiled at something Charlotte said, or noticed the way the morning light caught the auburn highlights in her dark hair, he told himself it was merely the novelty of a new face in their small community.

Nothing more significant than that.

THREE

Sarah took in the bustling main street of Silver Creek as Charlotte chattered enthusiastically beside her. Jack Montgomery walked slightly ahead, his bearing stiff and formal, nodding occasionally to townspeople who greeted him with a mixture of respect and wariness. She couldn't quite reconcile this stern businessman with the vulnerability she'd glimpsed at breakfast when he'd mentioned his absence from church.

"That's the general store," Charlotte was saying, pointing to a two-story building with a wide front porch. "Mr. Parker runs it with his wife Abigail. She's... well, she's very interested in everyone's business."

"Charlotte," Jack said warningly without turning around.

"I'm only being honest," Charlotte defended herself, then lowered her voice conspiratorially. "Mrs. Parker is the town's biggest gossip. Fair warning."

Sarah smiled despite herself. Charlotte's warmth was a welcome contrast to her brother's stiff demeanor and their mother's reserved politeness. "Thank you for the warning."

They paused as a wagon rumbled past, loaded with mining equipment. Sarah noticed how Jack's eyes tracked its progress, his brow furrowing slightly.

"Heading to the north claim," he murmured, more to himself than to them.

"Is that one of your mines?" Sarah asked.

Jack glanced at her. "Yes. We opened that tunnel last winter."

"Jack owns the largest mining operation in Silver Creek," Charlotte explained proudly. "Father discovered the original vein, but Jack has expanded the business considerably."

Sarah detected a note of strain in Jack's expression at the mention of his father. "It must be a great responsibility," she said carefully.

"It is," Jack replied curtly, then turned to continue walking.

The next stop was the post office, where Jack introduced her to Mr. Henley, the postmaster. The elderly man beamed when he learned she was the new teacher.

"My granddaughter Emma will be one of your students," he said warmly. "Bright as a button, that one. Been teaching herself from whatever books she can find."

"I look forward to meeting her," Sarah said sincerely. "How old is Emma?"

"Ten years old. Lost her mother two years back, lives with her pa now." Mr. Henley's expression grew sad. "Joseph does his best, but it's hard for a man alone."

Sarah felt a pang of sympathy. She knew too well the pain of losing a parent. "I'll pay special attention to Emma's education."

As they left the post office, Jack gave her an appraising look. "That was kind of you," he said.

"I meant it," Sarah replied. "Children who've experienced loss often need extra support."

Something flickered in Jack's eyes—understanding, perhaps, or recognition. But before he could respond, Charlotte was tugging them toward the next building.

"The church is just ahead," she said. "Reverend Wilson will be so pleased to meet you."

The white clapboard church stood at the end of the street, its simple steeple reaching toward the clear Colorado sky. Sarah noticed Jack's steps slowed as they approached.

"I have some business to attend to," he said abruptly. "Charlotte, you can introduce Miss Williams to the reverend."

"Jack—" Charlotte began, but he was already walking away.

Sarah watched his retreating figure, noting the tension in his shoulders. What had turned this man so completely from his faith?

"Don't mind him," Charlotte said . "He wasn't always like this. Before Father died, before the accident..." She trailed off, then brightened deliberately. "Come, let's find Reverend Wilson."

The church interior was simple but well-maintained, with wooden pews and plain glass windows that let in streams of golden light. Sarah paused in the doorway, breathing in the familiar scents of wood polish and old hymnals. How many Sundays had she spent in a similar church in Denver, sitting beside her mother?

"May I help you?"

A man emerged from a side door, dressed in simple black with a clerical collar. He appeared to be about sixty, with kind eyes behind wire-rimmed spectacles.

"Reverend Wilson," Charlotte said warmly. "This is Miss Sarah Williams, our new teacher."

"Ah, Miss Williams!" The reverend's face lit up. "We've been eagerly awaiting your arrival. Welcome to Silver Creek."

"Thank you, Reverend." Sarah shook his offered hand. "It's a pleasure to meet you."

"I hope the schoolhouse repairs progress quickly. The children have been without proper instruction for far too long."

"Yes, I'm eager to begin teaching as soon as possible," Sarah agreed. "Education is so important for young minds."

"Indeed! Education and faith go hand in hand. 'Train up a child in the way he should go, and when he is old, he will not depart from it.'" He smiled. "Proverbs, as I'm sure you know."

Sarah nodded. "My mother was fond of that verse. She believed strongly in the value of education."

"A wise woman. And I understand she recently passed? My condolences."

"Thank you." Sarah swallowed against the familiar tightness in her throat. "Her faith sustained her until the end."

"As I'm sure yours sustains you now," Reverend Wilson said gently. "Please know that our church family is here to support you in any way we can."

Charlotte had wandered toward the altar, ostensibly examining a flower arrangement, giving them a moment of privacy. Sarah appreciated the gesture.

"Reverend," she said hesitantly, "Charlotte mentioned that Mr. Montgomery doesn't attend services?"

A shadow crossed the reverend's face. "No, not for several years now. Not since the mining accident that took young Matthew Carter's life."

"Were they close?"

"Best friends since childhood. Jack blames himself for Matthew's death, though the investigation cleared him of any wrongdoing." The reverend sighed. "Grief and guilt can shake even the strongest faith."

Sarah thought of her own struggles after her mother's death, the nights she'd questioned God's plan. But her faith had ultimately sustained her, while Jack's seemed to have shattered entirely.

"We continue to pray for him," Reverend Wilson added. "God works in His own time, and I believe Jack will find his way back eventually."

Sarah nodded, then said, "I read a verse this morning in my Bible that stayed with me: 'Be still and know that I am God.'"

The reverend's expression warmed. "A timely reminder. That's one Charlotte often writes out and leaves around the house. She hopes Jack might see them now and again."

Sarah glanced at Charlotte, who was studying the stained glass window with polite interest. Quiet faith expressed in small, steady ways. A sister's love written in Scripture and hope.

"I hope that you will be a regular visitor to church yourself," Reverend Wilson said. "Perhaps we could discuss ways the church might support the school's mission."

"That's very kind of you," Sarah replied gratefully. "Any support would be most welcome. And yes, I will be here for Sunday services."

As they continued their conversation, Sarah found her thoughts drifting to Jack Montgomery. His abrupt departure at the church, the pain she'd glimpsed in his eyes, the way he'd stiffened at any mention of faith—all of it painted a picture of a man carrying a heavy burden.

Lord, she prayed silently, *please help me be a light in this place. And if it's Your will, help me to understand what has hurt Jack Montgomery so deeply.*

"Miss Williams?" Charlotte's voice drew her from her thoughts. "Is everything all right?"

"Yes, I'm sorry. I was just thinking about all that needs to be done before classes begin."

"Don't worry," Reverend Wilson assured her. "This community takes care of its own. You'll have more help than you know what to do with."

They spent another half hour in the church, with Reverend Wilson sharing information about the families whose children would attend school. Sarah made mental notes, already beginning to form pictures of her future students. As they emerged from the church into the afternoon sunshine, Sarah felt increasingly hopeful about her new position. Reverend Wilson's kindness and the promise of community support had eased many of her concerns about starting over in Silver Creek.

They had barely stepped outside when a woman hurried up the church path toward them, clearly intent on intercepting them before they could leave.

"Oh no," Charlotte murmured under her breath.

The woman was perhaps fifty years old, with graying hair pulled back severely and sharp eyes that immediately fixed on Sarah with undisguised curiosity. She carried herself with the purposeful air of someone accustomed to knowing everyone's business.

"Charlotte Montgomery!" the woman called out, slightly breathless from her quick pace. "Perfect timing. I was just coming to speak with Reverend Wilson about the Ladies' Aid meeting, but this is so much better."

"Mrs. Parker," Charlotte said with resigned politeness. "This is Miss Sarah Williams, our new schoolteacher. Miss Williams, may I present Mrs. Abigail Parker."

"How do you do," Sarah said, offering her hand.

Mrs. Parker shook it briefly while studying Sarah's face with the intensity of someone cataloging every detail. "My, you're quite young, aren't you? I do hope you have sufficient experience for our children." She tilted her head, her eyes narrowing slightly. "You know, there's something familiar about you. Your features... have we met before?"

Sarah felt a chill run down her spine. "I don't believe so, ma'am. I've never been to Silver Creek before."

"Hmm." Mrs. Parker continued to stare, her expression growing more puzzled. "It's the strangest thing. Your eyes, the shape of your face... you remind me of someone. Someone I met a few years back, though I can't quite place it." She shook her head in frustration. "It'll come to me eventually. It always does."

"I taught in Denver for several years," Sarah replied evenly, trying to keep her voice steady despite the woman's unsettling scrutiny.

"Denver!" Mrs. Parker's eyebrows rose, though her gaze remained fixed on Sarah's face. "How fascinating. And what brings you all the way to Silver Creek? Surely a young woman with city experience could find more... suitable employment closer to home?"

Sarah felt heat rise in her cheeks at the woman's probing, made worse by the continued examination. "I felt called to serve where I was needed most."

"Called, you say?" Mrs. Parker's tone suggested she found this explanation insufficient. "And your family? Do they approve of you traveling so far from home?" She paused, still studying Sarah's features. "What did you say your family name was again?"

"Williams," Sarah replied, her mouth suddenly dry.

"Williams..." Mrs. Parker repeated slowly, as if testing the name. "No, that's not it. But there's definitely something..." She trailed off, tapping her finger against her chin. "Well, no matter. I'm sure it'll come to me eventually. These things always do."

"Mrs. Parker," Charlotte interjected gently, "I'm sure Miss Williams would prefer to get settled before answering too many questions. And didn't you say you needed to speak with Reverend Wilson?"

"Oh yes, of course," Mrs. Parker said, though her expression suggested she was far from finished with her interrogation. "Miss Williams, you must come by the store soon. I'd love to hear more about your plans for the school. And your background, of course. It's so important for the community to know our new residents well."

"I'm sure we'll have many opportunities to speak," Sarah replied diplomatically.

Mrs. Parker finally stepped aside, allowing them to continue down the path, though Sarah could feel the woman's eyes following them even as she headed toward the church entrance.

"I'm sorry about that," Charlotte said quietly as they walked toward the main street. "Mrs. Parker means well, but she does tend to be rather... thorough in her inquiries."

"I gathered as much," Sarah said with a slight smile. "Though I suppose in a small town, everyone's naturally curious about newcomers."

As they turned onto the main street, Charlotte suddenly slowed her pace. "Speaking of people you should know about," she said in a lowered voice.

Sarah followed her gaze and saw a tall man walking toward them on the opposite side of the street. He was impeccably dressed in a fine wool coat and polished boots that seemed out of place in the dusty mining town. His dark hair was streaked with silver, and even from a distance, there was something about his bearing that commanded attention—and made Sarah feel inexplicably uneasy.

"That's Cyrus Blackwood," Charlotte said quietly. "Owner of Blackwood Mining."

The man's pale eyes swept the street with calculating interest, and when his gaze fell on them, Sarah noticed how it lingered on her with obvious curiosity. He touched his hat brim in acknowledgment but made no move to cross the street or approach them.

There was something in his manner that reminded Sarah of certain men in Denver—those who viewed everything and everyone as potential acquisitions. She instinctively moved closer to Charlotte as they continued walking.

"He seems..." Sarah paused, searching for the right word.

"Intimidating?" Charlotte suggested. "Yes, he has that effect on people. Successful, certainly, but there's been considerable tension between his mining interests and Jack's." She glanced around to ensure they wouldn't be overheard. "I probably shouldn't say more than that."

Sarah nodded, filing away the information. She was understanding that Silver Creek's pleasant exterior concealed undercurrents of conflict that she would need to navigate carefully as the new teacher.

They walked in companionable silence for a few minutes until Charlotte pointed ahead. "There's the schoolhouse. And look, Jack is waiting for us."

Sure enough, Jack stood near the damaged building, speaking with a middle-aged man in work clothes. Even from a distance, Sarah could see the tension in his posture as he gestured toward the collapsed roof.

Sarah's heart sank as she walked closer. She surveyed the building. The roof had partially caved in on one side, and debris was scattered around the entrance.

"Oh my," she breathed.

"I told you it was extensive," Jack said. "But my men are skilled. It will be repaired properly."

Sarah walked carefully around the building, peering through windows at the damaged interior. Through one window, she could see the teacher's quarters attached to the back. Her future home, currently uninhabitable.

Sarah took a slow step closer to the building, her eyes tracing the jagged break in the roofline and the crumpled wall beneath it. "I didn't expect the damage to be this bad," she said.

Charlotte nodded, pointing toward a blackened stump near the edge of the yard. "That oak took a direct hit. It snapped like kindling and came straight down on the roof."

"It's a mercy no one was inside," Sarah murmured.

Jack crossed his arms. "We haven't held classes in some time. The building's been empty since our last teacher left."

Sarah noticed movement near the damaged entrance and saw a small face peering around the doorframe. A girl with brown pigtails and curious eyes.

"Hello there," Sarah called gently.

The girl emerged shyly, followed by two boys who looked to be brothers. They appeared to range in age from perhaps eight to twelve.

"Are you the new teacher?" the girl asked.

"I am. I'm Miss Williams. And what's your name?"

"Emma Reynolds. Mr. Henley's my grandpa—he runs the post office."

Sarah smiled. "He said you were full of curiosity."

Emma grinned. "I like to know things. Grandpa says I was born with more questions than answers."

"I bet you explore a lot, too," Sarah said with a smile.

Emma nodded. "Sometimes I follow the wagons to see where they go. Grandpa says I can't sit still. I like to know what's happening. Nobody really sees me 'cause I'm little."

"This is Tom and Peter Garrett," Charlotte introduced the boys.

"Are you going to stay?" the older boy, Tom, asked, eyeing Sarah warily. "The last teacher left after a few months."

Sarah kneeled to meet his gaze. "I plan to stay as long as Silver Creek needs a teacher. And I'm very much looking forward to our classes together."

"Will we have actual books?" Peter, the younger boy, piped up. "We mostly just copied stuff from the Bible before."

"We'll have all sorts of books," Sarah promised with a warm smile. "Though the Bible will certainly be one of them. There are wonderful stories in it."

"Like David and Goliath?" Emma asked eagerly.

"Exactly like that."

Jack had been silent during this exchange, but Sarah noticed him watching her interaction with the children with an unreadable expression.

"You children should run along home," Charlotte said kindly. "Your parents will wonder where you are."

As the children scampered off, Emma called back, "When will school start, Miss Williams?"

"As soon as the school is repaired," Sarah replied. "If it takes awhile to fix the roof, I'll hold classes at the church hall. "

After the children left, Jack said, "You handled that well."

Sarah looked up at him, surprised by the compliment. "They seem like good children. Eager to learn."

"Most of them are. Though you'll have challenges with some of the older boys. Mining families don't always value education as they should."

"I've dealt with reluctant students before," Sarah said confidently.

Jack studied her for a moment. "I believe you have."

As they walked back toward the Montgomery house, Sarah reflected on the morning's encounters. Silver Creek was feeling less foreign, its people taking shape in her mind. She had much to learn about this community, but she felt a growing certainty that God had indeed led her here for a purpose.

"Thank you for showing me around," she said to both Montgomerys as they climbed the hill toward their home. "It's been very helpful."

"You'll meet more people at church on Sunday," Charlotte said. "Nearly the whole town attends."

Sarah noticed Jack's jaw tighten slightly at the mention of church, but he said nothing.

As they reached the house, he paused at the door. "Miss Williams, I hope you'll let us know if you need anything for your classes. Books, supplies, whatever you require."

"That's very generous, Mr. Montgomery."

He shrugged. "An educated population benefits everyone. It's good business."

But Sarah thought she detected something more than mere business interest in his offer. Perhaps there was more to Jack Montgomery than the stern, faithless exterior he presented to the world.

"I'll make a list," she said. "Thank you."

He nodded curtly and headed toward his office, leaving Sarah and Charlotte in the foyer.

"He likes you," Charlotte said quietly once Jack was out of earshot.

"I don't think your brother likes anyone very much," Sarah replied.

Charlotte smiled mysteriously. "You'd be surprised. I haven't seen him take such an interest in anyone in years."

Before Sarah could respond, Charlotte was already heading upstairs, humming softly to herself. Sarah stood alone in the foyer for a moment, pondering

Charlotte's words. Jack Montgomery was certainly a puzzle. He was a man of obvious intelligence and capability yet carrying such deep wounds that he'd turned from the very faith that might heal them.

Lord, she prayed silently, *help me be Your instrument in this place. Show me how to serve You here, with these children and this community. And if it's Your will, help me understand what You would have me do about Jack Montgomery.*

With that prayer in her heart, Sarah climbed the stairs to her room to prepare her first lessons for the children of Silver Creek, trusting that God would guide her steps in this new chapter of her life.

FOUR

J ack sat at his desk in the mine office, staring at the production reports without really seeing them. His mind kept returning to the morning's events—the town tour with Sarah Williams, his unexpected offer to accompany them, the way she had interacted with the children at the schoolhouse. There was something about her that didn't fit his initial impression of a desperate city woman seeking refuge in a small mining town.

He'd expected someone timid, perhaps even bitter about her circumstances. Instead, he'd found a woman with quiet confidence and genuine compassion. The way she'd spoken to Emma and the Garrett boys revealed a natural gift for connecting with children. And when she'd stood up to his questioning at breakfast, there had been a flash of spirit in those hazel eyes that had caught him off guard.

A knock at the door pulled him from his thoughts.

"Come in," he called, straightening in his chair and reaching for a pen to appear busy.

His foreman, August Hart, entered with a stack of papers. "Sorry to interrupt, Mr. Montgomery. I've got the reports on the north tunnel."

"Thank you, August." Jack took the papers, grateful for the distraction from his wandering thoughts. "Any problems to report?"

"Nothing serious. Had to shore up some supports in section three, but the veins looking promising. Could be as rich as your father's first strike."

Jack nodded, flipping through the reports. "And the men? Any complaints or concerns?"

"Just the usual grumbling about Blackwood's outfit trying to lure away our best workers with promises of higher wages." August hesitated, then added, "Though there's something else you should know. Some men are saying there've been strangers around the north claim after hours."

Jack looked up sharply. "Trespassers?"

"Maybe. Jenkins spotted someone near the equipment shed two nights ago. Couldn't get a good look at him in the dark." August crossed his arms. "Could be nothing, but with Blackwood so interested in that claim..."

"Increase the night security," Jack decided. "And let me know immediately if anything unusual happens."

"Yes, sir." August turned to leave but paused at the door. "If you don't mind my asking, how's the new schoolteacher settling in? Charlotte mentioned at church that she'd be staying with you until the schoolhouse is fixed."

Jack raised an eyebrow at the personal question, but August had been with the company since Jack's father's time and was more of a friend than employee.

"She seems capable," Jack said carefully. "Time will tell if she's up to the challenge of teaching in Silver Creek."

August gave him a knowing look. "Charlotte says she's pretty as a picture."

"I hadn't noticed," Jack lied, returning his attention to the reports.

August chuckled. "If you say so, Mr. Montgomery. I'll see to that extra security."

After August left, Jack put down the reports and rubbed his temples. The potential security issue with the north claim was concerning, especially with Blackwood circling like a vulture. The last thing he needed was complications with the mine on top of having a houseguest who was already complicating his thoughts far more than he'd expected.

Jack glanced at the small daguerreotype on his desk. It was a family portrait taken when he was eighteen, just before he left for college. His mother, born and raised in Baltimore, had insisted he attend university—just as the men in her family had for generations—believing that education was the surest mark of a gentleman, even out here in the wilds of Colorado. His father stood tall and proud in the center, one hand on Jack's shoulder, the other holding Charlotte, then just a girl of thirteen. His mother sat primly in front, her expression serene but distant, as it had been since the difficult birth of Charlotte that had rendered her unable to have more children.

Thomas Montgomery had been a hard man to please, but a good father. He'd built the Montgomery Mining Company from nothing, turning a lucky strike into a thriving enterprise that supported half the town. His faith had been as solid as the mountains themselves—unwavering, immovable. Jack had once envied that certainty, that absolute trust in God's plan.

Until the accident.

Jack pushed the memories away and focused on the work before him. The mine, the town, his family's legacy. These were the things that mattered. Not disturbing memories, not attractive schoolteachers with compassionate eyes. Just the responsibilities that had been his since his father's death.

By the time Jack returned home that evening, the sun was setting, painting the mountains with shades of gold and purple. He paused on the porch and took a moment to appreciate the view. Silver Creek sprawled below, the buildings casting long shadows as the day ended. In the distance, he could see the church spire catching the last rays of sunlight.

The door opened behind him, and Charlotte stepped out.

"I thought I heard you come up the walk," she said, joining him at the porch railing. "You're home earlier than usual."

"I wanted to check on our guest," Jack said, then hastily added, "Make sure she has everything she needs."

Charlotte smiled knowingly. "Sarah spent the afternoon helping me prepare for the Ladies' Aid Society meeting next week. She has a wonderful eye for detail."

Jack made a noncommittal sound, unwilling to encourage his sister's obvious interest in his reaction to Sarah.

"She also asked about father's library," Charlotte continued. "It seems she's quite the reader. I told her she was welcome to borrow any books she liked."

"That was generous of you," Jack said, though he felt a strange twinge at the thought of Sarah exploring his father's private sanctuary. The library had remained untouched since Thomas Montgomery's death, preserved like a shrine to the man who had built their fortune.

"Will you join us for dinner tonight?" Charlotte asked. "Or are you planning to hide in your office again?"

Jack gave her a stern look that had no effect whatsoever on his irrepressible sister. "I'll join you. As I said, I want to ensure Miss Williams is comfortable during her stay."

"Of course," Charlotte said innocently. "It's purely a matter of hospitality."

Jack ignored the implication in her tone. "I should change before dinner," he said, opening the door for her.

"Jack," Charlotte said, suddenly serious. "I think she might be good for Silver Creek. The children need someone like her."

"We'll see," Jack replied, but he hoped his sister was right.

As they entered the foyer, Jack heard the piano from the parlor—a simple melody, played with more enthusiasm than skill. He and Charlotte exchanged surprised glances. No one had played the piano since their mother had lost interest in music after Charlotte's birth.

They tiptoed to the parlor doorway. Sarah sat at the piano, her back to them, playing a hymn Jack recognized from his childhood. Emma Reynolds sat beside her on the bench, watching Sarah's hands with rapt attention.

"You try now," Sarah was saying, guiding Emma's small fingers to the keys. "Just like I showed you."

Emma played a simple scale, her face lighting up when she completed it without a mistake. "I did it, Miss Williams!"

"You certainly did," Sarah said warmly. "You're a natural, Emma. With practice, you'll be playing beautifully in no time."

"Pa says music is a waste of time," Emma said, her smile fading. "Says it won't put food on the table."

"Perhaps not," Sarah conceded. "But it feeds the soul, which is just as important. Don't you think?"

Emma nodded solemnly. "That's what my ma used to say. She sang all the time, even when she was sick."

Sarah placed a gentle hand on the girl's shoulder. "Then every time you play, you'll remember her. That's a gift beyond measure."

Jack felt a tightness in his chest at the exchange. His own mother had once told him something similar about music being food for the soul. It was a memory he hadn't recalled in years.

Charlotte cleared her throat, alerting them to their presence. Sarah and Emma turned, startled.

"I'm sorry," Sarah said, rising quickly. "I hope you don't mind. Emma came by for a visit, and when she saw the piano..."

"Not at all," Charlotte assured her. "It's lovely to hear Mother's piano being played again. It's been years."

Emma scrambled off the bench, suddenly shy in Jack's presence. "I should go, Miss Williams. Pa will wonder where I am."

"I'll walk you to the door," Sarah said, then glanced at Jack. "Unless you needed to speak with her, Mr. Montgomery?"

Jack shook his head. "No, but it's getting dark. Perhaps I should escort Emma home."

"Oh, you don't have to do that," Emma said quickly. "I know the way. I come up here all the time to get eggs from Mrs. Montgomery."

Jack gave a small nod, relieved. He never knew what to say to children. Their open faces and easy trust only made the weight on his chest press harder. "All right then," he said. "Just mind your step."

Emma nodded and followed Sarah to the front door. Charlotte excused herself to speak with the cook about dinner, leaving Jack alone in the parlor. He approached the piano, running his fingers lightly over the keys his mother had once played so beautifully.

"She's a thoughtful little thing," Sarah said from the doorway.

Jack nodded. "Mr. Henley says she's always got her nose in something—letters, maps, old almanacs."

Sarah smiled as she traced one of the worn keys. "She has that look in her eyes. Like the world's a book and she's just waiting to turn the page. Reminds me a little of myself when I was young."

"Were you raised in Denver?" Jack asked.

"Yes, though in much humbler circumstances than this," Sarah said, gesturing to the elegant parlor. "My father was a mining engineer before he left for the southern claims. My mother taught me at home until I was old enough for school."

"And now you're the teacher," Jack observed.

A small smile curved her lips. "Life has a way of coming full circle, doesn't it? Though I never imagined I'd end up in a place like Silver Creek."

"Are you disappointed?" The question slipped out before Jack could consider it.

Sarah looked surprised. "No, not at all. It's different from Denver, but there's something... honest about Silver Creek. The people seem genuine. In Denver, especially after mother fell ill, I often felt invisible. Here, I've been noticed, for better or worse."

"Small towns can be overly curious about newcomers," Jack warned. "Not always kindly."

"I've already gathered that from Mrs. Parker at the general store," Sarah said with a slight laugh. "She had quite a few questions about my background when Charlotte introduced us."

Jack grimaced. "Abigail Parker could extract information from a stone. I apologize if she made you uncomfortable."

"Not at all. I have nothing to hide," Sarah said, then hesitated. "Though I am curious about one thing."

"Yes?"

"The piano," she said, touching the polished wood. "Charlotte mentioned it belonged to your mother, but she seemed surprised to hear it being played. Does Mrs. Montgomery no longer play?"

Jack stiffened, uncomfortable with the personal question. "No, not for many years."

He expected Sarah to press for more details, as most would, but she simply nodded. "I hope my playing didn't bring up painful memories. It was presumptuous of me to use it without asking."

"It didn't," Jack said, though it wasn't entirely true. "And you're welcome to play it. It's sat silent for too long."

Sarah studied him for a moment, as if trying to determine the sincerity of his permission. "Thank you. Music has always been a comfort to me, especially when I was caring for my mother."

Something in her tone made Jack think there was more to that story, but before he could ask, Charlotte returned to announce dinner was ready.

Throughout the meal, Jack watched Sarah more carefully than he'd intended. She spoke easily with Charlotte about books and music, occasionally including his mother in the conversation with respectful questions about Silver Creek's history. To Jack's surprise, his mother seemed to warm slightly to Sarah, sharing stories about the town's early days when Thomas had first struck silver.

"It must have been challenging to build a life in such a remote location," Sarah said, her genuine interest clear.

"It was," Eleanor acknowledged. "But Thomas was determined to create not just a mine, but a community. He believed strongly in his responsibilities as an employer and a civic leader."

"That's admirable," Sarah said. "It's clear his vision lives on in Silver Creek. The town has a sense of purpose that many larger cities lack."

Jack felt a swell of pride at her words, though he knew the reality was more complicated. Silver Creek had its share of problems, many of which fell to him to resolve as the town's largest employer and most prominent citizen.

"Jack has continued his father's work," Charlotte said proudly. "The Montgomery Mine employs half the men in town, and Jack ensures they're treated fairly."

"Charlotte," Jack said warningly, uncomfortable with the praise.

"It's true," Charlotte insisted. "You should have seen how angry he was when he discovered Blackwood's mine wasn't providing proper supports in the tunnels. He reported them to the territorial inspector."

Jack noticed Sarah's interest piqued at the mention of Blackwood. "Is that the man who wanted to buy your north claim?" she asked.

"You've heard of him already?" Jack asked, surprised.

"Charlotte mentioned him this morning," Sarah explained. "I saw him in town today. Tall man, expensively dressed, with a rather intimidating manner?"

"Yes, that would be Cyrus Blackwood," Eleanor confirmed. "He arrived in Silver Creek five years ago and has been acquiring mining interests ever since."

"Not always by the most straightforward means," Jack added darkly.

"Jack," Eleanor admonished. "We shouldn't speak ill of our neighbors to Miss Williams. She'll think we're terrible gossips."

"It's not gossip if it's fact, Mother," Jack countered. "Blackwood has been trying to undermine our operation since he arrived. Miss Williams should know his character if she's to live in Silver Creek."

"It sounds as though there's quite a history there," Sarah observed carefully.

Jack hesitated, aware that he'd said more than he'd intended. "Business rivalries can become personal in a town this size," he said finally. "It's nothing for you to concern yourself with."

Sarah nodded, though Jack could see she was curious about the obvious tension the subject had created. Thankfully, Charlotte changed the topic to the upcoming church social, and the rest of the meal passed without incident.

After dinner, Jack excused himself to return to his work, retreating to his office where he could compose his thoughts. He hadn't meant to bring up Blackwood at dinner, but the man's name always triggered his anger. If August's report about strangers near the north claim was accurate, it would be just like Blackwood to resort to underhanded tactics to gain information about the new vein.

A soft knock interrupted his brooding. "Come in," he called, expecting Charlotte or his mother.

Instead, Sarah appeared in the doorway, a book clutched in her hands. "I'm sorry to disturb you," she said. "Charlotte said I might find you here."

Jack stood, surprised by her visit. "Is everything all right?"

"Yes, of course. I just..." She hesitated, then held up the book. "I found this in your father's library and wondered if I might borrow it. Charlotte said it would be fine, but since it's about mining, I thought I should ask you directly."

Jack recognized the leather-bound volume—one of his father's books on modern mining techniques. "You're interested in mining?" he asked skeptically.

"I thought it might help me better understand my students' lives," Sarah explained. "Many of them will follow their fathers into the mines. If I understand their world, perhaps I can make their education more relevant to their futures."

Jack was struck by her thoughtfulness. Most teachers he'd known focused solely on their prescribed curriculum, with little thought for how their students would apply that knowledge.

"Of course you may borrow it," he said, gesturing for her to enter. "Though it's rather technical in parts."

"I'm not unfamiliar with the subject," Sarah said, stepping into the office. "My father used to discuss his work with me. He believed girls should understand such things just as well as boys."

"An unusual perspective," Jack commented, genuinely intrigued.

"He was an unusual man," Sarah said, a hint of sadness in her voice. "Before he left, that is."

Jack indicated a chair across from his desk. "Would you like to sit? I actually have some simpler materials that might better serve your purpose."

Sarah hesitated, then took the offered seat. "I wouldn't want to take up your time."

"It's no trouble." Jack moved to a bookshelf and selected a slimmer volume with illustrations. "This explains the basic principles without the engineering details. My father used it to introduce me to the business when I was a boy."

He handed her the book, their fingers brushing briefly in the exchange. Jack was startled by the jolt he felt at the contact and quickly withdrew his hand.

"Thank you," Sarah said, apparently unaware of his reaction. She opened the book, examining an illustration of a mine shaft. "This is perfect. I can use these diagrams to show the children how the mining process works."

"They'll appreciate that," Jack said, resuming his seat. "Especially the boys who will likely work in the mines someday."

"Not all of them will become miners," Sarah said, looking up from the book. "Some might discover other talents or interests through their education."

"In Silver Creek, options are limited," Jack pointed out. "The mine is the lifeblood of this town."

"Perhaps," Sarah conceded. "But education opens doors that might otherwise remain closed. That's why I believe so strongly in making it accessible to all children, regardless of their circumstances."

Her passion for teaching was clear, reminding Jack of his father's equal passion for developing Silver Creek. There was something compelling about a person driven by genuine conviction.

"You speak as though from experience," he observed.

Sarah smiled slightly. "My mother believed education saved me from a life of servitude. When my father left and she became ill, I was able to support us through tutoring at Denver's Franklin School because of the education she'd insisted upon."

"She sounds like a remarkable woman."

"She was," Sarah said softly. "Her faith sustained her through everything, even at the end." She ran her fingers along the edge of the book. "I'm trying to honor that faith by making my own way now."

The mention of faith created a familiar tension in Jack's chest, but he found himself unwilling to close the conversation as he usually did when the subject arose.

"And you believe God led you to Silver Creek?" he asked, keeping his tone neutral.

"I do," Sarah said simply. "Though I admit I questioned His plan when I first arrived and found the schoolhouse in ruins."

A smile tugged at Jack's lips despite himself. "I can imagine that was discouraging."

"It was," Sarah admitted with a small laugh. "But my mother always said God works in mysterious ways. Perhaps there was a reason I needed to stay here, with your family, rather than move directly into the teacher's quarters."

That God might have orchestrated their meeting struck Jack as both presumptuous and oddly compelling. He'd rejected such notions of divine intervention after the accident, unable to reconcile a loving God with the tragedy that had claimed Matthew's life. Yet there was something in Sarah's quiet certainty that gave him pause.

Before he could respond, Charlotte appeared in the doorway. "There you are, Sarah! Mother and I were wondering if you'd like to join us for tea in the parlor."

"Of course," Sarah said, rising from her chair. She held up the book Jack had given her. "Thank you for this, Mr. Montgomery. It's exactly what I needed."

"You're welcome," Jack said, standing as well. "If you have questions about it, feel free to ask."

"I will," Sarah promised, then followed Charlotte from the room.

Jack remained standing for a moment after they left, struck by the unexpected turn the evening had taken. He'd intended to keep his distance from Sarah Williams, to view her merely as a temporary inconvenience until the schoolhouse was repaired. Instead, he found himself intrigued by her intelligence, her dedication to teaching, and the quiet strength that seemed to sustain her despite her losses.

It was precisely this kind of distraction he didn't need, with Blackwood circling the north claim and security concerns demanding his attention. Yet as Jack returned to his desk and the work waiting there, he wondered what other surprises the new schoolteacher might have in store during her stay in his home.

And, more troublingly, why he was looking forward to discovering them.

FIVE

Sarah woke early the next morning, eager to look at the damaged schoolhouse again, and then plan her lessons. After a quick breakfast alone, she gathered her notebook, pencils, and the mining book Jack had lent her, tucking them into a small satchel.

Mrs. Finch, the housekeeper, caught her at the front door. "Miss Williams, are you going out?"

"Yes, to the schoolhouse. I want to see what can be salvaged and begin organizing my classroom."

"But it's not safe there," Mrs. Finch protested. "The roof could collapse further."

"I'll be careful," Sarah promised. "I won't go into any damaged areas."

Mrs. Finch didn't look convinced but nodded reluctantly. "At least take an umbrella. There are clouds gathering to the west."

Sarah accepted the offered umbrella gratefully. "Thank you, Mrs. Finch. Please tell the Montgomerys not to worry if I'm not back for lunch. I have a lot to do."

The morning air was crisp as Sarah made her way down the hill toward town. Silver Creek was already bustling with activity—miners heading to their shifts, shopkeepers sweeping their storefronts, wagons delivering goods. Several people nodded or tipped their hats to her as she passed, and Sarah returned their greetings warmly. Despite her brief time in Silver Creek, she was already recognizing faces.

When she reached the schoolhouse, Sarah stood for a moment surveying the damage. In the clear morning light, it looked even worse than it had the day before. The roof had collapsed on the far side, and debris littered the yard. Still, the primary structure appeared sound, and the damage seemed confined to one section.

Sarah circled the building, looking for the safest entrance. The front door was partially blocked by fallen timber, but a side door near the teacher's quarters seemed accessible. She tried the handle and found it unlocked.

Inside, she found herself in a small hallway that connected the teacher's quarters to the main classroom. To her left was a door leading to what would be her future living space, and straight ahead, an open doorway led into the classroom proper.

Sarah stepped into the classroom first, where dust motes danced in the shafts of sunlight streaming through the windows. The room was in disarray—desks overturned, books scattered across the floor, water damage from the rain staining one wall. But it wasn't as bad as she'd feared. Much could be salvaged.

Sarah set her satchel on the teacher's desk, which remained intact, and began taking inventory. She found several readers still in usable condition, a box of slates that had been protected by a fallen shelf, and a cabinet of supplies that appeared untouched. She made notes in her notebook, creating lists of what could be used and what needed replacement.

After examining the classroom, Sarah ventured carefully toward the teacher's quarters. The door was stuck, requiring a firm push to open. Inside, she found a simple but comfortable space—a small sitting room with an adjoining bedroom and a tiny kitchen. This area had suffered minimal damage, mostly water stains on the ceiling where rain had leaked through the damaged roof.

"My future home," Sarah murmured to herself, running her hand along a dusty shelf. It wasn't luxurious by any means, but it was hers—a place where she could build her independence.

She returned to the classroom and began clearing debris, eager to make tangible progress. She was so absorbed in her work that she didn't hear the approach of footsteps until a small voice called out.

"Miss Williams?"

Sarah turned to find Emma standing in the doorway, her pigtails slightly askew and her dress smudged with dirt.

"Emma! What are you doing here?"

"I saw you come in," Emma said, shuffling her feet. "I wanted to help. Pa's at work in the mine, and I don't have any chores until later."

Sarah smiled warmly. "I'd welcome the help, but are you sure your father wouldn't mind?"

"He won't mind," Emma said confidently. "He said it's good I'm excited about school starting." She glanced around at the mess. "It sure is awful in here."

"It looks worse than it is," Sarah assured her. "Many things can be salvaged. Would you like to help me sort the books?"

Emma nodded eagerly, and they set to work, creating piles of books that could be cleaned and reused. As they worked, Sarah asked Emma about her interests and what she'd been learning before the previous teacher left.

"She mostly had us copy Bible verses and do sums," Emma said, carefully wiping dust from a reader. "She was nice but didn't make it interesting like you did with the piano yesterday."

"Well, I believe learning should be enjoyable as well as useful," Sarah said. "What subjects do you like best?"

"Reading," Emma answered promptly. "And stories about faraway places. Grandpa gives me newspapers from big cities sometimes. I like reading about what happens there."

"That's wonderful, Emma. A good reader can learn about the entire world." Sarah handed her another book to clean. "And what about your other subjects? Mathematics? Science?"

Emma wrinkled her nose. "Sums are hard sometimes. And we didn't do much science except for what's in the Bible about creation."

"Science helps us understand God's creation better," Sarah explained. "For instance, do you know why the rain falls or how plants grow?"

Emma considered this. "Pa says rain is God's way of watering His garden."

"That's a lovely way of thinking about it. And God created natural laws that govern how rain forms in clouds and falls to earth. Understanding those laws helps us appreciate His wisdom even more."

As they continued working, Emma told Sarah about the other children who would be her students. Besides the Garrett brothers, there were the Cooper twins who were always causing mischief, and Ethan Blackwood, the nephew of the mine owner who thought himself better that the other children.

"No one really likes Ethan," Emma confided. "He's mean sometimes, especially to the younger kids."

"Perhaps he's just unsure how to make friends," Sarah suggested, though she mentally noted this potential challenge. "Sometimes children who act unkindly are actually lonely or sad inside."

By midday, they had made significant progress. The classroom was cleaner, books and supplies were sorted, and Sarah had a better understanding of what would be needed for her lessons.

"Look, Miss Williams! I found a map!" Emma exclaimed, pulling a rolled paper from behind a bookshelf.

Sarah helped her unroll it, revealing a faded but still usable map of the United States. "This is perfect, Emma. We can use this for geography lessons."

A distant rumble of thunder interrupted their work. Sarah glanced out the window to see dark clouds gathering. "I think we should finish up soon. That storm is moving in quickly."

"Pa says the storms come fast in the mountains," Emma nodded, helping Sarah gather the salvaged books into a crate.

"Your father sounds very wise," Sarah said, closing her notebook. "I look forward to meeting him."

"He works hard in Mr. Montgomery's mine," Emma said proudly. "He's a blaster—that means he sets the explosives to break up the rock so they can get to the silver."

"That's an important job," Sarah said. "It must require great skill and care."

"Pa says it's dangerous but good pay," Emma replied matter-of-factly. "And Mr. Montgomery makes sure everything's safe. Not like Mr. Blackwood's mine where the men get hurt more."

Sarah was struck by the child's candid assessment of the two mine owners. "You seem to think highly of Mr. Montgomery."

"Everybody does," Emma said. "Well, except Mr. Blackwood. Pa says they don't get along 'cause Mr. Montgomery won't sell him the north claim where there's lots of silver."

Another rumble of thunder, closer now, punctuated Emma's words. Sarah gathered her satchel. "We should really get going before the rain starts."

They quickly finished organizing the salvaged materials, and Sarah made a final note of items she would need for teaching. The sky had darkened considerably by the time they were ready to leave.

"I'll walk you home first, Emma," Sarah said as they stepped outside. "Then I'll head back to the Montgomery house."

"I live on Cedar Street, near the livery," Emma said. "It's not far."

The first fat drops of rain fell as they hurried down the schoolhouse steps. Sarah opened the umbrella Mrs. Finch had given her, holding it over both of them. They had just reached the bottom step when the skies opened in earnest, rain pouring down in sheets.

"We should hurry!" Sarah called over the downpour.

In her haste, she didn't notice the slick mud at the base of the steps. Her foot slid suddenly, and she felt a sharp pain shoot through her ankle as it twisted beneath her. Sarah cried out, dropping the umbrella as she fell awkwardly to the ground.

"Miss Williams!" Emma exclaimed, kneeling beside her. "Are you hurt?"

Sarah tried to stand but gasped as weight on her injured ankle sent pain shooting up her leg. "I think I've twisted my ankle. It's nothing serious, just painful."

The rain continued to pour down, soaking them both. Sarah tried again to stand, using a railing for support, but her ankle protested sharply.

"I'll get help," Emma decided, her young face set with determination. "You stay here under the overhang."

"Emma, wait—" But the girl was already dashing off, pigtails bouncing as she ran through the downpour.

Sarah dragged herself back up the few steps to shelter under the schoolhouse overhang, wincing at the pain in her ankle. She felt foolish for having been so careless. What a fine impression she was making. The new teacher who couldn't even navigate a simple set of stairs!

The rain continued to pound down, creating rivulets that ran down the street. Sarah shivered in her damp dress, hoping Emma wouldn't go all the way to the Montgomery house for help. It would be too far for the child in this weather.

Just as she was considering attempting to limp to the nearest building, Sarah saw Emma returning accompanied by Jack Montgomery. He wore an oilskin coat and wide-brimmed hat, but even from a distance, Sarah could see the concern on his face.

"Miss Williams!" he called as they approached. "Emma says you've fallen."

Sarah felt heat rise in her cheeks despite the cool rain. "It's nothing serious, Mr. Montgomery. Just a twisted ankle. I was careless on the wet steps."

Jack kneeled beside her, his expression serious as he examined her ankle. "May I?" he asked, his hands hovering near her foot.

Sarah nodded, and he gently removed her boot, his touch careful and clinical. "Can you move your toes?" he asked.

She tried and winced slightly.

"That's good," he said. "It doesn't appear to be broken, but it's already swelling. You shouldn't walk on it." He glanced at the relentless downpour. "We need to get you out of this rain before you catch a chill."

"I can manage with some help," Sarah insisted, not wanting to be a burden.

Jack shook his head firmly. "Absolutely not. Putting weight on it now will only make it worse." Before Sarah could protest further, he turned to Emma. "Run to Dr. Martinez's office. Tell him Miss Williams has injured her ankle and ask him to come to the Montgomery house when he's able."

Emma nodded and dashed off again, seemingly unbothered by the rain.

"Now," Jack said, turning back to Sarah, "with your permission, I'm going to carry you home."

Sarah's eyes widened. "Mr. Montgomery, that's not necessary. Perhaps I could wait here until the rain subsides, or—"

"Miss Williams," Jack interrupted, his tone gentler than she'd heard from him before, "you're already soaked through, and that ankle needs proper attention. Please allow me to help you."

Something in his expression, a mix of concern and determination, made any further protest seem futile. Sarah nodded reluctantly.

Jack positioned himself beside her. "Put your arm around my neck," he instructed.

Sarah did as he asked, acutely aware of their proximity as he carefully lifted her into his arms. She was not a small woman, but he carried her with apparent ease, his arms secure around her.

"I apologize for the impropriety," he said as he stepped into the rain, sheltering her as much as possible with his body.

"Under the circumstances, I believe even the strictest etiquette would allow an exception," Sarah replied, trying to keep her tone light despite her discomfort—both physical and at their intimate position.

As Jack carried her through the rain-slicked streets, Sarah couldn't help but notice the strength in his arms and the careful way he moved to avoid jostling her injured ankle. For a man who presented such a stern facade to the world, his gentle handling surprised her.

Several townspeople stopped and stared as they passed, and Sarah felt her cheeks burn with embarrassment. What a spectacle they must make—the new schoolteacher being carried through town in the arms of Jack Montgomery!

"People are staring," she murmured.

"Let them," Jack replied simply. "Your well-being is more important than gossip."

The journey up the hill to the Montgomery house seemed endless. By the time they reached the front porch, both were thoroughly soaked despite Jack's rain gear. Mrs. Finch opened the door with a gasp.

"Goodness gracious! What happened?"

"Miss Williams took a fall at the schoolhouse," Jack explained, carrying Sarah inside. "Please prepare a fire in the downstairs guest room and bring hot water and clean towels."

Mrs. Finch hurried off to do as instructed while Jack carried Sarah to a small but comfortable room off the main hallway. He set her down carefully on a chaise lounge.

"Thank you," Sarah said, feeling oddly breathless. "I'm sorry to have caused such trouble."

"It's no trouble," Jack assured her, his usual reserve softened by concern. "I was inspecting damage to the mercantile roof when Emma found me. Fortunate timing."

Mrs. Finch returned with towels and a basin of hot water, followed by Charlotte, who exclaimed in distress at Sarah's condition.

"Oh, my goodness! Sarah, what happened? You're soaked through!"

"I slipped on the schoolhouse steps," Sarah explained. "Your brother was kind enough to bring me home."

"Jack, you should change out of those wet clothes," Charlotte said practically. "I'll help Sarah."

Jack nodded, but before leaving, he kneeled and carefully placed a small pillow under Sarah's injured ankle. "Keep it elevated," he instructed. "And don't try to walk on it until Dr. Martinez has examined it."

After Jack left, Charlotte helped Sarah change into a dry nightgown and robe, exclaiming over the swelling of her ankle. Mrs. Finch built up the fire, creating a cozy warmth in the small room.

"Such a fright you must have had," Charlotte said, brushing Sarah's damp hair. "But how fortunate Jack was nearby."

"Yes," Sarah agreed. "I don't know what I would have done otherwise."

"Jack may seem stern, but he's always been the first to help someone in need," Charlotte said, a hint of pride in her voice. "After father died, he took care of everything, including me and Mother."

Sarah was touched by Charlotte's obvious admiration for her brother. "He seems to take his responsibilities seriously."

"Too seriously, sometimes," Charlotte sighed. "He rarely allows himself any enjoyment. It's been that way since the accident."

Sarah remembered Reverend Wilson's mention of an accident that had taken Jack's best friend's life. Before she could ask more, there was a knock at the door.

"May I come in?" Jack called.

"Yes," Charlotte replied.

Jack entered, now dressed in dry clothes. He was accompanied by a gray-haired man carrying a medical bag.

"Miss Williams, this is Dr. Martinez," Jack introduced.

"I understand you've had a fall," the doctor said kindly, setting his bag down beside the chaise. "Let's have a look at that ankle, shall we?"

As the doctor examined her, Sarah noticed Jack hovering near the doorway, his expression concerned. His attentiveness moved her.

"A moderate sprain," Dr. Martinez pronounced finally. "Not severe, but you should stay off it for at least three days. Keep it elevated, apply cold compresses several times a day to reduce the swelling, and then warm compresses after the first day."

"Three days?" Sarah repeated, dismayed. "But I need to prepare for classes. The children—"

"Will still be there when you've healed," the doctor interrupted firmly. "Pushing yourself now will only prolong your recovery."

"Dr. Martinez is right," Jack said from the doorway. "The school preparations can wait."

Sarah wanted to argue, but knew they were right. "Very well," she conceded reluctantly.

Dr. Martinez prepared a tonic for pain and left additional instructions with Charlotte before departing. As Charlotte prepared to leave as well, promising to bring Sarah some books to pass the time, Jack stepped forward.

"A moment, if I may," he said to Sarah.

Charlotte gave them a curious look but left the room, closing the door partially behind her.

Jack approached the chaise, his expression unreadable. "How are you feeling?"

"Better, thank you," Sarah said. "Though I feel foolish for being so careless."

"Accidents happen," Jack said simply. "Even to the most careful among us."

The weight in his voice made Sarah think of what Reverend Wilson had told her about the mining accident and Jack's guilt. She chose not to press the painful subject.

"I understand you have some medical knowledge," she said. "You knew exactly what to check before Dr. Martinez arrived."

A shadow crossed Jack's face. "When you're responsible for a mine, you see your share of injuries. I've learned what to look for."

"It must be a heavy responsibility," Sarah said quietly.

Jack's gaze met hers, and for a moment, Sarah glimpsed vulnerability beneath his composed exterior. "Yes," he admitted. "Sometimes unbearably so."

The confession, simple as it was, seemed to surprise them both. Jack straightened, his expression closing once more. "You should rest. Ring the bell if you need anything. Mrs. Finch will hear it."

"Thank you again, Mr. Montgomery," Sarah said. "Not just for carrying me home, but for your kindness."

Jack paused at the door, looking back at her with an expression she couldn't quite interpret. "Few would describe me as kind, Miss Williams."

"Perhaps they haven't been paying proper attention," Sarah replied softly.

Something flickered in his eyes—surprise, perhaps, or a brief glimpse of the man beneath the stern exterior. Then he nodded once and left, closing the door gently behind him.

Sarah leaned back against the pillows, her ankle throbbing dully despite Dr. Martinez's tonic. The events of the day played through her mind—the damaged schoolhouse, Emma's helpful chatter, the sudden rainstorm, and most vividly, the feeling of being carried in Jack Montgomery's powerful arms.

She had come to Silver Creek to build a new life, to find purpose after her mother's death. A simple fall had shown her an unexpected side of Jack Montgomery's character—gentleness beneath his stern exterior.

"Lord," she prayed quietly, "thank You for Your constant care, even in unexpected forms. Please help me use this time of confinement wisely and guide me in understanding this place and these people You've brought into my life."

With that prayer on her lips, Sarah drifted into a restful sleep, the sound of rain against the windows creating a soothing rhythm to carry her into dreams.

Six

J ack sat at his desk, still thinking about the events of the past few days—Sarah's fall at the schoolhouse, carrying her home through the rain, the way she'd felt so fragile in his arms despite her obvious strength of character. Dr. Martinez had assured them the injury wasn't serious, but Jack found himself concerned about her recovery.

A knock sounded on the door, interrupting his thoughts. He looked up to find Sheriff Taylor standing in the doorway, his hat in hand and a frown etched deep into his weathered face.

"Jack," the sheriff said, stepping inside uninvited. "Got a moment?"

Jack gestured to the chair across from his desk. "Always. What's on your mind, Sam?"

The sheriff sat, glancing out the window toward the direction of the north claim. "I've been hearing things. Miners talking about strangers on your land at night. And this morning we had something concrete. Someone tampered with your pump system overnight. Jenkins reported it delayed work for three hours."

Jack leaned forward. "We've suspected sabotage for weeks. You told me you couldn't act without proof."

Taylor sighed. "I still can't arrest a man based on shadows and gossip. But I got something more today." He reached into his coat pocket and laid a small, twisted piece of metal on Jack's desk.

"What's this?"

"A fuse casing. Found near the supply shed after the pump incident. Not yours and definitely not standard issue for this region. My guess is it's Union stock, brought up from New Mexico or Arizona. Someone's importing blasting gear that doesn't belong."

Jack studied the casing, his pulse quickening. "Blackwood."

"Can't say that yet," the sheriff said cautiously. "But he's the only one with the motive and the money to get this kind of equipment out here quiet-like. With that schoolteacher of yours new in town, I'd keep an eye out. Someone with a fresh pair of eyes and no history here? She's liable to ask the wrong person the wrong thing, and Blackwood has a way of making curiosity cost."

Jack's jaw tightened. "He's trying to shake confidence in Montgomery Mining. Undermining the school, spreading rumors, and now this."

The sheriff stood. "That's why I'm telling you this now. I'm not ready to drag Blackwood in just yet, but I am assigning two deputies to keep an eye on the north claim. And if he makes another move, we'll be ready."

Jack nodded. "Thank you, Sam."

"Keep your people close, Jack. That includes Miss Williams. Blackwood plays dirty, and I don't think he'll mind dragging her name through the mud if it serves his end."

"He won't touch her," Jack said coldly.

Taylor gave him a sharp look, then pulled his hat back on. "See that he doesn't."

The moment the door shut behind the sheriff, Jack sat back, the fuse casing still on his desk. He turned it over once, the metal cool against his palm. Blackwood was making moves, and now the sheriff had confirmed it. Whatever came next, Jack had to be ready.

***

Jack stood at the edge of the damaged schoolhouse roof, watching as his workers installed new support beams. The sun beat down on his shoulders, but he barely noticed the heat. His mind was elsewhere—specifically, on the young woman currently recovering in his home.

"We'll have the roof sealed by tomorrow, Mr. Montgomery," Tony Jenkins, his head carpenter, called up to him. "But the interior repairs will take longer."

"How much longer?" Jack asked, his voice sharper than he'd intended.

Jenkins looked surprised at his tone. "At least ten days, maybe more. Unless..."

"Unless what?"

"Unless you want us to bring in more men from the mine. Could cut the time in half, but it would slow production."

Jack considered this, weighing the options. Normally, he would never divert workers from the mine for a town project. The mine was the priority—always had been, always would be. Yet he nodded.

"Do it. I want this completed as quickly as possible."

Jenkins raised his eyebrows but knew better than to question his employer. "Yes, sir. I'll make the arrangements."

Jack climbed down from the roof, brushing dust from his hands. He wasn't entirely sure why he'd made that decision. Was it truly to help Sarah begin her teaching duties sooner, or was it to hasten her move from his home? The question unsettled him, as did his preoccupation with her well-being.

It had been two days since her fall, and though Dr. Martinez reported her ankle was healing well, she had graduated from complete bed rest to spending her afternoons in the library or parlor with her foot elevated. Jack had stopped by more often than necessary, ostensibly to check on her progress but truthfully because her company offered a curious respite from his usual concerns.

As he walked back toward his house, Jack spotted August heading toward him from the direction of the mine.

"Mr. Montgomery," August greeted him. "I was just coming to find you. About this morning's incident at the north claim."

Jack's jaw tightened. "Any leads on who might be responsible?"

"Nothing concrete. Whoever did it knew what they were doing. They got in and out clean." August lowered his voice. "The men are saying it's Blackwood's doing."

"We need proof before making accusations," Jack said, though he harbored little doubt himself. "Double the night guard and install those new locks we ordered. The sheriff's promised to have some of his men keep an eye out, too."

"Already done," August assured him. "But there's something else. One of our men spotted Blackwood himself near our property line yesterday afternoon. Said he was studying our operation through a spyglass."

Jack's hands clenched. "Legal, unfortunately, as long as he stays on public land."

"Legal, maybe. Ethical, no." August shook his head. "The man's up to something, Jack. We both know it."

Jack nodded grimly. "Keep me informed of any further incidents. And August—" he hesitated, then continued. "I'm reassigning some miners to help with the schoolhouse repairs. We need it completed faster."

Surprise flickered across August's weathered face. "The schoolhouse? That's a change of priorities."

"It's important for the town," Jack said, avoiding his foreman's knowing gaze. "The children need their education."

"Of course," August agreed, though his slight smile suggested he understood more than Jack had said. "And nothing to do with a certain schoolteacher currently living in your home?"

"That will be all, August," Jack said firmly.

The foreman touched his hat respectfully, though amusement lingered in his eyes as he turned back toward the mine. Jack watched him go, irritated by the man's perception. Was he so transparent that even August could see his growing interest in Sarah Williams?

The thought troubled him all the way home. He had built careful walls around himself since Matthew's death, focusing solely on his responsibilities to the mine, his family, and the town. There was no room for personal entanglements, especially not with a woman who wore her faith as openly as Sarah did.

When he arrived home, the house was unusually quiet. His mother was visiting a friend, and Charlotte would likely be in the garden at this hour. Jack removed his hat and dusty coat, then found himself drawn toward the library where he suspected Sarah would be reading.

He paused in the doorway and found her settled in the large armchair near the window, her injured ankle propped on a footstool, a book in her lap. Afternoon sunlight streamed through the window, catching the auburn highlights in her hair. She looked peaceful, absorbed in her reading.

"I hope I'm not disturbing you," Jack said quietly.

Sarah looked up with a smile. "Not at all, Mr. Montgomery. I was just exploring your father's collection. He had excellent taste in literature."

Jack entered the room, noting the book in her hands—a volume of Tennyson's poetry. "Father was well-read for a mining man. Mother used to tease him about his 'impractical' interests."

"There's nothing impractical about feeding the mind and soul," Sarah said. "Some of the most successful people I've known have been those who read widely."

Jack took a seat in the chair across from her, maintaining appropriate distance. "How is your ankle feeling today?"

"Much better, thank you. Dr. Martinez says I should be able to walk normally by tomorrow, though I'm to avoid any strenuous activity for another few days." She gestured to the library around them. "I've been thoroughly enjoying this enforced leisure, actually. When did you last have time to simply sit and read for pleasure?"

The question caught Jack off guard. He couldn't remember the last time he'd read anything that wasn't related to mining reports or business correspondence. "It's been some time," he admitted.

"That's a shame. My mother always said that we become less than ourselves when we forget to tend our inner lives as well as our outer responsibilities."

There was something about her tone, not preachy or condescending, but genuinely concerned, that made Jack consider her words seriously. "It sounds like your mother was remarkably insightful."

"She was," Sarah agreed, a hint of sadness crossing her features. "Though I sometimes wonder if she was too trusting, too willing to believe the best of people."

Jack heard an undertone in her voice, but before he could probe further, Charlotte's voice carried from the hallway.

"Jack? Are you home?"

"In the library," he called back.

Charlotte appeared in the doorway moments later. "Oh good, you're both here. Jack, I was just speaking with Mrs. Harless. She wanted to know when school might start."

"The repairs should be completed within the week," Jack replied. "I've assigned additional workers to speed the process."

Sarah looked surprised. "Additional workers? Won't that affect operations at the mine?"

"The mine can spare them," Jack assured her. "The children's education is important to the town's future."

"That's very generous of you," Sarah said, her gaze direct in a way that made Jack wonder if she saw through his practical justification to the personal motivation beneath.

Charlotte glanced between them with barely concealed interest. "Sarah, you mentioned wanting to see Father's books on local history. Perhaps Jack could show you the section on Silver Creek's founding? It's quite fascinating."

"I'd like that," Sarah said, looking to Jack.

Jack rose and moved to a section of shelves near the window. "Father documented the early days quite thoroughly." He pulled down a leather-bound journal. "This contains his account of discovering the first silver vein."

As he handed her the book, their fingers brushed briefly. The contact was fleeting but sent an unexpected jolt through Jack. Sarah's eyes met his for a moment, and he wondered if she had felt it too.

"Thank you," she said softly, opening the journal carefully.

Charlotte cleared her throat. "I should check on dinner preparations. Jack, you'll keep Sarah company while she reads, won't you? These old books can be quite delicate."

Before Jack could protest, Charlotte had slipped out, leaving them alone but properly in an open room where anyone might enter. Her matchmaking efforts were becoming increasingly transparent.

"Your sister is determined to throw us together," Sarah observed with amusement.

Jack felt heat rise in his face. "Charlotte has romantic notions about everything. Please don't feel obligated—"

"I don't," Sarah interrupted gently. "I enjoy your company, Mr. Montgomery. You're not quite as stern as you pretend to be."

The observation surprised him. "Most people find me rather... disagreeable."

"Most people don't look past the surface," Sarah replied, turning a page in the journal. "Oh, this is fascinating. Your father's handwriting is so precise."

Jack found himself drawn to look over her shoulder at the entries. "He was meticulous about record-keeping. Mother used to say he treated that journal like a love letter to the mountain."

"I can see why," Sarah murmured, reading aloud. "'The silver lies like captured starlight in the dark stone, waiting for patient hands to bring it to the light.' He was quite poetic for a mining man."

"Father believed there was beauty in everything, even the hardest work," Jack said, then stopped, surprised by the personal revelation.

Sarah looked up at him. "You miss him very much."

It wasn't a question, and somehow that made it easier to answer honestly. "Every day. Sometimes I wonder if I'm living up to his expectations."

"I imagine he'd be very proud of what you've accomplished," Sarah said quietly. "Silver Creek is thriving, your workers speak of you with respect, and you've maintained his vision while making it your own."

Her words stirred something in Jack—a warmth he hadn't felt in years. "Thank you," he said simply.

They were interrupted by a sharp knock at the front door. Jack frowned, rising from his chair. "Excuse me. I should see who that is."

He left the library, oddly unsettled by the brief exchange. Sarah Williams had a directness about her that penetrated the careful distance he maintained with most people. It was disarming and dangerous to the control he'd maintained since Matthew's death.

Jack opened the front door to find the last person he wanted to see standing on his porch.

"Montgomery," Cyrus Blackwood greeted him with a smile that didn't reach his cold eyes. "I hope I'm not interrupting your evening."

Jack stiffened. "What brings you here, Blackwood?"

"Neighborly concern," Blackwood replied smoothly. "I heard about your... guest's unfortunate accident. I thought I'd pay my respects to the new school-teacher. Welcome her to Silver Creek properly."

Jack doubted Blackwood had ever done anything from "neighborly concern" in his life. "Miss Williams is recovering well, thank you. I'll convey your good wishes."

He began to close the door, but Blackwood placed his foot in the opening. "Actually, I'd prefer to convey them myself. I understand she's quite charming. And I have a nephew who will be in her class."

Jack knew refusing would only pique Blackwood's interest further. Reluctantly, he stepped aside. "A brief visit, then. Miss Williams needs her rest."

"Of course," Blackwood agreed, entering the foyer with the confident stride of a man who believed every door should open for him.

"This way," Jack said curtly, leading him to the library. "Miss Williams? You have a visitor."

Sarah looked up from the journal, her expression immediately becoming more guarded as she took in Blackwood's presence.

"Miss Williams, this is Cyrus Blackwood. He owns the Black Diamond Mine on the south side of town."

Blackwood stepped forward, removing his hat with a flourish. "Miss Williams, it's a pleasure to meet you. I've heard so much about Silver Creek's new teacher."

Sarah straightened in her chair, maintaining her dignity despite her awkward position with her foot elevated. "Mr. Blackwood. How kind of you to call."

"I couldn't let a newcomer to our town suffer without offering my sympathy," Blackwood said smoothly. "Especially one as important as our children's teacher." He turned to Jack. "Montgomery, perhaps some refreshment for your guest and myself?"

The presumption grated on Jack's nerves, but he maintained his composure. "I'll see what can be arranged."

He stepped into the hallway, signaling to Mrs. Finch to bring tea, but remained within earshot. He didn't trust Blackwood alone with Sarah, even for a moment.

"I understand you're from Denver, Miss Williams?" Blackwood was saying. "A considerable change, coming to a small mining town like ours."

"Change can be refreshing, Mr. Blackwood," Sarah replied. "And Silver Creek has been most welcoming."

"Particularly the Montgomerys, it seems," Blackwood observed with a chuckle. "Quite fortunate that Jack was nearby when you fell."

"Yes, it was," Sarah agreed, her tone revealing nothing.

"You must find your current accommodations more comfortable than the teacher's quarters would have been," Blackwood continued. "The Montgomery home is the finest in Silver Creek. A far cry from a schoolteacher's typical lodgings."

Jack detected the subtle condescension in Blackwood's tone, the implication that Sarah was enjoying luxuries above her station. To his surprise, Sarah responded with poised dignity.

"The Montgomerys have been gracious hosts during my recovery, but I look forward to establishing my own household at the schoolhouse. Independence has always been important to me, Mr. Blackwood."

Jack found himself impressed by her response. Neither defensive nor intimidated but firmly establishing her position.

"Independence can be overrated, my dear," Blackwood said with false concern. "A young woman alone in a frontier town... it can be dangerous. If you ever need assistance of any kind, my door is always open."

Jack reentered the room, unwilling to allow Blackwood's insinuations to continue. "Miss Williams has the entire town's support, Blackwood. She'll want for nothing."

Mrs. Finch arrived with tea, providing a momentary distraction from the tension in the room. As she served them, Blackwood turned the conversation to business matters.

"I was sorry to hear about the incident at your north claim today, Montgomery. Equipment failure, wasn't it?"

Jack's eyes narrowed. The tampering had only been discovered that morning, yet Blackwood already knew of it. "News travels fast," he observed.

"Silver Creek is a small town," Blackwood replied with a shrug. "Perhaps if you invested in better equipment, failures wouldn't occur."

"Perhaps if certain individuals respected property boundaries, there would be fewer incidents altogether," Jack countered.

Sarah glanced between them, clearly sensing the undercurrent of hostility. "Mr. Blackwood, have you lived in Silver Creek long?" she asked, deftly changing the subject.

"Five years," Blackwood replied, turning his attention back to her. "Though it feels like home now. I've established deep roots here." He sipped his tea. "Unlike some of our residents who arrive and depart with little warning."

Jack didn't miss the calculating look Blackwood gave Sarah. Was he fishing for information about her background? Did he plan to scare her off? The thought increased his unease.

"Silver Creek is fortunate to have attracted someone of Miss Williams' qualifications," Jack said firmly. "Her commitment to education will benefit the entire community."

"Indeed," Blackwood agreed, though his smile remained cold. "Education is so important, isn't it? Knowing who people really are, where they come from. The truth behind appearances."

Sarah's expression remained composed, though Jack noticed her grip tighten slightly on her teacup. "Truth is certainly valuable, Mr. Blackwood. As is discernment about the sources of our information."

Blackwood's eyes narrowed briefly at the subtle rebuke, then he laughed. "Touché, Miss Williams. I see our children will be learning more than just their letters and numbers under your tutelage."

He stood, placing his hat back on his head. "I've taken enough of your recovery time. I hope to see you at church on Sunday, if your ankle permits."

"Thank you for your visit, Mr. Blackwood," Sarah said politely.

Jack escorted Blackwood to the door, anxious to have him out of his house. At the threshold, Blackwood paused.

"She's quite charming, your little schoolteacher," he said in a low voice. "Though one wonders what brings a young woman of obvious breeding to a place like Silver Creek, especially with no family connections to speak of."

"Miss Williams' background is not your concern, Blackwood," Jack said coldly.

"Perhaps not," Blackwood conceded with a smile that sent a chill down Jack's spine. "But I've always been curious about people's motivations. Especially when they appear in the midst of our business disagreements."

"If you're implying—"

"I'm not implying anything, Montgomery," Blackwood interrupted smoothly. "Merely making an observation. Give your mother and sister my regards, won't you? I look forward to our next meeting."

With that, he descended the porch steps and walked toward his waiting carriage, leaving Jack with a growing sense of disquiet. Blackwood's interest in Sarah was troubling. The man had a talent for finding and exploiting weaknesses—and Jack was uncomfortably aware that he had already begun to care about Sarah's welfare in a way that could be perceived as a vulnerability.

When Jack returned to the library, he found Sarah staring thoughtfully out the window. She looked up as he entered, her expression concerned.

"Mr. Blackwood is an interesting man," she said carefully.

"That's one word for him," Jack replied, taking the seat he had vacated. "I apologize for his intrusion. He rarely does anything without ulterior motives."

"I gathered as much," Sarah said. "His questions appeared intended more for investigation than for simple conversation."

Jack hesitated, then decided she deserved a warning. "Be cautious around Blackwood, Miss Williams. He's not someone to trust."

"May I ask why?" Sarah inquired. "There was significant tension between you."

Jack considered how much to reveal. "We have competing business interests," he said finally. "And different views on how the mining industry should operate in Silver Creek."

"I sense it's more personal than that," Sarah observed quietly.

The perception was unsettling. "Blackwood arrived in Silver Creek shortly after my father's death," Jack explained reluctantly. "He immediately began acquiring smaller mining claims, often using methods that, while technically legal, were ethically questionable."

"And your paths have crossed repeatedly since then?"

"Unfortunately," Jack confirmed. "The Montgomery Mine has been his primary target for years. He particularly wants the north claim, which contains one of the richest silver veins discovered in recent years."

"And you won't sell to him?"

"Never," Jack said firmly. "That claim was my father's last discovery before his death. He was proud of it. I promised him I would develop it properly."

Sarah nodded, understanding in her eyes. "A promise to a parent carries tremendous weight."

Again, her perception caught him off guard. Few understood his sense of obligation to his father's legacy. "Yes, it does," he agreed quietly.

They sat in comfortable silence for a moment before Sarah spoke again. "Thank you for the warning about Mr. Blackwood. I'll be cautious."

"Good," Jack said, rising to leave. "You should rest now. Dr. Martinez mentioned you might be able to join us for dinner tomorrow if your ankle continues to improve."

"I'd like that," Sarah said with a smile that Jack found oddly warming. "Being confined, pleasant as your library is, has made me eager for more varied company."

"Your company has been..." Jack paused, searching for the right words. "Unexpectedly refreshing."

The admission surprised them both. Sarah's eyes widened slightly, and Jack felt heat rise in his face. "I should let you rest," he said quickly, moving toward the door.

"Mr. Montgomery," Sarah called as he reached the doorway. "Thank you for arranging extra workers for the schoolhouse. It means a great deal to me."

Jack nodded, unable to articulate the confusing mix of motives behind that decision. "Good evening, Miss Williams."

"Good evening, Mr. Montgomery."

As Jack left the library, he was troubled by the realization that Blackwood's visit had stirred protective instincts he'd thought long buried. The man's interest in Sarah was concerning, particularly given his talent for uncovering others' vulnerabilities.

More troubling still was Jack's growing awareness that Sarah Williams was becoming important to him in ways he couldn't quite define—and didn't dare examine too closely. He had spent five years carefully constructing barriers around his heart after Matthew's death. Now, a schoolteacher with thoughtful hazel eyes and unwavering faith was somehow finding cracks in those defenses.

SEVEN

"Try putting some weight on it now," Dr. Martinez instructed, supporting Sarah's elbow as she carefully rose from the chaise lounge. "Slowly."

Sarah gingerly placed her injured foot on the floor, wincing slightly as she shifted her weight onto it. The pain was there, but duller now. More of a persistent throb than the sharp agony of three days ago.

"Good," the doctor said approvingly. "The swelling has gone down considerably. You've been following my instructions well."

"Miss Williams has been a model patient," Charlotte said from the doorway. "Though she's champed at the bit to get back to her teaching preparations."

Sarah smiled at her newfound friend. Over the past three days, Charlotte had been a constant companion, bringing books, sharing town gossip, and helping Sarah prepare teaching materials while confined to the guest room. Her bright spirit and open heart had made Sarah's convalescence far more pleasant than it might have been.

"Am I free to move about now, Doctor?" Sarah asked hopefully.

"Yes, but with caution," Dr. Martinez replied, packing his medical bag. "Short walks only, preferably with support, and continue to elevate the ankle when sitting. No extended periods standing for at least another two days."

"And the church hall?" Sarah pressed. "I had hoped to begin setting it up for classes tomorrow."

Dr. Martinez shook his head firmly. "Not yet. Perhaps in three days, if the healing continues well. For now, limit yourself to the house and garden."

Sarah suppressed her disappointment. Every day delayed was another day the children of Silver Creek went without proper education. Still, she knew the doctor was right—rushing her recovery would only prolong it.

"Thank you, Dr. Martinez," she said. "I'll follow your instructions."

After the doctor left, Charlotte helped Sarah change into a day dress, then supported her as they slowly made their way to the dining room for lunch. It was Sarah's first meal outside the guest room since her accident, and she welcomed the change of scenery.

Eleanor was already seated at the table, her posture impeccable as always. "Miss Williams," she greeted Sarah. "Dr. Martinez tells me you're improving."

"Yes, thank you, Mrs. Montgomery," Sarah replied, carefully taking a seat. "I'm grateful for your hospitality during my recovery."

Eleanor nodded. "It's merely Christian charity."

Charlotte rolled her eyes at her mother's formal tone. "Mother, Sarah's been with us nearly a week now. Surely, we can dispense with some of the formality?"

"Proper manners are never dispensable, Charlotte," Eleanor replied, though her expression softened slightly. "But I suppose less formality might be acceptable within the family circle."

Sarah was surprised to be included, however obliquely, in the "family circle." Despite Eleanor's reserved manner, she seemed to be warming to Sarah's presence, if only marginally.

"Where is Jack?" Charlotte asked as Mrs. Finch served the soup. "He promised to join us for lunch today."

"Your brother sent word that he's delayed at the mine," Eleanor replied, a note of disapproval in her voice. "Again."

"He works too hard," Charlotte sighed, turning to Sarah. "Ever since Father died, Jack has carried the weight of everything—the mine, the town's affairs, our family. He rarely allows himself any rest."

"A Christian man would understand the importance of the Sabbath," Eleanor commented. "Your father always kept the Lord's day sacred, no matter how pressing the mine's concerns."

A flicker of tension crossed Charlotte's face at her mother's words. Sarah had noticed this pattern over the past few days—Eleanor's frequent references to church and faith, often in relation to the late Mr. Montgomery, and the discomfort these comments created in Charlotte.

The conversation shifted to other topics—plans for the church social the following week, news of a new family arriving in Silver Creek, Charlotte's progress with her watercolor painting. Throughout the meal, Sarah observed the complex dynamic between mother and daughter. There was obvious love, but also an undercurrent of strain that seemed to center around Jack and his absence from their conversation.

After lunch, Charlotte helped Sarah to the parlor, where they had been working on teaching materials. They spent a pleasant afternoon cutting letters from colored paper for the younger children and discussing lesson plans for different age groups.

"I think Emma Reynolds would benefit from more advanced reading," Sarah commented. "She's clearly capable of work beyond her grade level."

"Emma's a bright child," Charlotte agreed. "Such a shame about her mother. Her father does his best, but a girl needs feminine guidance."

Sarah nodded thoughtfully. "She mentioned her mother used to sing to her. Perhaps I could incorporate more music into the lessons. I noticed the schoolhouse has an old piano."

"That's a wonderful idea," Charlotte said. "Music was always my favorite subject." She hesitated, then added, "Jack used to play, you know. The piano. Mother taught him when he was young."

"Really?" Sarah couldn't quite imagine the stern mine owner sitting at a piano. "He doesn't seem the type."

"He was different before," Charlotte said softly. "Before Father died. Before the accident."

Sarah had been curious about the accident, but she had hesitated to ask directly. Now, seeing an opening, she ventured, "Can you tell me about the accident?"

Charlotte nodded, setting down her scissors. "It was five years ago, shortly after Father died. A section of tunnel collapsed. Three men were killed, including Matthew Carter, Jack's closest friend since childhood."

"How terrible," Sarah said softly.

"They grew up together," Charlotte continued, her eyes distant with memory. "Matthew's father worked for our father, and the boys were inseparable. Matthew became the mine foreman when Jack took over after Father's death."

"And Jack blames himself for the accident?" Sarah guessed, recalling Reverend Wilson's words.

"Yes, though the investigation cleared him of any negligence. It was his first major decision after taking over expanding that section of the mine. When the support structures failed..." Charlotte's voice trailed off. "Jack was never the same afterward. He stopped attending church, stopped playing the piano, stopped doing anything that wasn't directly related to the mine or his responsibilities."

"He turned away from his faith," Sarah said, understanding now the tension she'd observed between Jack and his mother.

"Completely," Charlotte confirmed. "He said he couldn't believe in a God who would allow such a tragedy. Mother was horrified, of course. She's never accepted his rejection of the church."

"And you?" Sarah asked gently.

A sad smile touched Charlotte's lips. "I pray for him. Every day. And I leave little Bible verses around where he might see them—notes in his books, cards on his desk. He pretends not to notice, but sometimes I see him reading them."

The tender image of Charlotte's faithful persistence moved Sarah deeply. "Your brother is fortunate to have such a loving sister."

"I just want him to find peace again," Charlotte said. "To forgive himself. To remember that God hasn't abandoned him, even if he's tried to abandon God."

Sarah reached across the table to squeeze Charlotte's hand. "Faith often returns in unexpected ways," she said. "Sometimes when we least expect it."

Charlotte brightened. "That's what I keep hoping. That something or someone will help Jack find his way back."

The pointed look Charlotte gave her made Sarah uncomfortable. "Charlotte, I'm just the schoolteacher."

"You're more than that," Charlotte insisted. "I've seen how he looks at you when he thinks no one notices. He's intrigued by you, Sarah. And you've already gotten him to talk more in a week than he usually does in a month."

Sarah felt heat rise in her cheeks. "I think you're imagining things."

"Am I?" Charlotte challenged with a knowing smile. "We'll see."

To Sarah's relief, Mrs. Finch entered with tea, ending the uncomfortable conversation. As they sipped their tea, Sarah found her thoughts turning to Jack despite herself. She had noticed a change in him since that first cool greeting—a softening, perhaps, or at least a growing civility. But Charlotte's implications went far beyond mere civility, suggesting an interest Sarah wasn't sure existed or should exist.

After tea, Charlotte excused herself to write letters, and Sarah decided to attempt a short walk in the garden as Dr. Martinez had suggested. The late afternoon sun cast long shadows across the grounds as she made her way carefully along the gravel path, leaning occasionally on the walking stick Dr. Martinez had provided.

The Montgomery garden was impressive. The formal beds near the house showed the fresh green shoots of emerging perennials and carefully tended rose bushes just beginning to leaf out. Beyond, fruit trees displayed the last of their delicate spring blossoms, and a small kitchen garden had been freshly prepared for planting. Sarah breathed deeply, appreciating the crisp mountain air after days confined indoors. Her ankle ached dully with each step, but the pain was manageable, and the freedom of movement was worth it.

As she rounded a bend in the path, Sarah was surprised to see Jack seated on a stone bench beneath an apple tree. He hadn't noticed her, his attention focused on something in his hands—a pocket watch, she realized, that glinted in the fading sunlight.

Sarah hesitated, not wanting to intrude on what seemed like a private moment. Before she could retreat, however, Jack looked up and saw her.

"Miss Williams," he said, quickly pocketing the watch. "Should you be walking unassisted?"

"Dr. Martinez said short walks were permissible," Sarah replied, approaching slowly. "And I have this." She held up the walking stick.

"Still, you should be careful on the gravel," Jack said, rising to offer his arm. "The footing can be treacherous, even for those with two good ankles."

Sarah accepted his support, touched by his concern. "Thank you. I confess I was eager for fresh air after being indoors for so long."

"Understandable," Jack said, guiding her to the bench. "Though our Colorado evenings can grow cool quickly."

As they sat together on the stone bench, Sarah was acutely aware of his proximity. Jack was not a man who seemed comfortable with casual physical contact, yet he had offered his arm without hesitation.

"It's a beautiful garden," Sarah said, breaking the momentary silence. "Did your mother design it?"

"My father, actually," Jack replied. "He believed a proper home needed a proper garden. The roses were my mother's addition after they married."

"Your father sounds like he was a remarkable man."

"He was," Jack agreed, his tone warming with evident respect. "Strong but fair. Demanding but generous. The kind of man who expected much because he gave much."

"Charlotte speaks of him often," Sarah said. "It's clear how much she admired him."

"We all did," Jack said. His hand moved unconsciously to his pocket where he'd placed the watch.

Sarah hesitated, then ventured, "Was that his watch?"

Jack looked surprised, then shook his head. "No. It belonged to Matthew Carter. His father gave it to me after... after the accident."

"I'm sorry," Sarah whispered. "Charlotte told me about your friend."

Jack's expression closed immediately. "Charlotte talks too much."

"She cares about you. As does your mother, in her way."

"By constantly reminding me of my spiritual failings?" Jack's tone was bitter. "Mother believes faith is the answer to everything, just as Father did."

"And you don't?"

Jack turned to look at her directly, his eyes intense. "What do you believe, Miss Williams? You've lost your mother, your father has abandoned you, yet you still cling to your faith. Why?"

The directness of the question caught Sarah off guard, but she answered honestly. "Because it's all that sustained me through those losses. When Mother was dying, her faith never wavered. She told me that God doesn't promise an absence of suffering, only that He will be with us through it."

"Cold comfort for those left behind," Jack commented.

"Perhaps," Sarah acknowledged. "But I've found it to be true, nonetheless. In my darkest moments, when I felt most alone, I sensed God's presence. Not removing my pain but sharing it. Bearing it with me."

Jack was silent for a long moment, his gaze distant. "I felt no such presence after the accident," he finally said. "Only absence. Silence."

"Sometimes silence is an answer too," Sarah said gently. "When my father left and we heard nothing for months, I questioned everything—why he had gone, whether he still loved us, if he was even alive. The silence was excruciating."

"How did you bear it?" Jack asked, genuine curiosity in his voice.

"Prayer, at first," Sarah admitted. "Then, when that brought no answers, I simply continued living. Caring for my mother. Teaching my students. And gradually, I saw small moments of grace that I might have missed if everything had gone according to my expectations."

"Grace?" Jack repeated skeptically.

"Yes," Sarah said. "The kindness of our landlady when we couldn't pay full rent. A student's mother bringing soup when my mother was too ill to cook. Even finding the teaching position here in Silver Creek, just when I needed it most."

She looked at him directly. "Sometimes I think God places signs in our path—people, opportunities, even challenges—to guide us, though we may not recognize them as such in the moment."

Something flickered in Jack's eyes. Discomfort, perhaps, or recognition. He looked away, fidgeting with his cuff. "A convenient interpretation that credits God for coincidences and human kindness."

"Perhaps," Sarah conceded. "Or perhaps what we call coincidence is actually divine guidance, if only we have eyes to see it."

Jack stood abruptly. "It's getting cold. You should return inside before you catch a chill."

The conversation was clearly over, but Sarah felt she had glimpsed something important in their exchange—a crack in Jack's carefully maintained facade of indifference toward matters of faith.

"Of course," she said, accepting his offered arm once more for the walk back to the house. "Thank you for indulging my questions, Mr. Montgomery."

They walked in silence for several steps before Jack spoke again. "Why do you care?" he asked suddenly. "About my spiritual state. You barely know me."

Sarah considered her answer carefully. "I care about the well-being of those around me. And I've seen how the weight of the past burdens you, just as it once burdened me."

"Our situations are hardly comparable," Jack said stiffly.

"No," Sarah agreed. "But pain is pain, Mr. Montgomery. And faith can heal even the deepest wounds, if we allow it."

They had reached the house, and Jack paused at the door. "My wounds aren't your concern, Miss Williams."

"Perhaps not," Sarah conceded. "But as your guest, your well-being naturally concerns me. And as a Christian, I believe we're called to bear one another's burdens."

Jack's expression remained guarded, but something in his eyes softened. "Your faith is admirable, even if I don't share it."

"Thank you," Sarah said simply. "And thank you for the company in the garden. It was a pleasant change from the guest room walls."

"You're welcome," Jack replied formally, opening the door for her. "Good evening, Miss Williams."

"Good evening, Mr. Montgomery."

As Sarah made her way slowly to her room, she reflected on their conversation. Jack Montgomery presented himself as a man unmoved by faith, yet she had sensed an undercurrent of longing beneath his skepticism—a desire, perhaps, for the certainty he had once possessed and lost.

Charlotte's words came back to her: "I just want him to find peace again." Sarah found herself sharing that wish, though she knew Jack's spiritual journey was his own. All she could do was offer understanding and, perhaps, when appropriate, gentle reminders of the faith he had abandoned.

In her room, Sarah opened her mother's Bible to the passage that had comforted her most during her mother's illness: "Come to me, all you who are weary and burdened, and I will give you rest."

"Lord," she prayed softly, "please open Jack's heart to Your peace. Help him to see the signs of Your presence in his life, even when he feels most alone. And guide me to be a light, however small, in this place where You have led me."

As she closed the Bible, Sarah was struck by the realization that in just one week, Silver Creek had felt less like a temporary refuge and more like a place she might truly belong. The Montgomery home, initially so intimidating, now felt almost familiar. Charlotte had become a friend, and even Eleanor was gradually warming to her presence.

And Jack... Jack remained a puzzle, but one Sarah increasingly felt drawn to understand. Not merely out of Christian charity, as she had told herself, but because there was something compelling about the man beneath the stern exterior—a depth of feeling and principle that called to her despite their differences.

The thought was unsettling. Sarah had come to Silver Creek to begin a new life as a teacher, not to develop feelings for a man who had renounced the faith that was the cornerstone of her life. Yet as she prepared for bed, she couldn't deny that her conversation with Jack in the garden had affected her more deeply than she cared to admit.

"One day at a time," she reminded herself, echoing her mother's favorite advice. Whatever God's plan might be for her in Silver Creek, it would unfold in His time, not hers. Her task was simply to remain faithful to her calling and open to His guidance, even if that guidance came in unexpected forms.

EIGHT

Jack stood in the doorway of the newly repaired schoolhouse, surveying the work with critical eyes. The workers had done an admirable job—better than he'd expected in such a short time. The collapsed roof had been completely rebuilt, the damaged walls repaired and freshly painted, windows re-glazed, and floors sanded smooth. Even the teacher's quarters at the back had a fresh coat of whitewash.

"It looks perfect, Mr. Montgomery," Tony Jenkins said, wiping sawdust from his hands as he approached. "Just as you requested."

"You and your men did good work," Jack acknowledged with a nod. "The town council will be pleased."

"And the new teacher? Think she'll approve?"

Jack thought of Sarah's face when he'd told her the repairs were complete—her eyes bright with excitement, a smile transforming her features. She'd spent the past two days gathering supplies and preparing lessons, eager to begin her teaching duties now that her ankle had healed sufficiently.

"I believe she will," he said simply.

Jenkins grinned. "The men were happy to help. Miss Williams made quite an impression when she visited the site yesterday. Brought us fresh lemonade and thanked each man personally."

Jack wasn't surprised. In the two weeks since Sarah's arrival in Silver Creek, she had demonstrated a genuine warmth that won people over despite her outsider status. Even his mother had begun to soften toward her, impressed by Sarah's knowledge of scripture and her willingness to help with Eleanor's church committee work.

"The celebration begins at noon," Jack reminded Jenkins. "Make sure your men know they're invited. The town council wants to thank everyone involved in the repairs."

"We'll be there," Jenkins promised. "Wouldn't miss it."

As the carpenter departed, Jack took a last look around the empty schoolroom. Soon it would be filled with children's voices, with Sarah at the front, sharing her knowledge and enthusiasm. The thought brought an unexpected sense of satisfaction and an equally unexpected pang of regret. With the schoolhouse repaired, Sarah would move from his home to the teacher's quarters today, after the celebration.

It was the outcome he'd worked toward, expediting repairs specifically for this purpose. Yet now that the moment had arrived, Jack found himself strangely reluctant to see her go. Her presence had brought a lightness to the Montgomery house that had been absent for years. Charlotte was happier, more animated. Even his mother seemed less severe lately.

And he'd grown accustomed to their conversations over breakfast, to encountering her in the library selecting books, to hearing her laugh with Charlotte in the parlor. The house would seem emptier without her.

"Foolishness," he muttered to himself, turning abruptly to leave. Sarah Williams was the schoolteacher, nothing more. Her departure from his home was the natural order of things, the arrangement always intended.

Yet as he walked back toward town, Jack couldn't deny that something had shifted during Sarah's stay. She had somehow penetrated the careful distance he maintained with most people, drawing him into conversations that ventured beyond the superficial, challenging his long-held positions with gentle but persistent questions.

Most unsettling were her comments about faith—about God sending signs that might go unrecognized. The words had lingered in his mind for days, surfacing at odd moments. Last Sunday, he'd paused outside the church as the congregation sang hymns, listening for several minutes before continuing on his way. And twice this week, he'd picked up one of Charlotte's Bible verse cards from his desk instead of immediately discarding it as was his habit.

"Mr. Montgomery!"

Jack looked up to see August approaching from the direction of the mine. His foreman's expression was troubled. "What's wrong?" Jack asked immediately.

"We've got multiple situations brewing," August replied grimly. "Blackwood's men have been making rounds to several of our workers' homes, asking pointed questions about their property holdings and family finances. And there's something else—strange equipment deliveries to his operation after dark. Heavy crates that don't look like standard mining gear."

Jack frowned. This was escalating beyond Blackwood's usual underhanded tactics. "What kind of equipment?"

"Can't say for certain, but the night watchman at Peterson's store said it looked like blasting supplies. More than any legitimate operation would need." August lowered his voice. "And word is that Blackwood's been meeting with men from outside Silver Creek. Rough types, not miners."

A familiar anger stirred in Jack's chest, mixed now with genuine concern. "Any of our workers seem particularly worried?"

"Joseph Reynolds looked shaken when I saw him this morning. Mentioned something about unexpected visitors, but clammed up when I pressed for details." August glanced toward the town square. "He's planning to attend the celebration today, but he seemed nervous about it."

"I'll keep an eye on the situation," Jack decided. "And have a word with Sheriff Taylor about Blackwood's increasingly aggressive methods."

"Good luck with that," August said skeptically. "Taylor's never been eager to cross Blackwood, especially now that the man's got territorial connections."

"Territorial connections?"

"Claims he's got backing from investors in Denver. Big money, from what I hear. The kind that buys influence with officials." August shook his head. "Makes him feel untouchable."

Jack couldn't disagree with August's assessment, but the sheriff still needed to be informed. "Nevertheless, he should be aware of the pattern. This isn't just business competition anymore."

They walked together toward the town square, where preparations for the celebration were underway. Tables had been set up for a community luncheon, and a small platform constructed for the official speeches. Women bustled about, arranging flowers and food, while men hung bunting and a banner that read "WELCOME TO OUR NEW TEACHER - MISS SARAH WILLIAMS."

"Quite the reception," August commented. "The town hasn't been this excited since the Fourth of July picnic."

"Silver Creek has been without a teacher for months," Jack pointed out. "The parents are relieved their children's education will resume."

"And the new teacher being pretty as a picture doesn't hurt," August added with a knowing smile.

Jack gave him a stern look. "Miss Williams' appearance is irrelevant to her qualifications."

"Of course," August agreed, though his expression remained amused. "Speaking of Miss Williams, I hear she's moving to the teacher's quarters after the celebration. Your household returns to normal today."

"Yes," Jack said shortly.

"Well, I'd better check on those equipment deliveries I mentioned," August said. "Want to get a closer look at what Blackwood's really up to. Something tells me today's celebration might be interrupted if we're not careful."

As August departed, Jack surveyed the growing crowd in the town square. He was worried by Blackwood's escalating aggression, particularly given the north's unexpectedly lucrative claim. The rival mine owner had made three separate offers for the property in the past month alone, each more generous than the last. His persistence suggested he knew something about the claim that Jack didn't or was growing desperate.

Jack spotted Charlotte and Sarah near the schoolhouse, surrounded by a group of children eager to see their new classroom. Sarah wore a simple green gingham dress with a matching green ribbon that complemented her chestnut hair, which was arranged more elaborately than usual for the occasion. She moved with only the slightest hint of a limp, her recovery nearly complete.

As if sensing his gaze, Sarah looked up and met his eyes across the square. She smiled and waved, gesturing for him to join them. Jack hesitated, then made his way toward the schoolhouse.

"Jack!" Charlotte called as he approached. "Sarah's showing the children their new classroom. Isn't it wonderful?"

"It looks very nice," he agreed, noting the pride in Sarah's expression as she surveyed her domain.

"The children are excited to begin lessons on Monday," Sarah said. "Aren't you, Emma?"

Emma nodded enthusiastically. "Miss Williams says we're going to learn geography with a real map of the whole United States!"

"And reading from actual books, not just the Bible," added Peter Garrett. "Though Miss Williams says we'll still have Bible lessons too."

"A balanced education is important," Sarah explained to Jack. "Spiritual and practical knowledge are both necessary."

Before Jack could respond, a commotion at the edge of the square drew everyone's attention. Joseph Reynolds had arrived, a livid bruise darkening his left cheek. Beside him stood a burly man Jack recognized as one of Blackwood's mine supervisors, Howard Simmons.

"You've got three days, Reynolds," Simmons was saying loudly enough for nearby people to hear. "Mr. Blackwood's been more than patient."

"There is no debt," Joseph insisted, his voice tight with anger. "I never borrowed a cent from Blackwood or anyone associated with him."

"That's not what the promissory note says," Simmons sneered. "Signed by your own hand."

"It's a forgery, and you know it!"

Emma clutched Sarah's skirts, her small face crumpling with distress. "Pa?"

Sarah immediately kneeled beside the girl, putting a comforting arm around her shoulders. "It's all right, Emma. Your father's just disagreeing with that man. Why don't you stay here with Charlotte while I go see if I can help?"

"I'll handle this," Jack said firmly. "Please keep the children away."

He strode toward the confrontation, which was drawing increasing attention from the gathering crowd. As he approached, he could see Joseph's hands clenched into fists at his sides, his face flushed with anger.

"Is there a problem here, gentlemen?" Jack asked, positioning himself between Joseph and Simmons.

"This doesn't concern you, Montgomery," Simmons said dismissively. "This is between Reynolds and Mr. Blackwood."

"Any disturbance at a town celebration concerns me," Jack replied coolly. "Especially when it involves one of my employees."

"Your employee has an outstanding debt to Mr. Blackwood," Simmons insisted. "Fifty dollars plus interest, due by the end of the week."

"I told you, there is no debt!" Joseph exclaimed. "I never signed anything."

Jack turned to Joseph. "Do you have any idea what he's talking about?"

"None," Joseph said firmly. "Blackwood approached me last month about selling my father's claim north of town. I refused. Next thing I know, this snake is claiming I borrowed money against the property."

Jack had seen this tactic before. Blackwood creating false debts to pressure landowners was a new low, but not an entirely surprising one. "Where is this promissory note?" he asked Simmons.

"Mr. Blackwood has it in safekeeping," Simmons replied, a little too quickly. "Reynolds can see it when he comes to settle his debt."

"Convenient," Jack observed. "Tell your employer that if he wishes to pursue this matter, he can do so through proper legal channels. Until then, I suggest you leave Mr. Reynolds alone."

Simmons's face darkened. "You're making a mistake, Montgomery. Mr. Blackwood isn't a man you want to cross."

"Neither am I," Jack said quietly. "Now, I believe Sheriff Taylor has arrived. Shall I call him over to discuss this further?"

Simmons glanced toward the sheriff, who was indeed making his way through the crowd, then back at Jack. With a final glare at Joseph, he turned and stalked away.

"Thank you, Mr. Montgomery," Joseph said, the tension visibly easing from his shoulders. "I don't know what would have happened if you hadn't stepped in."

"It's nothing," Jack assured him. "But be careful, Joseph. Blackwood doesn't give up easily when he wants something."

"My father's claim isn't much," Joseph said, "but it's all I have to leave Emma someday. I won't sell it, no matter what pressure he applies."

"I understand," Jack said, thinking of his own determination to preserve his father's legacy. "If Simmons or anyone else bothers you again, let me know immediately."

As Joseph nodded gratefully, Jack became aware of Sarah approaching, her expression concerned. "Is everything all right?" she asked.

"Just a misunderstanding," Jack said, not wanting to worry her. "It's resolved now."

"Emma was quite upset," Sarah said. "She's with Charlotte by the school-house."

Joseph's face fell. "I didn't mean for her to see that. She worries enough as it is."

"She's a sensitive child," Sarah agreed. "But also remarkably resilient. Why don't you go to her? I'm sure seeing you will calm her fears."

As Joseph hurried toward the schoolhouse, Sarah turned to Jack. "What was that really about?"

Jack hesitated, then decided she deserved the truth. "Blackwood is claiming Joseph owes him money—a debt Joseph insists doesn't exist. It's likely a tactic to pressure him into selling his small claim."

"That's despicable," Sarah said, her hazel eyes flashing with indignation. "Using a man's financial vulnerability against him, especially when he's raising a child alone."

"Blackwood has few scruples where business is concerned," Jack said grimly. "And Joseph isn't the first to face such tactics."

Sarah glanced toward the schoolhouse, where Joseph was now kneeling beside Emma, whispering to the girl. "Poor Emma. She adores her father. The thought of him in trouble must be terrifying for her."

"You seem to have developed quite a bond with her," Jack observed.

"She has such a bright spirit despite everything she's endured," Sarah said. "No child should have to shoulder such loss."

Before Jack could inquire further, Mayor Watkins approached, his round face beaming. "Mr. Montgomery! Miss Williams! We're ready to begin the ceremony if you'd join us at the platform."

The official portion of the celebration was mercifully brief. Mayor Watkins gave a flowery speech about the importance of education, Jack spoke briefly about the community effort behind the schoolhouse repairs, and Reverend Wilson offered a blessing for the school year ahead. Throughout it all, Jack was acutely aware of Sarah standing nearby, her quiet dignity evident as she thanked the town for their welcome.

After the speeches, the community luncheon began. Jack found himself drawn into conversations with various townspeople, discussing everything from mine operations to the likelihood of a late spring snow. He noticed Sarah moving among the tables, engaging easily with parents and children alike, her natural warmth drawing people to her.

At one point, he spotted her sitting with Emma, who appeared calmer now, though still clinging to her father's hand. Jack couldn't hear their conversation from his position, but he could see the gentle way Sarah spoke to the girl, and how intently Emma listened in response.

As the celebration began to wind down in the late afternoon, Jack found himself helping to carry Sarah's belongings from his home to her new quarters. Charlotte had organized a small procession of volunteers, each carrying books, teaching supplies, or the few personal items Sarah had brought from Denver.

"You really don't need to help with this, Mr. Montgomery," Sarah protested when she saw him lifting her trunk.

"It's no trouble," Jack assured her, surprising himself with the sincerity of his words. "It's the least I can do after you've endured two weeks of Montgomery hospitality."

A smile touched her lips. "Hardly endured. Your family has been most kind."

"Charlotte will miss having you in the house," Jack said as they walked toward the schoolhouse. "She's enjoyed having a companion closer to her age."

"I'll miss her too," Sarah replied. "And your mother. Even Mrs. Finch."

Jack noticed she didn't mention missing him and felt an irrational twinge of disappointment. "The teacher's quarters are rather small compared to what you've become accustomed to."

"They're perfect for my needs," Sarah assured him. "And I'm looking forward to establishing my own household, modest though it may be."

They reached the small apartment attached to the back of the schoolhouse. It consisted of just three rooms—a tiny parlor, an even smaller bedroom, and a compact kitchen—but the space was clean and bright, with simple but sturdy furniture.

Jack set the trunk down in the bedroom, noting the narrow bed and plain dresser. "If you need anything—additional furniture, supplies—don't hesitate to ask."

"You've already been more than generous," Sarah said, arranging her mother's Bible on the bedside table. "I can't thank you enough for expediting the repairs."

"It was in the town's interest," Jack said automatically.

Sarah gave him a knowing look. "Of course."

There was something in her tone—a gentle skepticism, perhaps—that made Jack feel strangely transparent, as if she could see past his practical justifications to the more personal motivations beneath. It was disconcerting to feel so easily read by someone who had known him such a short time.

Charlotte and several other volunteers arrived with the rest of Sarah's belongings prevented further conversation. Soon the small quarters were filled with people arranging books, hanging curtains, and offering suggestions for organization.

Jack retreated to the doorway, watching as Sarah graciously directed the enthusiastic help. She seemed in her element, building connections with the townspeople while gently maintaining her authority. It was a delicate balance, one Jack had observed her navigate with surprising skill during her two weeks in Silver Creek.

As the helpers gradually departed, Jack lingered, reluctant to leave despite having no obvious reason to stay. Charlotte noticed his hesitation and gave him a meaningful look before announcing that she would walk home with Mrs. Parker, leaving Jack to say his goodbyes alone.

"Well," he said awkwardly when only he and Sarah remained in the small parlor. "I suppose you're officially settled now."

"Yes," Sarah agreed, looking around at her new home with evident satisfaction. "It feels good to have a place of my own again, small as it is."

"If you need anything—"

"I know where to find you," Sarah finished with a smile. "Thank you, Mr. Montgomery. For everything."

Jack nodded, suddenly unsure what to do with his hands. "Good evening, then, Miss Williams."

"Good evening, Mr. Montgomery."

He turned to go, then paused at the door. "The celebration went well today. The town has clearly embraced you as their teacher."

"I hope to prove worthy of their trust," Sarah said.

"You already have," Jack said simply, and left before he could say anything more revealing.

The walk home felt longer than usual, the evening shadows stretching across his path as the sun set behind the mountains. Jack found his thoughts returning to the image of Sarah comforting Emma during the confrontation with Simmons. There had been such understanding in her expression, such genuine empathy.

Later, after a quiet dinner with his mother and Charlotte, Jack found himself restless, unable to settle to his usual evening routine of reviewing mine reports.

The house felt different somehow—the absence of their guest more noticeable than he had expected.

He wandered to the library, running his fingers along the spines of books Sarah had borrowed during her stay. She had eclectic tastes—novels by Dickens and Eliot, poetry collections, histories of America, and several volumes on education theory. Her curiosity seemed boundless, her mind open to new ideas and perspectives.

It was that openness, perhaps, that had allowed her to connect so quickly with the people of Silver Creek despite being an outsider. Jack had observed her today, moving easily among the townspeople, remembering names and personal details, showing genuine interest in their lives. Even his mother, initially so reserved toward Sarah, had been drawn into conversation with her about the church altar cloths.

Jack selected a book Sarah had been reading, a collection of poetry by Tennyson, and opened it to a marked page. "In Memoriam," a poem about grief and faith after the death of a beloved friend. The parallel to his own experience with Matthew's death was impossible to miss.

Had she left the marker there intentionally for him to find? Another of her "signs" meant to guide him back to faith? The thought should have irritated him, yet he found himself oddly touched by the possibility.

Unable to settle in the library, Jack decided to check on some paperwork in his study. As he passed the guest room where Sarah had stayed, he noticed the door was ajar. On impulse, he stepped inside.

The room had already been cleaned and prepared for future guests, all traces of Sarah's occupation removed. Yet something caught his eye on the windowsill—a small card with Charlotte's handwriting. One of her Bible verses, no doubt.

Jack picked it up, intending to return it to his sister, when the words caught his attention: "Be still, and know that I am God." The same verse Charlotte had placed in his study last week—and the week before that, if he recalled correctly. His sister's persistence was remarkable, if ineffective.

As he turned to leave, voices from the garden below drew his attention to the window. Charlotte and Emma stood near the rose bushes, Emma clutching a small basket.

"I'm sure Miss Williams will love these for her new home," Charlotte was saying. "The yellow roses are particularly lovely this time of year."

"She said yellow was her favorite color," Emma replied. "Do you think it's too late to take them to her tonight?"

"Perhaps," Charlotte said gently. "But we can bring them first thing tomorrow. I'm sure she'll appreciate the thought whenever she receives them."

"She's been so kind to me," Emma said, her small face earnest in the fading light. "She understands about Pa."

"What do you mean, dear?" Charlotte asked.

"About worrying for him," Emma explained. "After the man was mean to Pa today, I was scared. Miss Williams told me she knows what it's like to worry about a father. She said her father went away two years ago and she still worries about him every day."

"That must be very difficult for her," Charlotte said softly.

Emma nodded solemnly. "She said sometimes when we can't understand why bad things happen, we have to trust that God has a plan, even if we can't see it yet." The child carefully selected another rose. "Do you think God has a plan for Pa and me, Miss Charlotte?"

"I'm certain of it," Charlotte assured her. "Just as He has a plan for Miss Williams and for all of us."

Jack stepped back from the window, Emma's words echoing in his mind. Sarah's father had been gone for two years, yet she still worried about him daily. This wasn't just theoretical compassion she offered Emma—it was understanding born from her own ongoing pain.

Yet despite that pain, she maintained her faith in God's plan. The dichotomy troubled Jack. How could someone who had experienced such profound loss still believe so firmly in divine guidance?

He returned to his study, but the mining reports failed to hold his attention. Instead, his mind kept returning to Sarah's words: "Sometimes I think God places signs in our path—people, opportunities, even challenges—to guide us, though we may not recognize them as such in the moment."

Was Sarah herself such a sign in his life? For five years, he had maintained careful distance from matters of faith. Yet in just two weeks, Sarah Williams had somehow slipped past his defenses, challenging his worldview with her quiet faith and genuine compassion.

Jack finally gave up on work and prepared for bed. As he changed into his nightclothes, he caught sight of Matthew's pocket watch on his dresser. He picked it up, running his thumb over the engraved initials.

"What would you think of her, Matthew?" he asked quietly. "This school-teacher who speaks of faith as if it were as natural as breathing?"

Matthew had been a believer, like Jack's father. After his return from college and his father's death, it had been Matthew who encouraged Jack to find solace in faith rather than shouldering his burdens alone.

"I'm still carrying them alone, old friend," Jack murmured. "Though perhaps a bit less heavily these past two weeks."

He placed the watch back on the dresser and extinguished the lamp. In the darkness, Jack found his thoughts returning to Sarah—her compassion for Emma, her gentle challenges to his skepticism, her resilience in the face of loss. If God truly did place signs in people's paths, as Sarah believed, could she have been sent to Silver Creek for a purpose beyond teaching its children? The question followed Jack into uneasy dreams.

NINE

Sarah woke before dawn on her first morning in the teacher's quarters, momentarily disoriented by the unfamiliar surroundings. The small bedroom was nothing like the spacious guest room at the Montgomery house—the ceiling lower, the furniture simpler, the bed narrower. Yet as her eyes adjusted to the dim light filtering through the thin curtains, a sense of satisfaction settled over her. This place was hers, modest though it might be.

She rose and lit the lamp, shivering slightly in the morning chill. The quarters lacked the multiple fireplaces and coal stoves of the Montgomery house, relying instead on a small stove in the parlor that had gone cold overnight. Sarah quickly dressed, wrapped a shawl around her shoulders, and set about rekindling the fire.

As she waited for the stove to warm the small space, Sarah prepared a simple breakfast of tea and toast. The silence struck her forcefully—no sounds of Mrs. Finch bustling about the kitchen, no Charlotte chattering about her plans for the day, no distant murmur of Jack's voice as he discussed mining business with August Hart over coffee.

"You're being foolish," Sarah chided herself aloud. "You knew living alone would be... well, solitary."

Yet she couldn't deny that she missed the Montgomery household more than she had expected. During her two-week stay, she had grown accustomed to the rhythm of their family life, finding unexpected comfort in the routine and companionship they provided.

Pushing aside these thoughts, Sarah focused on the day ahead—her first as Silver Creek's schoolteacher. She had prepared meticulously, organizing lessons for children ranging from six to sixteen years of age, with widely varying levels of previous education. It would be challenging, but Sarah felt equal to the task. This was, after all, what she had come to Silver Creek to do.

After breakfast, she crossed from her quarters into the schoolroom, surveying the space with a critical eye. The repairs had been expertly done, with no trace remaining of the storm damage that had delayed her beginning. The wooden desks were arranged in rows facing her larger desk at the front. Bookshelves lined one wall, sparsely filled with the salvaged readers and texts she had found. A large slate blackboard dominated the front wall, its surface freshly cleaned and ready for use.

Sarah began writing the day's lessons on the blackboard, her chalk moving smoothly across the slate surface. She had just finished when a knock at the schoolhouse door startled her.

"Hello?" she called, setting down her chalk and brushing dust from her hands.

The door opened to reveal Jack Montgomery, carrying what appeared to be a large framed object wrapped in burlap. Behind him stood two mine workers with several wooden crates.

"Good morning, Miss Williams," Jack said formally. "I hope we're not intruding."

"Not at all," Sarah replied, surprised by his unexpected appearance. "School doesn't begin for another hour."

Jack nodded to the men, who brought the crates inside and set them near her desk. "A few items I thought might be useful," he explained. "The town budget for school supplies is rather limited."

"That's very thoughtful," Sarah said, curious about the contents.

Jack gestured to the burlap-wrapped frame. "This first."

As he unwrapped it, Sarah gasped with delight. It was a new chalkboard, larger than the existing one and mounted in a handsome wooden frame. "It's wonderful! But surely this was expensive."

"It's an investment in the town's future," Jack said matter-of-factly. "Education benefits everyone in Silver Creek."

"Still, this is incredibly generous," Sarah insisted, running her fingers along the smooth surface of the new board. "Thank you."

Jack seemed momentarily discomfited by her gratitude. "The crates contain books and supplies," he continued briskly. "Nothing elaborate, but they should help fill your shelves."

Sarah opened the nearest crate to find it packed with readers, arithmetic primers, geography texts, and history books—many of the titles she had mentioned hoping to get during conversations with Charlotte. "These are exactly what I needed," she said, looking up at Jack. "How did you know?"

"Charlotte may have mentioned your wish list," Jack admitted. "And I added a few titles I thought might be useful based on my own education."

The workers mounted the new chalkboard beside the existing one, then departed with a respectful nod to Jack. As Sarah examined the books more carefully, she discovered many were recent editions, not the outdated texts often sent to frontier schools.

"These are wonderful quality," she observed. "Where did you find such excellent materials?"

"Many are from my father's library," Jack said, his tone deliberately casual. "He believed in maintaining a comprehensive collection, and these were just sitting unused. I thought they might serve a better purpose in the classroom."

Sarah studied him, suspecting there was more to the story than he was admitting. Jack Montgomery was not a man who did things halfway. If he had decided to provide supplies for her school, he would have ensured they were the best available—even if it meant parting with his family's valuable books. "Well, whatever the circumstances, I'm grateful," she said sincerely. "The children will benefit tremendously from these resources."

Jack nodded, seeming relieved that she didn't press for further explanation. "I should let you finish preparing for your students," he said, moving toward the door. "Good luck with your first day, Miss Williams."

"Thank you, Mr. Montgomery. For everything."

After Jack left, Sarah continued unpacking the crates, marveling at the thoughtfulness of the gift. Alongside the textbooks were slates for each student, colored chalks, maps, a globe, and even a small set of scientific specimens—rock samples, pressed leaves, and butterfly specimens under glass. It was a far more comprehensive collection than she had dared hope for, rivaling the resources of many Denver schools.

As she arranged the new materials, Sarah reflected on Jack's generosity. He had claimed it was merely good business to support the town's education, but she suspected his motives were more personal than he cared to admit. Despite his gruff exterior and professed indifference to matters beyond business, Jack Montgomery clearly cared deeply about Silver Creek and its residents.

By the time the first students began arriving, Sarah had arranged the new supplies and prepared the classroom for the day's lessons. Emma was the first to enter, her eyes widening at the sight of the new books and materials.

"Miss Williams, where did all this come from?" she asked in wonder, running her fingers along the spine of a colorful geography text.

"Mr. Montgomery brought them this morning," Sarah explained. "A gift to help us begin our school year properly."

"Mr. Montgomery must like you an awful lot," Emma observed with the directness of childhood. "Pa says he's not normally so generous."

Sarah felt a blush rising in her cheeks. "Mr. Montgomery is concerned with the town's welfare," she corrected gently. "And you children and your education, in particular."

Emma gave her a knowing look that seemed far too mature for her ten years, but thankfully other students began arriving, preventing further discussion of Jack Montgomery's motives.

By nine o'clock, twenty children of various ages had assembled in the classroom, regarding Sarah with expressions ranging from curiosity to boredom to outright skepticism. She recognized many from the schoolhouse celebration, but there were several she hadn't met, including an arrogant-looking boy of about fourteen who slouched in a back-row seat.

"Good morning, children," Sarah began, smiling warmly. "I'm Miss Williams, your new teacher. I'm delighted to meet all of you and to begin our learning journey together."

She proceeded with introductions, asking each child to stand and tell her their name and one thing they hoped to learn this year. Most responded readily, though with varying degrees of enthusiasm. When she reached the sullen boy in the back, he remained slouched in his seat.

"And you are?" Sarah prompted.

"Ethan Blackwood," he replied with a smirk. "And I don't need to learn anything from you."

A ripple of whispers spread through the classroom. Sarah maintained her composure, though the name Blackwood immediately put her on alert. This must be the nephew Charlotte had mentioned.

"Everyone has something to learn, Ethan," Sarah said calmly. "Even those who already consider themselves well-educated. Please stand and introduce yourself properly."

The boy's smirk widened. "My uncle says you are just a charity case Montgomery took in. Says you don't have proper qualifications and won't last a month."

Sarah felt heat rise in her cheeks but kept her voice steady. "Your uncle is entitled to his opinion. However, in this classroom, I expect all students to show respect to me and to their fellow students. Now, please stand and introduce yourself properly, or you may wait in the corner until you're prepared to participate."

For a moment, the boy looked startled, as if he hadn't expected to be challenged. Then, with obvious reluctance, he stood. "Ethan Blackwood. Fourteen years old. And I don't see why I need to be here at all when Uncle Cyrus says I'll be helping run his mines soon."

"Thank you," Sarah said. "I hope our time together will help prepare you for those future responsibilities. Even mine managers benefit from knowledge of reading, mathematics, and history."

With introductions complete, Sarah divided the students into groups based on age and previous education, assigning independent work to the older children while she assessed the younger ones' reading abilities. Despite Ethan's initial disruption, the morning proceeded smoothly, with most children responding well to Sarah's gentle but firm guidance.

At midday, Sarah dismissed the students for lunch, watching as they scattered to the schoolyard or headed home for their meal. She went to her room for a quick lunch, reviewing which students needed extra help and what teaching methods worked best that morning.

The afternoon brought new challenges. As the novelty of a new teacher wore off, several of the older boys began testing boundaries. Tom Garrett passed notes when he thought she wasn't looking. The Cooper twins whispered constantly, dissolving into poorly suppressed giggles. But it was Ethan Blackwood who presented the greatest challenge, deliberately contradicting Sarah's instructions and making dismissive comments just loud enough for other students to hear.

When Ethan began distracting Emma during her reading exercise, Sarah decided more direct intervention was necessary.

"Ethan," she said firmly. "Since you seem to have completed your arithmetic problems already, perhaps you would be kind enough to help Emma with her reading."

Ethan looked up, startled. "What?"

"You clearly have time to whisper to Emma, so I assume your own work is finished," Sarah said. "Therefore, you can assist her with her reading passage. Please come to the front."

Trapped by his own behavior, Ethan reluctantly approached, his face flushed with embarrassment. To Sarah's surprise, once paired with Emma, he actually showed patience and a natural ability to explain concepts clearly. Emma responded well to his guidance, and by the end of the exercise, Ethan seemed almost to be enjoying the role of tutor.

"Thank you," Sarah said when they finished. "You have a gift for teaching. Perhaps you could assist some of our younger students regularly."

A flicker of genuine pleasure crossed Ethan's face before he remembered his affected disdain. "Whatever," he muttered, returning to his seat. But for the rest of the afternoon, his disruptive behavior ceased.

By the end of the day, Sarah was exhausted but satisfied. Despite the challenges, she felt she had connected with most of the children and established a foundation of respect that would serve them well in the coming weeks. As the last student departed with a shy "Goodbye, Miss Williams," Sarah sank into her chair with a sigh of relief.

Her solitude was short-lived. A knock at the door revealed Charlotte, bearing a basket covered with a checkered cloth.

"I thought you might be too tired to cook after your first day," she said, bustling in with characteristic energy. "Mrs. Finch sent chicken pie and apple tart. She says you're too thin."

Sarah laughed, genuinely touched by the gesture. "Please thank her for me. I am rather exhausted."

Charlotte set the basket on Sarah's desk and perched on a nearby student desk. "Well? How was it? Did they behave? Did they like the new books? Jack was up at dawn having those crates delivered from the station."

"The books are wonderful," Sarah confirmed. "And the children were... mostly well-behaved. I had some challenges with Ethan Blackwood."

Charlotte rolled her eyes. "That boy has been spoiled rotten since his parents sent him to live with his uncle. Cyrus lets him run wild, filling his head with nonsense about his future as a mining magnate."

"He's actually quite bright," Sarah observed. "Just undisciplined and arrogant."

"Like his uncle," Charlotte said wryly. "Though Ethan might still be salvageable. He's young."

They chatted about the day's events as Charlotte helped Sarah tidy the classroom. Sarah relished the company after the intensity of her first day teaching.

"You must come for dinner on Sunday," Charlotte declared as she prepared to leave. "Mother insists. She claims she needs to ensure you're eating properly, but I think she actually misses having you around. We all do."

Sarah felt a warmth spread through her at Charlotte's words. "I'd love to come. Please thank your mother for the invitation."

"Wonderful! After church, then."

As Charlotte departed, Sarah returned to her quarters, where she gratefully served herself a generous portion of the chicken pie. Mrs. Finch's cooking was as excellent as ever, reminding Sarah of the comforts she had left behind at the Montgomery house.

The rest of the week followed a similar pattern. Each day brought minor victories and new challenges in the classroom. Sarah gradually learned each child's strengths and weaknesses, adjusting her teaching approach accordingly. Even Ethan Blackwood became marginally more cooperative, especially after Sarah continued to enlist his help with younger students, capitalizing on his previously untapped leadership abilities.

By Friday, Sarah had established a routine that seemed to work for most of the children. The new books and materials had helped to keep them engaged, particularly the older students who might otherwise have resented returning to school. Sarah made a mental note to thank Jack again for his generosity when she saw him on Sunday.

The thought of seeing Jack again created an unexpected flutter in her stomach, which Sarah firmly suppressed. Her growing fondness for the Montgomery family was natural, given their kindness during her stay with them. It would be foolish to attribute special significance to her anticipation of seeing Jack specifically.

When Sunday morning arrived, Sarah dressed with particular care in her best dress—a deep green that complemented the green flecks in her eyes. She had attended services the previous Sunday with Charlotte and Eleanor, meeting a good deal of townspeople she hadn't yet encountered. This second visit to Silver Creek's church felt more comfortable, with friendly faces greeting her as she entered the simple wooden building.

Charlotte waved from the Montgomery family pew near the front, and Sarah joined her and Eleanor, exchanging polite greetings with Mrs. Montgomery before the service began. As the congregation settled, Sarah couldn't help glancing around, noting which of her students were present and which families apparently didn't prioritize church attendance.

It was during this casual survey she spotted a tall figure slipping into the very last pew—Jack, looking uncomfortable in a formal suit, his expression guarded. Sarah blinked in surprise, certain she must be mistaken. According to Charlotte, he hadn't attended church in five years, not since Matthew's death.

But there was no mistake. Jack sat rigidly at the end of the back pew, his gaze fixed straight ahead, his posture suggesting he might bolt at any moment. Sarah turned to Charlotte, whose wide eyes confirmed that this was indeed an unexpected development.

"Is that—?" Sarah whispered.

Charlotte nodded, her expression a mixture of shock and hope. "I can't believe it," she breathed. "What could have made him—?"

Eleanor hushed them as Reverend Wilson approached the pulpit, though Sarah noticed the older woman casting an astonished glance toward her son at the back of the church.

The service proceeded normally, with hymns and prayers followed by Reverend Wilson's sermon—a thoughtful discussion of redemption and second chances based on the parable of the Prodigal Son. Sarah found herself only half-listening, acutely aware of Jack's presence behind her. She resisted the urge to turn and look at him again, though she wondered what had prompted this sudden return to church after so many years.

When the service concluded, Sarah joined the congregation in a final hymn, her clear voice blending with the others. As the last notes faded, she turned, hoping to catch Jack's eye, but found his seat empty. Through the open church door, she glimpsed his tall figure striding rapidly down the street, clearly having departed before the final benediction.

Charlotte approached, her eyes still wide with wonder. "I can't believe it," she whispered. "Jack was here!"

"I saw," Sarah confirmed. "I wonder why he came?"

Charlotte shook her head. "He said nothing about it at breakfast. In fact, he left before Mother and I, saying he had business to attend to." She clasped Sarah's hands excitedly. "This must be a sign. He's beginning to change."

"Perhaps," Sarah cautioned, not wanting to encourage unrealistic expectations. "Attending a single service doesn't automatically mean he's returned to his faith."

"Jack doesn't do anything out of mere curiosity," Charlotte insisted. "And he certainly doesn't attend church without a significant reason." She lowered her voice further. "Something is changing in him, Sarah. I've seen it these past weeks ever since you came to Silver Creek."

Before Sarah could respond to this unsettling suggestion, Eleanor joined them. "Was that your brother I saw slipping out before the benediction?" she asked Charlotte.

"Yes, Mother. Isn't it wonderful? Jack came to church!"

Eleanor's expression was more reserved than her daughter's. "We shall see if it was a momentary impulse or something more meaningful," she said. "In any case, Miss Williams, we look forward to having you for dinner today. Shall we walk home together?"

As they left the church, Sarah found her thoughts returning to Jack's unexpected appearance. What had drawn him back to church after so many years? And why had he left before the service ended?

Charlotte's suggestion that his attendance was connected to Sarah's arrival in Silver Creek seemed far-fetched. Yet she couldn't deny that Jack had shown signs of softening during their time together at the Montgomery house. Their conversations about faith, while often strained, had revealed a man wrestling with profound questions rather than someone who had rejected belief entirely.

The possibility that she might have influenced Jack's spiritual journey, even marginally, was both thrilling and intimidating. Sarah had never considered herself especially eloquent or persuasive in matters of faith. She simply lived her beliefs as best she could, trusting in God's guidance through life's joys and sorrows.

Had that quiet faith somehow spoken to Jack more effectively than his sister's earnest Bible verses or his mother's pointed references to church attendance? The thought was humbling and somewhat frightening in its implications.

As Sarah walked with the Montgomery women toward their home on the hill, she offered a silent prayer for Jack, wherever he had gone after his hasty departure from church. If he was indeed taking tentative steps back toward faith, she prayed for his journey to continue, with or without her influence.

"A penny for your thoughts, Sarah," Charlotte said, linking her arm through Sarah's as they walked. "You're very quiet."

Sarah smiled, pushing aside her musings about Jack. "I was just thinking about my first week of teaching. It's been more rewarding than I expected, despite the challenges."

"And there have been challenges, I understand," Eleanor commented. "Charlotte mentioned the Blackwood boy has been disruptive."

"Ethan has a strong personality," Sarah said diplomatically. "But he's shown improvement already. I believe he simply needs positive direction for his considerable energy and intelligence."

Eleanor raised an eyebrow. "You're more charitable than most would be in your position. Cyrus Blackwood has encouraged that boy's worst tendencies since his sister sent him to Silver Creek."

"Children often act out when they feel unwanted or insecure," Sarah observed. "Being sent away from his parents couldn't have been easy for Ethan."

"You have insight beyond your years, Miss Williams," Eleanor said, with what seemed like genuine approval. "Silver Creek is fortunate to have you as its teacher."

The compliment, unexpected from the typically reserved Eleanor, warmed Sarah considerably. As they continued toward the Montgomery house, Sarah found herself looking forward to dinner with these women who had become important to her in such a short time.

Yet her thoughts kept returning to Jack, who had slipped away from church before she could speak with him. Would he be at dinner? And if so, what had prompted his unprecedented return to church after five years of absence?

Despite her best efforts to focus on the conversation with Charlotte and Eleanor, Sarah couldn't quite suppress the hope that she might have played some small part in Jack's apparent reconsideration of faith. The possibility was both daunting and deeply moving—a reminder that God often worked through unexpected channels to reach those who had turned away from Him.

"Sarah?" Charlotte's voice broke through her reverie. "We're home. Are you certain you're all right? You seem distracted."

"I'm fine," Sarah assured her with a smile. "Just a little tired from my first week of teaching. I'm looking forward to a pleasant afternoon with friends."

As they approached the Montgomery house, Sarah glanced up at the second-floor window that she knew belonged to Jack's study. Was he there now, perhaps wrestling with the implications of his return to church? Or had he retreated to the solitude of the mine, where the practical concerns of business might drown out the spiritual questions raised by Reverend Wilson's sermon?

Either way, Sarah sensed that Jack Montgomery's journey back to faith had begun, however tentatively. And for reasons she wasn't quite ready to examine, that knowledge filled her with a quiet joy that lingered as she followed Charlotte and Eleanor into the house for Sunday dinner.

TEN

J ack stood alone on the rocky hillside overlooking Silver Creek, the town spread out below like a model village in the warm afternoon light. From this distance, the white steeple of the church gleamed against the mountain backdrop—a beacon he had once looked to for hope, now a symbol of everything he had lost.

He hadn't meant to go inside.

When he'd left the house that morning under the pretense of business, he'd intended to walk off a restless feeling that had clung to him since sunrise. But then the bells rang, and the familiar melody of an old hymn floated on the breeze. His feet, unbidden, had carried him up the church steps and through the back door.

Even now, the memory made his stomach twist. Sitting in the rear pew, watching Sarah's composed profile as she sang, hearing Reverend Wilson preach about prodigal sons and undeserved mercy—it had stirred up things he thought long buried.

He hadn't stayed for the benediction.

He'd slipped out before the last hymn ended, the walls suddenly too close, the air too heavy. The ache in his chest at the sound of Matthew's favorite hymn had driven him out like a man escaping a mine just before collapse.

Now, hours later, he still hadn't returned home. The quiet of the hillside offered space to think—or at least to try. But the silence only echoed the questions he wasn't ready to answer.

A soft breeze stirred the pine branches overhead, and Jack turned toward the path down the hill, squaring his shoulders as he descended. He didn't have answers, but there was always work to be done.

By the time he reached his office at the mine, the sun was lower in the sky, casting golden light through the windows. He had just settled behind his desk when a knock at the door pulled him from his thoughts.

"Come in," he called.

His mother entered, her posture as rigid as ever, but her expression surprisingly uncertain.

"Mother," Jack said, setting down his pen. "This is unexpected."

"I won't take much of your time," Eleanor said, seating herself across from his desk. "I wanted to speak with you about your attendance at church yesterday."

Jack suppressed a sigh. He'd been expecting this conversation since his impulsive decision to attend services. "It was merely a visit, Mother. Don't make more of it than it was."

"Was it?" Eleanor asked, studying him with an intensity that reminded Jack uncomfortably of his childhood. "You haven't set foot in church since Matthew's funeral."

"Perhaps I was curious to hear Reverend Wilson's sermon."

"Perhaps," Eleanor said, clearly unconvinced. "Or perhaps Miss Williams has had more influence on you than you care to admit."

Jack stiffened. "This has nothing to do with Miss Williams."

"Doesn't it?" His mother raised an eyebrow. "Your behavior has changed remarkably since her arrival in Silver Creek. You've become more... engaged. Less withdrawn."

"I've been occupied with mine business and the schoolhouse repairs," Jack said dismissively. "Nothing more significant than that."

Eleanor's expression softened slightly. "Jack, I'm not criticizing. I'm hopeful. You've been carrying the weight of Matthew's death for five years. If Sarah—Miss Williams—has somehow helped ease that burden, I'm grateful."

Using Sarah's first name startled Jack. His mother was typically formal with newcomers, especially those she considered beneath their social standing.

"You seem to have developed a high opinion of Miss Williams," he observed cautiously.

"She's a remarkable young woman," Eleanor acknowledged. "Her faith has sustained her through significant hardships, yet she remains compassionate and optimistic. Such strength of character is rare."

Jack couldn't disagree, though he was surprised to hear his mother express such sentiments. "She's certainly dedicated to her teaching," he said neutrally.

"And to her faith," Eleanor added pointedly. "Something you once valued as well."

Jack tensed again, anticipating a lecture, but his mother rose to leave.

"I won't press you further," she said. "But I want you to know that your father would be proud of the man you've become, Jack, even with your spiritual reservations. And he would have admired Miss Williams greatly."

The unexpected reference to his father's approval left Jack momentarily speechless. Before he could respond, Eleanor was gone, leaving him with troubling thoughts about his impulsive church attendance and its apparent effect on his family.

Jack hadn't planned to attend services. He'd risen early as usual, completed some paperwork, and walked toward town with no particular destination in mind. When the church bells rang, he'd stopped outside, listening to the familiar hymns that had once been such a part of his life.

Almost against his will, he'd entered, slipping into the back pew just as Reverend Wilson approached the pulpit. He'd spotted Sarah immediately, sitting with Charlotte and his mother near the front, her chestnut hair neatly arranged, her posture attentive.

The sermon about the Prodigal Son had struck uncomfortably close to home. Though Jack hadn't squandered his inheritance like the son in the parable, he had certainly turned away from the faith his father had valued so deeply. Reverend Wilson's words about forgiveness and second chances had stirred emotions Jack had long suppressed.

But it was the final hymn—Sarah's clear voice rising above the congregation—that had finally driven him from the church before the benediction. The familiar melody had transported him back to Sundays before the accident, when Matthew had stood beside him in the family pew, singing the same hymn with unabashed enthusiasm despite his limited musical talents.

The memory had been too much to bear. Jack had fled, striding past the mine to the hillside where he'd spent the rest of the morning, trying to make sense of the conflicting emotions the service had stirred in him.

Now, facing his mother's hopeful assessment, Jack felt even more unsettled. Had Sarah truly influenced his decision to attend church? And if so, what did that say about her growing importance in his life?

A second knock at his door provided a welcome interruption.

"Mr. Montgomery?" August entered, looking uncharacteristically concerned. "There's a situation at the north claim you should see."

Jack rose immediately. "What's happened?"

"Someone's tampered with the new support beams in tunnel three. Not enough to cause immediate danger, but if it had gone unnoticed..."

Jack grabbed his hat. "Let's go."

***

The damage was subtle but potentially catastrophic—strategic weakening of support beams in one of the most active sections of the mine. Without August's vigilance, it might have gone undetected until a collapse occurred.

"This was deliberate," Jack said grimly, examining a beam that had been partially sawed through. "And done by someone with mining knowledge. They knew exactly where to weaken the structure for maximum effect."

"Blackwood?" August suggested, his voice low to avoid being overheard by the workers reinforcing the compromised beams.

"Who else?" Jack ran a hand through his hair in frustration. "But this had to be done from the inside. Someone with legitimate access to this section."

"You think one of our own men did this?" August's face darkened with the implications.

"Not willingly," Jack said, thinking of Joseph Reynolds and the false debt Blackwood had manufactured.

"But if Blackwood's been pressuring our workers with threats against their families, fabricated debts, or other coercion..."

"That would explain how they got past the guards," August said grimly. "The deputies are watching for outsiders, not our own people being forced to do his dirty work."

Jack nodded, the full scope of Blackwood's manipulation becoming clear. "We need to speak with the men privately, find out who's been approached or threatened. And August—we can't trust anyone with access to the tunnels until we know who's been compromised."

"That will slow production to a crawl," August warned.

"I'd rather have slow production than dead miners," Jack said firmly. "And send word to Sheriff Taylor. He needs to know that Blackwood's using coercion against our workers."

As they emerged from the tunnel into the late afternoon sunshine, Jack spotted a familiar figure near the mine office—Sarah Williams, apparently deep in conversation with Henry Carter. The sight of her there, so unexpectedly, momentarily distracted him from the sabotage.

"Miss Williams," he called, crossing to where they stood. "This is an unexpected visit."

Sarah turned, smiling when she saw him despite his dusty appearance. "Mr. Montgomery. I was just speaking with Mr. Carter. Emma wrote a composition about mining that showed such insight, it stirred my own curiosity. I realized I'd never actually seen the workings of a mine up close."

Henry held up the paper proudly. "The girl has talent, Mr. Montgomery. Takes after her mother with her writing skills."

"I'm glad to hear it," Jack said sincerely. "Emma is fortunate to have such an excellent teacher."

A faint blush colored Sarah's cheeks at the compliment. "Thank you. But the credit belongs to Emma's natural intelligence and curiosity."

Henry excused himself to return to work, leaving Jack and Sarah alone.

"Your visit could have waited until tomorrow," Jack said.

"True," Sarah admitted with a small smile. "But after reading Emma's composition, I wanted to see the place through her eyes—and perhaps better understand what so many of her classmates' families do every day."

"I'm glad they're useful," Jack said, acutely aware of August watching them with poorly concealed interest from the mine office doorway. "Would you care to walk back to town? I have business there anyway."

They fell into step together, the late afternoon sun casting long shadows across the path. Jack was conscious of the proper distance between them as they walked, careful not to brush against her skirts inadvertently.

"I saw you at church," Sarah said after a few moments of silence.

Jack tensed. "Briefly."

"It meant a great deal to Charlotte," Sarah continued. "And to your mother, I think, though she's less expressive."

"As I told Mother, it was merely curiosity," Jack said, more sharply than he'd intended. "Reverend Wilson has a reputation as a compelling speaker."

"He is," Sarah agreed mildly. "Though I suspect it was more than curiosity that brought you there after five years of absence."

Jack stopped walking, turning to face her directly. "Miss Williams, while I appreciate your concern for my spiritual welfare, my reasons for attending church, or not attending, are my own."

Sarah met his gaze steadily. "Of course they are. I apologize if I seemed presumptuous."

Something in her calm acceptance of his rebuke made Jack ashamed of his harshness. "No, I apologize for my tone. You meant no offense."

They resumed walking, the silence between them now somewhat strained. Jack searched for a neutral topic to ease the tension.

"How are you finding the teacher's quarters now that you've had a week to settle in?" he asked finally.

"Quite comfortable, thank you," Sarah replied. "Though I confess I sometimes miss the company at your house. Living alone is quiet."

"You're welcome to visit whenever you wish," Jack said. "Charlotte would be delighted to have you more often, and even Mother has commented on your absence."

"That's kind of them," Sarah said. "And of you to extend the invitation."

They had reached the edge of town, where their paths would naturally diverge—Sarah toward the schoolhouse, Jack toward the sheriff's office. Yet neither moved to part ways immediately.

"I was impressed by how you handled Ethan Blackwood," Jack said suddenly. "Charlotte mentioned you've channeled his disruptive tendencies in a more positive direction."

Sarah looked surprised at the change of subject. "Ethan is actually quite bright. He simply needs appropriate challenges and responsibilities."

"Most people would have simply disciplined him," Jack observed.

"Discipline has its place," Sarah acknowledged. "But understanding often achieves more lasting results. Ethan is starved for positive attention and genuine responsibility. I suspect his uncle treats him either as an annoyance or as a miniature version of himself, neither of which serves the boy well."

Jack was struck again by Sarah's insight and compassion—the same qualities that had drawn him to their conversations during her stay at his home.

"You have a gift for seeing beyond surface behaviors to the person beneath," he said quietly.

Her eyes widened slightly at the unexpected compliment. "I try to see people as God sees them with all their potential and worth, despite their flaws or mistakes."

The statement hung between them, freighted with meaning that extended beyond their discussion of Ethan Blackwood. Did Sarah see Jack, too, with such compassionate clarity? The thought was both appealing and terrifying.

"I should report this afternoon's incident to Sheriff Taylor," Jack said, reluctantly breaking the moment. "And you likely have lessons to prepare."

"Yes," Sarah agreed, though she made no immediate move to leave. "Mr. Montgomery... Jack. I'm glad you came to church yesterday, whatever your reasons. And I hope you'll come again."

Something in the way she said his name, gentle, without presumption, stirred an emotion Jack couldn't name. Before he could respond, Sarah continued, her voice soft but clear.

"Faith isn't about certainty, you know. It's about trusting even during doubt and questions. I think you have more faith than you realize."

With that, she turned and walked toward the schoolhouse, leaving Jack staring after her, unsettled by her words and by the unfamiliar warmth her presence had stirred in him.

***

Jack's meeting with Sheriff Taylor proved frustrating but unsurprising. The sheriff promised to "look into" the sabotage but offered little hope of finding concrete evidence against Blackwood or his men.

"You know how it is, Jack," Taylor said, leaning back in his chair. "Without witnesses or proof, I can't make accusations against a man of Blackwood's standing."

"Someone could have been killed," Jack insisted. "This goes beyond our business rivalry."

"I understand that," Taylor sighed. "But all I can do is increase patrols near the mines and warn Blackwood that I'm watching his activities. Without evidence, my hands are tied."

Jack left the sheriff's office dissatisfied but resigned. He'd known Taylor wouldn't take decisive action—the man was too cautious by nature and too wary of Blackwood's influence in the territorial government.

The evening shadows were lengthening as Jack made his way home, crickets beginning their nightly chorus in the warming air. A meadowlark's liquid song echoed from the hillside, one of the first he'd heard this season. Usually, such signs of spring's progress brought him a measure of peace, but tonight his mind was too troubled—by the sabotage, by his mother's hopeful assessment of his church attendance, and most of all, by Sarah's parting words. *Faith isn't about certainty... It's about trusting even during doubt and questions.*

The concept challenged Jack's long-held position that faith required a certainty he could no longer maintain after Matthew's death. He had always framed the issue in stark terms: either God controlled everything, making Him responsible for tragedies like the mine collapse, or He controlled nothing, making faith pointless.

Sarah's understanding seemed more nuanced. A trust that persisted despite unanswered questions, and a relationship rather than a philosophical position. It was an approach to faith Jack had never seriously considered.

As he reached home, Jack paused on the porch, watching the last light fade from the sky. A small bird was building a nest in the eaves, carrying twigs and bits of straw with determined efficiency. The sight reminded him of the bird nest at the church and of Matthew's love for these small creatures.

"Another sign?" Jack murmured to himself, half mocking, half wondering.

"Did you say something, sir?" Mrs. Finch asked, opening the door to admit him.

"Nothing important," Jack replied, removing his hat. "Is dinner ready?"

"Yes, sir. Miss Charlotte and your mother are already seated."

Jack washed quickly and joined his family in the dining room, where the conversation inevitably turned to Sarah.

"She's doing wonders with those children," Charlotte enthused. "Even Mrs. Cooper commented on the improvement in her twins' behavior, and they've always been terrors."

"Miss Williams has a natural authority that children respond to," Eleanor observed. "Firm but kind—the mark of an excellent teacher."

Jack ate silently, letting their praise of Sarah wash over him. It was deserved, certainly. She had already made a significant impact on Silver Creek in her short time there, but their obvious admiration reminded him uncomfortably of his own growing regard for her.

"Jack, you're very quiet," Charlotte said, breaking into his thoughts. "Is something wrong at the mine?"

He considered whether to mention the sabotage, then decided against worrying them needlessly. "Nothing unusual. Just a busy day."

"Will you be attending church again next Sunday?" Eleanor asked with studied casualness.

Jack set down his fork, meeting his mother's hopeful gaze directly. "I haven't decided."

"Sarah would be pleased if you did," Charlotte said. "I could tell she was watching for you yesterday."

"Charlotte," Eleanor admonished. "Don't embarrass your brother."

"I'm merely stating facts," Charlotte replied innocently. "Sarah asks about Jack frequently."

This revelation caught Jack's attention despite his attempt to appear indifferent. "What does she ask?"

Charlotte smiled triumphantly at having engaged his interest. "About your work, mostly. And whether you've always been so serious or if the accident changed you. She seems quite interested in understanding you better."

"Charlotte, that's enough," Eleanor said firmly. "Your brother's relationship with Miss Williams is his own business."

"Relationship?" Jack repeated, alarmed by the word. "There is no relationship beyond neighborly acquaintance."

"Of course," Charlotte agreed, her tone making it clear she believed otherwise. "Though most 'neighborly acquaintances' don't give away their father's valuable books for someone else's classroom."

Jack felt heat rise in his face. "The school needed proper resources. Those books were sitting unused when they could serve a practical purpose."

"Naturally," Charlotte said, her eyes twinkling with mischief. "Father's precious library that you've guarded so carefully for five years. But one conversation with Sarah about her needs, and suddenly you're happy to part with his treasured collection."

"The books serve the community better in a classroom than gathering dust on shelves," Jack said defensively.

"True," Charlotte said, her eyes twinkling with mischief. "Just as your church attendance was merely 'curiosity' about Reverend Wilson's sermon."

"Charlotte, that's quite enough teasing," Eleanor intervened, though Jack thought he detected amusement in her tone as well. "Your brother has had a long day."

Jack excused himself as soon as politeness permitted and retreated to his study. He attempted to focus on mining reports, but Charlotte's revelation that Sarah asked about him frequently kept intruding on his thoughts, along with Sarah's parting words: *I think you have more faith than you realize.*

Unable to concentrate, Jack abandoned the reports and moved to the window. In the distance, he could just make out the silhouette of the schoolhouse where Sarah was presumably preparing tomorrow's lessons.

"This is madness," Jack muttered, turning away from the window.

With the sabotage escalating at the mine, he couldn't afford distractions. His men depended on his vigilance and practical solutions, not romantic entanglements with the schoolteacher. Hard work and attention to detail would protect his workers far better than prayer ever had.

Sarah Williams deserved someone who shared her unwavering faith, not a man who'd learned that the only reliable salvation came through one's own efforts. Whatever Charlotte might imagine, and despite the undeniable attraction he felt, there could be no future in his growing feelings for Sarah.

The sooner he accepted that truth and focused solely on the mine's security, the better for everyone involved.

Eleven

"Very good, Emma," Sarah said, smiling as the girl recited her multiplication tables without hesitation. "You've made remarkable progress."

Emma beamed at the praise. "Pa and I practice every night after supper. He says mathematics will help me manage my own business someday."

"A wise perspective," Sarah agreed, glancing at the classroom clock. "That's all for today, children. Remember to read chapter three in your history books tonight."

As the students gathered their things, Sarah noticed Ethan lingering at his desk, seemingly reluctant to leave. Over the past two weeks, he had become less disruptive, occasionally even helpful with younger students, though his demeanor remained guarded.

"Is there something I can help you with, Ethan?" she asked when the other children had gone.

He shifted uncomfortably. "Uncle Cyrus wants me to quit school," he blurted. "Says I don't need book learning to run the mines someday."

Sarah's heart sank. "I see. And what do you think about that?"

Ethan looked up, surprise flashing across his face as if no one had ever asked his opinion before. "I..." he hesitated. "I'd rather stay. At least until I finish my geography project."

"The one about mining regions? You've done excellent research," Sarah said encouragingly.

"Uncle won't care about that." Ethan's shoulders slumped. "He just wants me to follow him around the mine office, learning 'real business.'"

Sarah weighed her response. Antagonizing Cyrus Blackwood would do Ethan no favors, but she couldn't simply watch the boy's education be sacrificed to his uncle's ego.

"Perhaps we could compromise," she suggested. "You could attend school in the mornings and work with your uncle in the afternoons. That way, you'd learn both academic subjects and practical business."

Hope flickered in Ethan's eyes. "You think Uncle Cyrus would agree to that?"

"I'd be happy to discuss it with him," Sarah offered. "Education and practical experience together would make you even more valuable to your uncle's business in the future."

"Would you really talk to him?" Ethan asked, his typical bravado momentarily replaced by genuine vulnerability.

"Of course. I believe in your potential, Ethan."

The boy ducked his head, but not before Sarah caught the pleased flush on his face. "Thanks, Miss Williams."

After Ethan left, Sarah began preparing the classroom for tomorrow's lessons, her mind troubled. Confronting Cyrus Blackwood about Ethan's education would be uncomfortable at best, potentially disastrous at worst. From everything she'd heard about the man—and her own limited interactions with him—Blackwood was not someone who accepted opposition gracefully.

A light knock at the classroom door interrupted her thoughts. Sarah looked up to find Jack standing in the doorway, hat in hand, looking somewhat out of place among the small desks and children's artwork.

"Mr. Montgomery," she said, her pulse quickening inexplicably. "This is a surprise."

"Miss Williams." He nodded formally, though his eyes held a warmth that belied his stiff greeting. "I was passing by and thought I'd check on how the repairs to the building are holding up."

"Everything seems quite solid," Sarah assured him, setting down the chalk she'd been holding. "The children love the new windows. They let in so much more light for reading."

Jack stepped further into the classroom, his tall frame making the space seem suddenly smaller. "Good. We can't have our students straining their eyes."

"Were you really 'just passing by,' Mr. Montgomery?" Sarah asked with a slight smile, noticing a smudge of dust on his coat that spoke of time spent at the mine.

A faint flush colored his cheeks. "Actually, I wanted to discuss the possibility of a mine tour for your older students. August suggested it might be educational, given how many of them will likely work there someday."

"What a splendid idea," Sarah said, genuinely pleased. "The children would be fascinated to see where their fathers work."

"I thought we might arrange it for next week, if that suits your schedule." Jack moved closer to her desk, his attention caught by the stack of composition books. "Are these the children's assignments?"

"Yes, their essays on Silver Creek's history." Sarah gestured to the top book. "Emma's is particularly good. She has a natural talent for storytelling."

Jack picked up Emma's composition, his fingers brushing against Sarah's as he did so. The brief contact sent a surprising jolt through her, and she quickly withdrew her hand, hoping he hadn't noticed her reaction.

"Joseph must be proud," Jack commented, leafing through Emma's careful handwriting. "She writes well for her age."

"She's quite bright," Sarah agreed, acutely aware of Jack's proximity as he stood beside her desk. The faint scent of pine and leather that seemed to accompany him filled her senses.

Jack returned the composition book, his expression thoughtful. "We've never had a teacher who took such interest in the children's individual talents. The previous teacher was competent but uninspired."

"Every child has unique gifts," Sarah said. "Part of teaching is helping them discover those gifts."

Jack's eyes met hers directly. "You have a gift yourself, Miss Williams. For seeing the best in people, even when they don't see it themselves."

The intensity of his gaze made Sarah's cheeks warm. "I simply believe everyone has value and potential, Mr. Montgomery. Even those who may have lost sight of it temporarily."

Something flickered in Jack's expression—recognition, perhaps, that her words might apply to him. Before he could respond, the classroom door opened again, revealing Cyrus Blackwood's imposing figure.

"Miss Williams," Blackwood said, his smile not reaching his cold eyes. "I hoped to find you here." His gaze shifted to Jack, hardening noticeably. "Montgomery. Always turning up where you're not expected."

"Blackwood." Jack's voice had cooled considerably. "School business brings me here. And you?"

"The same, of course." Blackwood stepped further into the classroom, his expensive suit and gold watch fob speaking of wealth that stood in stark contrast to the modest schoolroom. "I've come to withdraw my nephew from school effective immediately."

Sarah felt her heart sink. "Mr. Blackwood, surely that's premature. Ethan has shown remarkable improvement in his studies."

"A waste of time," Blackwood dismissed. "The boy needs practical education in business and mining, not fairy tales about literature and arithmetic."

"Education is never wasted," Sarah said firmly. "Ethan is at a crucial stage. Depriving him of proper schooling would limit his future prospects, even in business."

Blackwood's eyebrows rose at her boldness. "You presume to tell me what's best for my nephew, Miss Williams?"

"I presume to advocate for my student's education," Sarah replied evenly. "As is my duty as his teacher."

Jack moved subtly closer to Sarah, his stance protective though his expression remained neutral. "Miss Williams has significantly improved Ethan's behavior and academic performance. Perhaps there's merit in allowing him to continue."

Blackwood's eyes narrowed, shifting between Jack and Sarah with calculating interest. "How touching. The mine owner and the schoolteacher, so devoted to my nephew's welfare." His pause was deliberate, loaded with suggestion. "Such personal attention to one's students is quite intensive, Miss Williams. I'm sure the good people of Silver Creek appreciate how thoroughly you involve yourself in their children's education."

Sarah felt heat rise in her cheeks at the veiled implication, her stomach churning at what the townspeople might think if such rumors spread. Jack spoke before she could respond, his voice dangerously quiet.

"Miss Williams conducts herself with complete propriety, Blackwood. Any suggestion otherwise reflects poorly on the one making it."

"Of course," Blackwood agreed with false innocence. "I merely observe that she seems to inspire such passionate defense of her methods." His smile turned predatory. "One wonders what other subjects receive such dedicated instruction."

Jack's jaw clenched, his hand tightening at his side. Sarah quickly intervened before the situation could escalate further.

"Perhaps we could discuss a compromise regarding Ethan's education?" she suggested, her voice steadier than she felt. "Partial attendance might allow him both academic instruction and practical experience."

Blackwood considered this, his calculating gaze never leaving her face. "How accommodating of you, Miss Williams. Very well—mornings only. The boy can spend afternoons learning actual skills."

"That seems reasonable," Sarah agreed, though she worried about the damage his insinuations might already have done to her reputation.

"How fortunate for young Ethan to have such attentive advocates," Blackwood said, his tone making the innocent words sound sordid. "I can see why you've made such an impression on our community, Miss Williams. Well, I won't keep you further. Good day, Miss Williams." He nodded curtly to Jack. "Montgomery."

After Blackwood departed, the classroom seemed suddenly larger, though the tension lingered in the air between them.

"I apologize for his behavior," Jack said quietly. "Blackwood delights in making others uncomfortable."

"There's no need to apologize," Sarah assured him. "You're not responsible for Mr. Blackwood's actions."

Jack's expression darkened. "Perhaps not. But his interest in you concerns me. Blackwood rarely pays attention to anyone unless he sees a potential advantage."

"I doubt I'm of any strategic value to his business plans," Sarah said, trying to lighten the moment.

"Don't underestimate yourself," Jack replied seriously. "You've become well-respected in Silver Creek already. That alone would interest Blackwood, who craves the town's approval despite his methods."

Sarah was touched by Jack's concern, though she tried not to read too much into it. "I'll be careful in my dealings with him."

Jack nodded, seemingly satisfied with her response. "About the mine tour—would next Friday morning suit your schedule?"

"Perfectly," Sarah said, grateful for the return to their original conversation. "The children will be thrilled."

"I'll make the arrangements then." Jack hesitated, as if wanting to say more, then settled for a formal nod. "Good afternoon, Miss Williams."

"Good afternoon, Mr. Montgomery."

As Jack turned to leave, Sarah found herself reluctant to see him go. "Mr. Montgomery," she called impulsively.

He paused at the door, turning back with a questioning look.

"Thank you," she said simply. "For your support with Mr. Blackwood. And for the mine tour. It means a great deal to the children and to me."

Something softened in Jack's expression. "You're welcome, Sarah."

The warmth in his voice sent an unexpected thrill through her, but before she could respond, he was gone, leaving her standing amid the empty desks with a flutter in her stomach that had nothing to do with her confrontation with Blackwood.

***

Sunday morning dawned clear and bright, the late spring sunshine warming the mountain air. Sarah dressed with care for church, selecting a deep blue dress that Charlotte had once admired. As she pinned her hair, she found herself wondering if Jack would attend services again.

His absence the previous Sunday had disappointed her more than she cared to admit. Though he had never promised to return to church regularly, Sarah had hoped their conversation about faith amid doubt might have prompted further exploration on his part.

At the church, Charlotte waved enthusiastically from the Montgomery pew. "Sarah! We saved you a seat."

As Sarah joined Charlotte and Eleanor, she couldn't help glancing toward the back of the church. The last row remained empty, dampening her spirits slightly.

"Looking for someone?" Charlotte whispered with knowing eyes.

"Just seeing who's here today," Sarah replied, feeling a blush rise in her cheeks.

Charlotte's smile suggested she wasn't fooled. "Jack said he might be late. Mine business this morning."

Sarah's heart quickened at this information, though she tried to maintain a neutral expression. "I'm sure Reverend Wilson will understand if business keeps him away."

"Oh, I think he'll make an appearance," Charlotte said confidently. "He specifically asked what time services began."

Eleanor shushed them gently as Reverend Wilson approached the pulpit to begin the service. The familiar rhythm of prayers and hymns soothed Sarah, though she remained distracted, her ears attuned to any sound from the back of the church.

It was during the second hymn that she heard it—the soft creak of the rear door opening. Sarah resisted the urge to turn around, forcing herself to focus on the hymnal in her hands. Only when the congregation sat for the sermon did she allow herself a quick glance backward.

Jack stood at the end of the last pew, his expression solemn as he listened to Reverend Wilson's words. Their eyes met briefly across the distance, and Sarah offered a small smile of encouragement before turning her attention back to the sermon.

Reverend Wilson spoke that day on Psalm 46:10: "Be still, and know that I am God." He discussed the challenge of finding stillness in a busy, often troubling world, and the importance of quiet reflection in recognizing God's presence in daily life.

"Sometimes," he said, "we're so busy questioning why God allows certain events that we fail to notice the ways He's working in our lives. Signs of His grace surround us—in nature, in unexpected encounters, in the kindness of strangers who become friends. But we must be still enough to recognize them."

The words resonated deeply with Sarah, reminding her of her conversations with Jack about signs from God. She wondered if they might have similar impact on him, sitting quietly in the back pew.

When the service ended, Sarah half-expected Jack to slip away early as he had before. Instead, she was surprised to see him lingering in the churchyard, engaged in conversation with Henry Carter. As she descended the church steps with Charlotte and Eleanor, Jack looked up, his gaze finding hers immediately.

"Sarah," Charlotte whispered excitedly, "Jack's waiting. He never stays after service. Never."

"He's likely just being polite," Sarah demurred, though her pulse quickened as they approached the two men.

"Ladies," Henry greeted them warmly. "A fine sermon today, wasn't it?"

"Quite thought-provoking," Eleanor agreed. "Stillness is something we too rarely practice in our busy lives."

Henry nodded sagely. "Reminds me of what my son Matthew used to say—that sometimes you need to stop talking at God and start listening to Him." He glanced at Jack. "That boy always had a way of cutting straight to the heart of things."

A shadow crossed Jack's face at the mention of Matthew, but it passed quickly. "He did," he agreed quietly. "Though I wasn't always the best listener."

"None of us are," Sarah said gently. "That's why the reminder is so necessary."

Jack's eyes met hers, a silent understanding passing between them. "Indeed."

"Well, I should be getting home," Henry said, adjusting his hat. He nodded respectfully to the group. "Good day to you all."

As Henry departed, another familiar figure approached from the direction of the post office. Mr. Walter Henley, Emma's grandfather, walked toward them with his characteristic unhurried pace, his kind eyes crinkling with pleasure as he spotted them gathered outside the church.

"Miss Williams," Mr. Henley said warmly, "would you and the Montgomerys join us for Sunday dinner? Nothing fancy, but Joseph makes a fine venison stew, and Emma's been hoping to show you her pressed flower collection."

"We'd be delighted," Eleanor answered before Sarah could respond. "Wouldn't we, Jack?"

Jack seemed momentarily startled by his mother's inclusion of him in the acceptance. "Of course," he said after a slight hesitation. "If you're certain there's room for all of us."

"Always room at our table," Mr. Henley assured him. "Emma will be beside herself with excitement. Two of her favorite people at once—Miss Williams and Mr. Montgomery."

Charlotte raised an eyebrow at this. "Emma's fond of Jack?"

Mr. Henley chuckled. "Ever since he fixed her doll last Christmas. The leg had come clean off, and Jack carved a new one, good as new. Never seen a child so grateful."

Sarah glanced at Jack, touched by this previously unknown kindness. He looked slightly embarrassed by Mr. Henley's revelation.

"It was nothing," he said. "Just a simple repair."

"Not to Emma," Mr. Henley said. "Small kindnesses matter most to children. They remember who sees them when they're hurting."

The observation hung in the air, carrying more weight than perhaps Mr. Henley had intended. Sarah thought of Jack's loss of faith after Matthew's death—a profound hurt that had shaped him for years. Who had seen his pain? Who had offered him the kindness and understanding he needed?

As if reading her thoughts, Jack's gaze found hers again, something vulnerable flickering in his blue eyes before he quickly masked it.

"Shall we walk together to the Reynolds house?" Eleanor suggested, breaking the moment.

As they set off, Sarah found herself walking beside Jack, a few paces behind the others. The spring sunshine filtered through the changing leaves, dappling the path with golden light.

"I was glad to see you at church today," Sarah said quietly, keeping her tone conversational. Eleanor and Charlotte walked with Mr. Henley, close enough to be in sight, but far enough away to give them privacy for conversation.

"The sermon was relevant," Jack admitted. "More so than I expected."

"Reverend Wilson has a gift for speaking to individual hearts while addressing the congregation," Sarah observed. "I often feel he's speaking directly to my situation."

"And what situation might that be?" Jack asked, genuine curiosity in his voice.

Sarah considered the question. "Learning to trust God's plan, even when it seems to lead in unexpected directions. Silver Creek was not where I imagined myself a few months ago."

"Do you regret coming here?" There was something in his tone—a hint of concern, perhaps—that warmed Sarah.

"Not at all," she assured him. "I believe I'm exactly where I'm meant to be, even if the path that led here was difficult."

Jack was silent for a moment, contemplating her words. "Your faith gives you certainty," he observed finally. "Even in uncertainty."

"Not certainty," Sarah corrected gently. "Trust. There's a difference."

A fallen branch lay across their path. Jack automatically offered his arm to help Sarah step over it, his touch firm and steadying through the fabric of her sleeve. The brief contact sent a flutter through her stomach, and she was acutely aware of his nearness, the clean scent of his shaving soap, the strength in his arm beneath her gloved hand.

"Thank you," she murmured, reluctantly releasing his arm once they'd navigated the obstacle.

"You're welcome." His voice sounded slightly rougher than usual, and he cleared his throat. "You were saying about trust versus certainty?"

Sarah gathered her thoughts, distracted by the lingering warmth where his arm had supported hers. "Certainty suggests knowing all outcomes, having all answers. Trust acknowledges that we can't know everything, but we can still believe in God's goodness despite the unknowns."

Jack considered this, his profile strong against the spring landscape. "That's a more subtle viewpoint than most people offer."

"Faith often exists in the nuances," Sarah said with a small smile. "In the questions as much as the answers."

"An unusual position for a devout Christian," Jack observed, though his tone held no criticism.

"Perhaps." Sarah watched a leaf spiral down from a nearby aspen. "But I've found that acknowledging questions strengthens faith rather than weakens it. Blind certainty is fragile. It shatters when confronted with tragedy or suffering. Trust, built on both joy and sorrow, is more resilient."

Jack fell silent again, and Sarah wondered if she had once again overstepped. Religious discussions were always delicate, particularly with someone whose faith had been so deeply wounded.

They had nearly reached the Reynolds house when Jack spoke again, his voice low enough that only she could hear. "Your perspective is thought-provoking, Sarah. Not what I expected when you first arrived in Silver Creek."

The use of her first name again, so rare from his lips, sent a pleasant warmth through her. "What did you expect, Mr. Montgomery?" she asked, unable to resist a small smile.

A hint of answering warmth touched his eyes. "Someone less challenging, certainly. Less perceptive."

Before Sarah could respond, Emma burst from the house, her face alight with excitement. "Miss Williams! Mr. Montgomery! You came!" She rushed toward them, pigtails flying. "I set the table all by myself, and Pa made his special stew, and Grandpa baked bread yesterday!"

Sarah laughed at the child's enthusiasm. "It sounds wonderful, Emma. Thank you for inviting us."

"Come see my flower collection!" Emma grabbed Sarah's hand, then reached for Jack's without hesitation. "I kept all the ones you helped me identify, Mr. Montgomery!"

As Emma tugged them both toward the house, their free hands brushed momentarily, sending a jolt of awareness through Sarah. Jack's eyes met hers over Emma's head, and something unspoken passed between them—a shared tenderness for the child's innocent joy, perhaps, or a deeper connection neither was ready to name.

The moment passed as quickly as it had come, but its effect lingered as they entered the Reynolds home, Emma still chattering between them, their faces warmed by more than just the sunshine.

TWELVE

J ack was reviewing the morning production reports when August knocked on his office door, his weathered face creased with concern.

"Come in," Jack called, setting down his pen. "What's troubling you, August?"

"It's about the school, Jack. We've got a problem." August closed the door behind him and took the chair across from Jack's desk. "Three families pulled their children out this week."

Jack felt his stomach tighten. "Which families?"

"The Morrisons, the Kellys, and young Ethan hasn't been attending either." August's expression grew grim. "All families with ties to Blackwood's operation."

"What reason did they give?"

"That's where it gets interesting." August leaned forward. "Mrs. Morrison said she'd heard troubling things about what Miss Williams is teaching. Said she doesn't want her daughter getting 'inappropriate ideas' about her place in the world."

Jack's jaw clenched. "What kind of inappropriate ideas?"

"According to the talk going around, Miss Williams is too progressive. Filling the girls' heads with notions about life beyond Silver Creek, teaching them to look down on traditional family roles." August shook his head. "Kelly said much the same—that his boy was coming home with ideas about workers' rights and questioning authority."

"And where are these accusations coming from?"

"Can't say for certain, but the rumors all seem to trace back to conversations at Blackwood's mine. His foremen have been asking pointed questions about the school curriculum, wondering aloud if Miss Williams is really suitable for a community like ours."

Jack stood abruptly, pacing to the window. Below, he could see workers preparing for the afternoon shift—good men with families who depended on honest work and stable community institutions. If Blackwood was poisoning their minds against Sarah...

"How are our families responding?" Jack asked.

"That's what worries me. Some are asking questions. Bill Hudson mentioned his wife is concerned about what young Lucy is learning. Even Walter Henley seemed troubled when I spoke with him this morning. And..."

Jack turned from the window, his attention sharpening. "And?"

"Bill Hudson's been acting strange ever since we discovered the damaged supports. Won't meet my eyes, keeps finding excuses to avoid any discussion about mine safety. When I asked him directly if he'd noticed anything unusual in that section, he got defensive, said he couldn't be expected to watch every beam in the mine."

"Hudson's been with us for three years," Jack said thoughtfully. "He's always been reliable."

"That's what worries me. If Blackwood can get to a man like Hudson—threaten his family, manufacture debts, whatever pressure he's applying—then none of our workers are safe from coercion. And now with his allegations about Sarah, he's got another foothold."

Jack felt anger building in his chest. Sarah had been nothing but dedicated to her students, working tirelessly to provide them with a solid education. To suggest she was undermining family values was not only false but deliberately malicious.

"There's more," August continued reluctantly. "Word is that Blackwood's been suggesting Miss Williams' background isn't what it seems. Hints about her reasons for leaving Denver, questions about her family's... circumstances."

"What kind of questions?"

"Nothing specific, but enough to plant doubt. You know how it is in a small town—people start wondering why a refined young woman would end up teaching in a place like Silver Creek unless something drove her here."

Jack's hands clenched into fists. Blackwood was attacking Sarah on multiple fronts—her professional competence, her moral character, and her personal history. It was a calculated campaign designed to destroy her reputation and force her to leave.

"I'm going to speak with Blackwood," Jack said grimly.

"Jack, be careful. The man's clever, and he's got support among his workers. If this turns into an open confrontation—"

"It already is an open confrontation," Jack interrupted. "He's just been fighting it in shadows. Time to bring it into the light."

***

Jack found Blackwood in the Silver Creek Hotel's restaurant, dining alone at his usual corner table. The man looked up with feigned surprise as Jack approached, his pale eyes glittering with amusement.

"Montgomery! What an unexpected pleasure." Blackwood gestured to the empty chair across from him. "Join me for coffee?"

"I'll stand," Jack said curtly. "This won't take long."

Blackwood chuckled, setting down his coffee cup with deliberate precision. "Straight to business, then. I admire directness in a man."

"Stop spreading lies about Miss Williams," Jack said without preamble. "Whatever game you're playing ends now."

"Lies?" Blackwood raised an eyebrow in mock innocence. "My dear Montgomery, I've done nothing but express concern for our community's children. Surely you want them to receive proper education?"

"There's nothing improper about Miss Williams' teaching."

"Isn't there?" Blackwood leaned back in his chair, his expression calculated. "I've heard troubling reports about her methods. Filling young girls' minds with ideas above their station, encouraging children to question their parents' values. Hardly appropriate for a frontier community."

"Those reports are fabricated, and you know it."

"Are they? I only repeat what concerned parents have told me." Blackwood's smile was cold. "Of course, one might question why a woman of Miss Williams' apparent breeding would teach in a place like Silver Creek. Usually such dramatic changes in circumstance have compelling explanations."

Jack leaned forward, his voice low and dangerous. "Let me be clear, Blackwood. If you continue spreading rumors about Miss Williams, you'll answer to me personally."

"How gallant," Blackwood murmured. "The mine owner defending the schoolteacher's honor. Tell me, Jack, what do you really know about your dear Miss Williams? About her family's circumstances? Her father's... associations?"

A chill ran down Jack's spine at the implication in Blackwood's tone. "What are you suggesting?"

"Nothing at all. Merely observing that people's pasts have a way of catching up with them. Especially when they've tried so hard to bury uncomfortable truths."

Jack straightened, fighting the urge to grab Blackwood by the throat. "This conversation is over. But remember what I've said. Leave Miss Williams alone."

"Of course, Montgomery. Though I should mention—concerned citizens have every right to question who's teaching their children. And if those questions reveal troubling answers..." Blackwood shrugged eloquently. "Well, sometimes communities must make tough decisions about who truly belongs among them."

The veiled threat hung in the air between them. Jack met Blackwood's gaze steadily. "You'd be wise not to test me on this matter."

With that, he turned and left the hotel, Blackwood's soft laughter following him onto the street.

***

Jack's mood remained dark as he made his way back toward the mine, Blackwood's implications gnawing at him. What did the man think he knew about Sarah's past? And how far would he go to drive her from Silver Creek?

As he walked, Jack noticed several townsfolk who would normally greet him warmly now offering only polite nods. Word of the school controversy was spreading, dividing the community along lines that hadn't existed before Sarah's arrival.

At the mine office, Henry was waiting for him, his weathered face troubled.

"Jack, we need to talk about what's happening with the school."

"I've just spoken with Blackwood about it," Jack said grimly.

"Then you know the situation is serious. Some of our best families are wavering about keeping their children enrolled." Henry removed his hat, turning it in his hands. "My own neighbors are asking questions I don't know how to answer."

"What kind of questions?"

"About Miss Williams' qualifications, her background, whether she's really suitable for our children." Henry's voice was heavy with concern. "Jack, I've seen her teach. She's dedicated and capable. But perception can be as damaging as truth in a place like this."

Jack felt the weight of responsibility settling on his shoulders. As the town's primary employer and most influential citizen, his opinion carried significant weight. How he handled this crisis could determine Sarah's future in Silver Creek.

"Henry, I need you to speak with the men. Make it clear that the Montgomery Mine supports Miss Williams and the school. Any family that withdraws their children based on unfounded rumors will answer to me."

Henry nodded slowly. "I'll do what I can. But Jack, if Blackwood has actual information about Miss Williams' past—information that could damage her reputation—we need to be prepared."

"Then we'll face it when it comes. Until then, we support her."

As Henry departed, Jack stood alone in his office, grappling with emotions he couldn't quite name. His defense of Sarah had been instinctive, driven by more than just a sense of justice. Somewhere along the way, her welfare had become important to him in ways that went beyond mere community responsibility.

The realization troubled him. He'd built careful walls around his heart after Matthew's death, determined never again to care so deeply that loss could devastate him. But Sarah Williams had somehow slipped past those defenses, her quiet strength and unwavering faith touching something he'd thought permanently buried.

A soft rustling sound drew his attention upward. In the rafters above his desk, a small bird was methodically building a nest, carrying twigs and bits of straw with determined efficiency. The sight reminded him of Sarah herself—taking whatever materials life provided and creating something beautiful and purposeful.

For the first time in years, Jack hoped rather than merely enduring. Whatever Blackwood threatened, whatever storms lay ahead, he would stand between Sarah and those who sought to destroy her. She had brought light back into his world, and he would not let that light be extinguished without a fight.

The question now was whether his protection would be enough, and whether Sarah would want it when she learned the full extent of the forces arrayed against her.

Thirteen

Sarah noticed the empty desks immediately. Three seats that should have been occupied by Ethan, young Timothy Morrison, and Katie Kelly, sat vacant as she called roll for the morning's lessons. She glanced at the clock—eight-thirty, well past the time when all her students usually arrived.

"Emma," she said, trying to keep her voice casual, "have you seen Ethan or the Timothy this morning?"

Emma shifted uncomfortably in her seat, her usual bright expression clouded with something that looked like worry. "No, Miss Williams. But..."

"But what, dear?"

Emma glanced around at the other children, then lowered her voice. "I heard Pa talking to Mr. Henderson last night. They were saying things about the school."

Sarah's stomach clenched, but she kept her expression calm. "What kind of things?"

"That maybe you're teaching us wrong things. Mr. Kelly said his Katie was getting ideas above her station, and Mr. Morrison said..." Emma's voice grew smaller. "He said you were making the children question their parents."

A murmur rippled through the classroom as the other students exchanged worried glances. Sarah felt heat rise in her cheeks, but she forced herself to speak steadily.

"I see. Well, children, let's begin our arithmetic lesson, shall we?"

But as the morning progressed, Sarah found it increasingly difficult to concentrate. Three families had kept their children home based on rumors about her teaching methods. What if more parents felt the same way? What if she lost her position before she'd even truly established herself?

By lunch break, Emma lingered after the other children had scattered to their midday meal.

"Miss Williams?" the girl's voice was small and uncertain. "You're not going to leave, are you? Like the other teachers did?"

Sarah kneeled beside Emma's desk, her heart breaking at the fear in the child's eyes. "Why would you think that, sweetheart?"

"Because that's what happens. Teachers come and then they go away when people get angry." Emma's lower lip trembled. "I don't want you to go. You're the best teacher we've ever had."

"I'm not going anywhere," Sarah said firmly, though privately she wondered if that promise was one she could keep. "Sometimes people worry about things they don't understand. That's normal."

After Emma left, Sarah remained in her empty classroom, staring at the three vacant desks. For the first time since arriving in Silver Creek, doubt crept into her heart like a cold fog. Was she truly making a difference here, or was she simply another outsider who would eventually be driven away?

Lord, she prayed silently, *I thought this was where You wanted me. But if I'm failing these children, if I'm causing division in this community...*

The prayer felt hollow, lacking her usual certainty. Perhaps her mother's unwavering faith had been easier to maintain because she'd never had to face such direct challenges to her calling.

Sarah squared her shoulders and gathered her shawl. If rumors were circulating about her teaching methods, she needed to understand exactly what was being said. And there was only one person in Silver Creek who would know every detail of the town's gossip.

Mrs. Parker looked up from her inventory ledger as Sarah entered the general store, her round face brightening with obvious interest. "Miss Williams! How lovely to see you, dear. What brings you in today?"

"I need some additional slate pencils for the children," Sarah said, noting how Mrs. Parker's expression immediately sharpened with curiosity.

"Of course, of course. Though I suppose you might not need quite so many now." Mrs. Parker's tone carried the weight of someone bursting to share important information.

"Oh? Why is that?"

Mrs. Parker glanced around the empty store, then leaned closer conspiratorially. "Well, my dear, I hate to be the bearer of troubling news, but there's been talk. About the school. About your teaching methods."

Sarah forced herself to look puzzled rather than defensive. "My methods? I'm afraid I don't understand."

"Now, I'm not saying I believe a word of it," Mrs. Parker said quickly, "but some folks are saying you're perhaps a bit too progressive for our community. Filling the girls' heads with ideas about life beyond Silver Creek, encouraging children to question their elders."

"How interesting," Sarah said thoughtfully. "I wonder what gave them that impression? I've been focusing primarily on reading, arithmetic, and geography. Just this week we studied the western territories and their natural resources."

Mrs. Parker's expression grew uncertain. "Well, yes, but... that is, I heard you were telling the girls they could aspire to more than keeping house."

"I mentioned that education opens doors," Sarah agreed calmly. "For instance, young Emma has such a gift for mathematics that she might help her father with bookkeeping for his mining work. That would certainly help their family, don't you think?"

"Oh." Mrs. Parker blinked. "Well, yes, that would be helpful."

"And when the Morrison boy struggled with his reading, I used mining terminology to help him practice. His father's work became a pathway to learning rather than something separate from it." Sarah selected her slate pencils carefully. "I believe education should strengthen family bonds, not weaken them."

Mrs. Parker's face was growing redder by the moment. "But surely... that is, I heard you were encouraging the children to question authority."

"I encourage them to ask questions about their lessons," Sarah said with a gentle smile. "Yesterday, Katie Kelly asked why silver was more valuable than copper. We had a wonderful discussion about scarcity and market forces. Her father's expertise in mining made her question quite insightful."

"Oh, my." Mrs. Parker was now looking thoroughly flustered. "That does sound educational."

"Mrs. Parker, I wonder if you might help me understand something." Sarah's voice carried just the right note of confused concern. "Where are these impressions about my teaching coming from? I'd hate for parents to worry unnecessarily about their children's education."

"Well... that is... I believe some of the talk originated from..." Mrs. Parker glanced around nervously. "Perhaps from families associated with the Black Diamond Mine. You know how Mr. Blackwood can be protective of traditional values."

"I see." Sarah nodded thoughtfully. "How fortunate that you've heard the truth directly from me. I do hope you'll help set minds at ease if you encounter these misconceptions again."

Mrs. Parker straightened, her expression now indignant on Sarah's behalf. "Oh, I will! The very idea that you would undermine family values when you're clearly supporting them. Why, just look at how much Emma has improved since you arrived!"

As Sarah paid for her supplies, Mrs. Parker was already mentally composing her corrections to the rumors she'd helped spread. By evening, Sarah knew, half the town would hear Mrs. Parker's passionate defense of the schoolteacher's proper methods and devotion to strengthening family bonds.

Walking back to the school, Sarah felt some of her confidence returning. She'd faced the crisis head-on rather than letting fear paralyze her. Mrs. Parker would set the record straight about the rumors, and perhaps the missing families would reconsider their hasty decisions.

But as she entered her empty classroom, the silence pressed against her like a weight. Three vacant desks served as stark reminders that her position in Silver Creek was more precarious than she'd realized. The afternoon light streaming through the windows seemed somehow colder, less welcoming than it had that morning.

Sarah moved to her desk and pulled out the letter from Denver that had arrived that morning. She'd been too shaken by the missing students to read it properly, but now, in the quiet classroom, she unfolded Mrs. O'Grady's familiar handwriting.

Dear Sarah,

I hope this letter finds you well settled in Silver Creek. I have news that may interest you, though I'm uncertain whether it will bring you joy or sorrow. Three days ago, I saw your father at your old boarding house room, speaking with the current tenant. He appeared to be looking for you, asking questions about where you had gone. He looked older, thinner than when he left, and seemed quite distressed to learn you were no longer in Denver.

I did not speak with him directly, as I was across the street when I observed this, but I thought you should know of his return. Whether you choose to contact him is, of course, your decision.

With warm regards and prayers for your happiness, Mrs. O'Grady

Sarah's hands trembled as she read the letter a second time. Her father—the man who had abandoned them when her mother was dying, who had left without a word of explanation or promise of return—was now looking for her. After two years of silence, he wanted to find her.

But where had he been when she'd sat by her mother's bedside, watching her fade away day by day? Where had he been when Sarah had sold everything they owned to pay for medicine that didn't work? Where had he been when she'd stood alone at her mother's graveside, with no family left in the world?

The letter blurred as tears filled her eyes. The day that had begun with missing students and whispered rumors now included this ghost from her past, this reminder of abandonment and broken promises. Sarah sank into her chair, feeling suddenly overwhelmed by the weight of fighting battles on multiple fronts.

Perhaps, she thought with uncharacteristic bleakness, *some people are simply meant to be alone.*

The thought surprised her with its bitterness. She'd always believed that God had a plan, that difficulties were part of His larger design. But sitting here in her empty classroom, facing challenges from her past and present, that faith felt more fragile than she cared to admit.

What if the rumors about her teaching were just the beginning? What if more families withdrew their children? What if her father's return somehow complicated her new life in Silver Creek? What if she lost everything she'd worked so hard to build?

The silence of the classroom seemed to echo with her doubts. For the first time since arriving in Silver Creek, Sarah Williams felt truly, utterly alone.

FOURTEEN

A week had passed since Jack's confrontation with Blackwood at the hotel, and he was pleased to see that the crisis at the school had largely resolved itself. August had reported that the Morrison and Kelly families were considering re-enrolling their children, having heard from other parents that Miss Williams was an excellent teacher who emphasized traditional values.

Jack sat in his study looking at his ledgers when Charlotte burst through the door with her characteristic enthusiasm.

"Jack! Have you heard the wonderful news about the school?"

"What news?" he asked, setting down his pen.

"Enrollment is back up! Mrs. Parker has been singing Sarah's praises all over town, and even Mrs. Morrison admitted she may have been hasty in her judgment." Charlotte settled into the chair across from his desk.

Jack felt a swell of satisfaction. His public defense of Sarah had clearly worked. The townspeople had rallied around her, and Blackwood's malicious rumors had backfired spectacularly.

"I'm glad to hear it," he said, already planning how he might casually mention his role in resolving the crisis when he next saw Sarah.

"You should stop by the school," Charlotte suggested with barely concealed matchmaking intent. "I'm sure Sarah would appreciate knowing you've heard about her success."

Jack found himself drawn to the idea. He'd deliberately kept his distance this past week, wanting to give Sarah space to handle the situation without his interference being too obvious. But now that the crisis had passed, she would welcome his visit.

That afternoon, Jack made his way to the schoolhouse, noting with satisfaction the sounds of children's laughter echoing from the playground. Classes were clearly back to normal, with a full complement of students engaged in their lessons.

He found Sarah in her classroom, working with young Emma on arithmetic while several other children practiced their penmanship. The scene reinforced his conviction that his intervention had been necessary and successful.

"Mr. Montgomery!" Emma called out when she spotted him. "Look how well I can do my sums now!"

"Very impressive, Emma," Jack said warmly, then turned to Sarah. "Miss Williams, I hope I'm not interrupting."

"Not at all," Sarah replied. "Children, please continue with your work while I speak with Mr. Montgomery."

As the children bent over their slates, Sarah moved toward the windows, gesturing for Jack to follow.

"I understand congratulations are in order," Jack said, keeping his voice low. "Charlotte tells me enrollment has recovered completely."

"Yes, it has," Sarah agreed. "The children are back where they belong."

Jack waited for her to acknowledge his role in the resolution, perhaps to thank him for his public defense. When no such recognition came, he found himself prompting gently.

"I'm glad the community came to its senses about Blackwood's rumors."

"Indeed. Mrs. Parker was helpful in setting the record straight." Sarah's gaze remained fixed on her students rather than meeting his eyes. "She's quite influential with correcting misinformation."

Before Jack could respond, Eleanor appeared in the doorway.

"Oh, wonderful!" Eleanor said, spotting them together. "I wanted to thank you both for how well you handled that unpleasant business with the school rumors."

"Mother," Jack said quickly, sensing dangerous territory.

But Eleanor continued, clearly pleased with the outcome. "Jack, your confrontation with that dreadful Mr. Blackwood was exactly what the situation required. Sometimes a man must step forward to protect a lady's reputation, regardless of the personal cost."

Jack felt heat bloom in his neck, a blush rising as Sarah's sharp, disapproving look pierced him. Her pleasant demeanor quickly turned angry.

"I see," Sarah said, her voice carrying an edge he'd never heard before. "How... gallant."

Eleanor, oblivious to the tension she'd created, beamed at them both. "Yes, it was quite the romantic gesture, don't you think? Like something from a novel."

"Mother," Jack said more urgently, but the damage was already done.

Sarah's cheeks had flushed pink. Whether from embarrassment or anger, Jack couldn't tell. "If you'll excuse me," she said with icy politeness, "I need to attend to my students."

She turned and walked back toward her desk, her spine rigid with controlled emotion. Eleanor looked between them with growing confusion.

"Did I say something wrong?" she whispered to Jack.

Before Jack could answer, Sarah addressed the class with forced brightness. "Children, please gather your things. It's time for afternoon recess."

As the students filed out chattering among themselves, Sarah remained at her desk, organizing papers with unnecessary intensity. Eleanor took the hint and departed, leaving Jack alone with a woman who suddenly seemed like a stranger.

"Sarah," he began carefully.

"Miss Williams," she corrected without looking up.

"Miss Williams," he amended, stung by the formality. "I believe there's been a misunderstanding."

"Has there?" Sarah finally raised her eyes to meet his, and Jack was surprised by the steel in her gaze. "Please enlighten me about what I've misunderstood."

Jack found himself in the uncomfortable position of defending actions he'd thought were obviously justified. "Blackwood was spreading malicious rumors about your character. Someone needed to speak up."

"Someone," Sarah repeated. "And you appointed yourself to that role without consulting me?"

"You were dealing with the enrollment crisis. I thought—"

"You thought I was incapable of handling my own problems," Sarah interrupted, her voice remaining level despite the anger flashing in her eyes. "You thought I needed a man to fight my battles for me."

"That's not what I thought at all," Jack protested, though even as he said it, he wondered if there was truth in her accusation. "I was trying to help."

"By making a public spectacle that confirmed every suspicion about improper familiarity between us?" Sarah set down her papers with deliberate calm. "By ensuring that your mother now views our acquaintance as some sort of romantic drama?"

Jack felt his own temper beginning to rise. "I defended your character against false accusations. I cannot see how that was inappropriate."

"Because it wasn't your place to defend me," Sarah said firmly. "I had already begun addressing the situation through proper channels. Mrs. Parker and I had an excellent conversation that resolved the misunderstandings far more effectively than your confrontational approach."

"My confrontational approach?" Jack's voice sharpened. "I stood up to a bully who was trying to destroy your reputation."

"And in doing so, you confirmed every whisper about your personal interest in the schoolteacher." Sarah's composure finally cracked slightly. "Do you have any idea how that undermines my professional authority? How it makes me appear to be some helpless female who requires masculine protection rather than a competent educator?"

Jack stared at her, realizing for the first time how his actions might have appeared from her perspective. He'd been so focused on defeating Blackwood's challenge that he hadn't considered how his public defense might affect Sarah's standing in the community.

"I never intended—" he began.

"I'm sure you didn't," Sarah said, her anger giving way to something that looked almost like disappointment. "But intent doesn't negate impact, Mr. Montgomery."

The use of his formal name felt like a physical blow. Jack struggled to understand how his well-intentioned actions had created such a rift between them.

"What would you have had me do?" he asked quietly. "Stand by while Blackwood slandered you?"

"I would have had you trust me to handle my own affairs," Sarah replied. "I would have had you believe that I could defend myself without needing rescue. Or you would have come to me first."

Jack felt something cold settle in his chest. "I see."

"Do you?" Sarah moved to the window, gazing out at the children playing in the schoolyard. "Mr. Montgomery, I'm grateful for your family's kindness and support. But I cannot accept a friendship that requires me to be diminished in order for you to feel heroic."

The words hit him like a slap. Jack had thought himself chivalrous, protective, honorable. To learn that Sarah viewed his actions as diminishing rather than supportive shook something fundamental in his understanding of their relationship.

"I should go," he said stiffly.

"Perhaps that would be best," Sarah agreed without turning from the window.

Jack walked out of the schoolhouse feeling as though the ground beneath his feet had shifted. A week ago, he'd thought himself Sarah's protector and champion. Today, he'd discovered she viewed him as an interfering obstacle to her independence.

As he mounted his horse and rode back toward the mine, Jack found himself questioning everything he thought he understood about Sarah Williams. More troubling still, he began to question his own motives. Had he really defended her out of noble principle, or had there been an element of possessiveness in his actions? Had he stepped forward to protect her reputation, or to stake a public claim on her affections?

The questions followed him home, leaving him to wonder if he'd damaged something precious beyond repair through his misguided attempts at chivalry. For the first time since meeting Sarah, Jack Montgomery felt truly uncertain about his place in her life—and whether she wanted him to have a place at all.

Fifteen

Sunday morning arrived with the weight of unfinished business pressing against Sarah's chest. Three days had passed since her confrontation with Jack in the classroom, and she questioned whether she'd been too harsh. As she carefully pinned her simple straw hat in place, her thoughts churned with conflicting emotions.

Perhaps she had overreacted. Jack's intentions had clearly been good, even if his methods were misguided. The memory of his confused expression when she'd dismissed his help haunted her quiet moments.

But then she thought of her mother, waiting faithfully for her father's return, growing smaller and more diminished with each passing month of silence. How many times had Sarah watched her mother make excuses for a man who had abandoned his responsibilities? How many times had she seen her mother's strength ebb away as she defined herself by someone else's choices?

I will not become that woman, Sarah told herself firmly, smoothing her blue Sunday dress. *I will not be diminished by dependence on masculine protection.*

A gentle knock interrupted her thoughts. "Sarah, dear, are you ready?" Charlotte's voice carried through the door, though it seemed more tentative than usual.

"Coming!" Sarah called, gathering her mother's worn Bible. As she stepped outside, she found Charlotte and Eleanor waiting, both looking somewhat subdued.

"Good morning," Eleanor said politely, though her warmth seemed forced. "I hope you slept well."

The careful distance in Eleanor's manner told Sarah that word of her disagreement with Jack had reached the family. She felt heat rise in her cheeks as they walked toward town, the silence stretching uncomfortably between them.

"The weather is lovely today," Charlotte ventured, clearly trying to ease the tension.

"Yes, quite beautiful," Sarah agreed, grateful for the neutral topic.

As they approached the white clapboard church, Sarah's gaze automatically swept the surrounding area, looking for any sign of Jack's solitary presence. Would he still come to watch from the shadows after their harsh words? The possibility that she might have driven him away entirely made her stomach clench with regret.

Inside the sanctuary, Sarah tried to focus on Reverend Wilson's sermon about forgiveness and the complexity of human relationships. His text came from Matthew 18:21-22, about forgiving not seven times but seventy times seven.

"Forgiveness," the reverend said, "is not about condoning wrong actions, but about freeing ourselves from the burden of anger. It requires us to see beyond the offense to the heart of the person who has wounded us."

Sarah thought of Jack's wounded expression, the way he'd walked away with his shoulders set in lines of dejection. Had she seen beyond his misguided interference to his genuine desire to protect her? Or had she been too quick to condemn?

After the service, as the congregation lingered in the sunshine, Sarah spotted a familiar figure at the edge of the churchyard. Jack stood partially hidden behind the old oak tree, dressed in his finest dark suit but maintaining his usual careful distance from the gathered worshippers.

Their eyes met across the space, and Sarah felt her breath catch. Even from this distance, she could see the wariness in his posture, the way he seemed ready to flee at the first sign of further rejection. The sight made her heart ache with remorse.

"I noticed him too," Charlotte murmured softly beside her. "He's been coming every Sunday, but he looks so... lost."

"Reverend Wilson," Mrs. Patterson was saying nearby, "we're so grateful for Sarah's offer to teach Sunday school. The children need additional Bible instruction."

"Indeed," the reverend replied warmly. "Miss Williams, would you like to begin today? The children are already quite excited about the prospect."

Sarah tore her gaze away from Jack's distant figure. "Of course. I'd be honored."

Twenty minutes later, Sarah found herself in the church's small back room with eight eager children, their faces bright with anticipation. She'd chosen the parable of the mustard seed, hoping its message about small beginnings might speak to her own troubled heart.

"Now then," she began, settling into a chair, "who can tell me about the mustard seed?"

Emma's hand shot up immediately. "It's the smallest of all seeds!"

"That's right. And what happens to this tiny seed?"

"It grows into an enormous bush!" Tommy Patterson declared. "Big enough for birds to nest in!"

As Sarah guided the children through the parable, movement outside the window caught her attention. Jack had moved closer to the building, standing beneath a cottonwood tree where he could see into the room. Their eyes met through the glass, and this time neither looked away immediately.

Something in his expression, longing mixed with uncertainty, made Sarah's heart clench with recognition. He was like a lost soul seeking sanctuary but afraid he might be turned away.

"Miss Williams?" Emma's voice drew her attention back. "How big does faith have to be to work?"

"That's a wonderful question, Emma." Sarah kept her voice steady despite Jack's proximity outside. "Jesus said that faith as small as a mustard seed could move mountains. Sometimes the tiniest acts of faith or forgiveness can grow into something beautiful."

The word 'forgiveness' seemed to hang in the air between her and the figure watching from outside. When Sarah glanced toward the window again, Jack had vanished, leaving only the swaying branches of the cottonwood.

After dismissing the children, Sarah walked slowly back toward the schoolhouse, her mind heavy with the memory of Jack's solitary figure. Charlotte had gone ahead to help Eleanor with Sunday dinner preparations, leaving Sarah alone with her troubled thoughts.

That evening, as purple shadows lengthened across her small parlor, Sarah opened her mother's Bible seeking guidance. The book fell naturally to a passage in Proverbs 27:5-6: "Open rebuke is better than secret love. Faithful are the wounds of a friend; but the kisses of an enemy are deceitful."

Sarah read the verses twice, considering their meaning. Had her rebuke of Jack been faithful correction, or had she wounded someone who genuinely cared for her? The distinction seemed crucial, yet increasingly unclear.

She thought of her father again, of how his prolonged absence had slowly drained the light from her mother's eyes. Even on her deathbed, Mama had whispered his name, still believing he might return. But was Jack's protective instinct the same as her father's... what? Sarah realized she didn't even know what to call it. Abandonment seemed too harsh when Mama had never stopped hoping. Selfishness felt wrong when they still didn't know his reasons for leaving.

The uncertainty troubled her, suggesting that perhaps her reaction to Jack had been colored by unresolved pain rather than clear understanding. She'd been so afraid of becoming like her mother—waiting, hoping, diminishing herself for a man who might never return—that she'd pushed away someone who had actually chosen to stay and fight for her.

The comparison made her chest tighten. Her father had left them to face Mama's illness alone, true. But Jack had stepped forward to defend her reputation when he could have remained safely silent. The situations weren't the same at all, yet her wounded heart had reacted as if they were.

Lord, she prayed silently, *give me wisdom to see clearly. If I have wounded someone who meant only kindness, help me find the courage to make amends. But help me also to maintain the independence You've given me.*

Outside her window, the evening star appeared in the darkening sky. Sarah chose to see it as she'd taught the children to see the mustard seed—a small sign of hope, a reminder that even the most complicated situations could grow into something beautiful with patience and faith.

Perhaps tomorrow she would find an opportunity to speak with Jack again, to bridge the gulf her harsh words had created. The thought both comforted and frightened her, for she was understanding that her feelings for Jack Montgomery were far more complex than simple gratitude or friendship.

Whatever those feelings might become, she owed him at least an honest conversation about the misunderstanding between them. The question was whether he would listen, or if her rejection had driven him too far away to reach.

As she prepared for bed, Sarah hoped next Sunday would find Jack still standing beneath the cottonwood tree, still seeking something he couldn't quite name. If God granted her that mercy, she would try to offer him the same grace she hoped to receive in return.

Sixteen

The morning sun cast long shadows across Silver Creek Cemetery as Jack dismounted from his horse, his boots crunching softly on the gravel path. He'd avoided this place for weeks, but something about yesterday's church service had drawn him here despite his reluctance. As he'd been walking away from the church grounds, he'd caught fragments of Sarah's voice drifting through the open window of the back room—her gentle explanation of the mustard seed parable, the children's eager responses. The sound of her teaching, filled with such warmth and faith, had stirred something in him that he couldn't quite name.

His father's grave sat beneath a spreading cottonwood, the simple granite headstone bearing the inscription: "Thomas Montgomery, 1821-1868. A man of faith, father, and friend." Jack had chosen those words himself, though lately they felt like an indictment of how far he'd strayed from his father's example.

"Hello, Pa," Jack said quietly, removing his hat as he stood before the weathered stone. "I suppose you're wondering what's become of your eldest son."

The question hung in the morning air, unanswered but somehow present. Jack could almost hear his father's gentle voice, the way he'd always listened without judgment before offering his counsel.

"I've been attending church again," Jack continued, feeling foolish for talking to empty air yet unable to stop. "Well, standing outside it, anyway. There's this woman—Sarah Williams. The new schoolteacher." He paused, running his fingers through his hair. "You'd like her, Pa. She's got that same quiet faith you always admired. The kind that doesn't waver when storms come."

Jack kneeled beside the grave, pulling away some weeds that had grown around the base of the headstone. "I think I've made a mess of things with her, though. Tried to help when she didn't want helping. Mother always said I had more good intentions than good sense."

The irony wasn't lost on him he was here seeking guidance from a man who'd died five years ago, while avoiding the very woman whose wisdom he desperately needed. His father had always been direct about such matters—when you've wronged someone, you make it right.

After a few more minutes of silent reflection, Jack rose and brushed the dirt from his knees. As he walked back toward his horse, movement near the edge of the cemetery caught his attention. A figure in a blue dress was kneeling among the wildflowers that grew in the meadow beyond the fence.

Sarah.

Jack hesitated, his earlier resolve wavering. She hadn't noticed him yet, focused as she was on handpicking flowers from the natural garden that bordered the cemetery grounds. Her movements were gentle, deliberate, as if each bloom required consideration.

Before he could retreat, Sarah looked up and saw him. They stared at each other across the distance, neither moving for a long moment. Then, as if drawn by some invisible thread, Jack walked toward her.

"Miss Williams," he said softly as he approached, noting how she tensed at his presence.

"Mr. Montgomery." Her voice was carefully polite, but he could see the wariness in her eyes. She clutched a small bouquet of purple and yellow wildflowers against her chest like a shield.

An uncomfortable silence stretched between them. Jack searched for the right words, aware that this unexpected meeting might be his only chance to repair the damage his thoughtless actions had caused.

"Sarah," he began, then caught himself. "Miss Williams, I owe you an apology."

She blinked in surprise, clearly not having expected that opening.

"I've been thinking about what you said," Jack continued, his words coming faster now that he'd begun. "About my interference in your affairs. You were right to rebuke me. I overstepped my bounds, and I did so without considering how my actions might affect you."

Sarah's grip on the flowers loosened slightly. "Mr. Montgomery—"

"Please, let me finish." He took a careful step closer, encouraged when she didn't retreat. "You accused me of not trusting you to handle your own problems, and that struck deeper than you might know. Because you were absolutely correct. I saw Blackwood as a threat to be defeated rather than trusting in your capability to address the situation properly."

The morning breeze stirred the surrounding grass, carrying the sweet scent of wildflowers and the distant sound of church bells from town.

"I suppose," Jack said quietly, "I'm more like other men than I care to admit. Always thinking we need to charge in and fix things rather than allowing others the dignity of fighting their own battles."

Sarah's expression had softened during his speech, and now she looked down at the flowers in her hands. "I owe you an apology as well," she said so quietly he had to lean forward to hear her. "I was harsher than the situation warranted. Your intentions were noble, even if your methods were misguided."

A rueful smile tugged at Jack's lips. "Misguided. That's a diplomatic way of putting it."

"I've been thinking too," Sarah continued, meeting his gaze again. "About what my mother used to say regarding good people making poor choices. She believed that a person's heart mattered more than their mistakes, provided they will learn from them."

"Your mother understood people well."

"She did." Sarah's voice grew wistful. "She loved flowers. Said they were God's way of painting the world beautiful." She held up her small bouquet. "I was gathering these for my classroom. I thought a few wildflowers on my desk might brighten the room for the children."

Jack studied the purple blooms among her collection, recognizing mountain lupine—the same flowers that grew wild around his father's grave each spring. "Those are lovely choices. The children will appreciate the gesture."

"I hope so." Sarah hesitated, then added, "I noticed you visiting the cemetery. I hope I'm not intruding on a private moment."

"Not at all. I was visiting my father's grave. I... I find myself seeking his counsel more often lately." Jack paused, wondering how much to reveal. "He was a man of deep faith. I think he would have appreciated your commitment to the children's spiritual education."

"You heard yesterday's lesson?"

"Fragments of it. The parable of the mustard seed seemed to resonate with the children."

Sarah smiled, and Jack felt something tight in his chest loosen. "They're eager learners. It's a joy to watch them discover new ideas."

They stood there in the morning sunshine, the earlier tension between them gradually fading. Jack realized this was the first genuine conversation they'd shared since that disastrous day in her classroom.

"Miss Williams," he said carefully, "I wonder if we might start over. Not forget what happened, but perhaps move forward with better understanding between us."

Sarah considered this, her fingers absently arranging the wildflowers in her hands. "I would like that, Mr. Montgomery. But I need you to understand—I value my independence. Not because I don't appreciate kindness or support, but because I've worked hard to become the person I am."

"I'm beginning to understand that," Jack replied. "And I respect it, even if my actions haven't always reflected that respect."

"Then perhaps we can be friends," Sarah said, extending her free hand. "Proper friends, with mutual understanding and regard."

Jack took her offered hand, noting how small and warm it felt in his own. "Friends," he agreed, though the word felt inadequate for the complex emotions she stirred in him.

As they shook hands, a child's laughter carried on the breeze from the direction of town, reminding them both of the day's responsibilities ahead.

"I should return to prepare for the week's lessons," Sarah said, though she seemed reluctant to end their conversation.

"And I have mining reports that won't read themselves," Jack replied with equal reluctance.

They walked together toward the path that led back to town, an easy silence settling between them. As they reached the point where their paths would diverge—his toward the mine office, hers toward the schoolhouse—Sarah paused.

"Jack? Thank you for the apology. It couldn't have been easy to admit fault."

Jack studied her earnest face, noting the way the morning light brought out golden highlights in her brown hair. "Admitting fault is simple, Miss Williams. Learning from it is the challenge."

As they parted ways, Jack walked with lighter steps than he'd felt in days. The conversation hadn't erased the complexity of his feelings for Sarah, but it had given him something equally valuable—hope that they might find their way to understanding each other.

Perhaps that was enough for now. Perhaps friendship was the foundation upon which something deeper might eventually grow, if God willed it. The thought no longer frightened him quite as much as it once had.

Behind him, the wildflowers swayed in the morning breeze, and Jack could almost imagine his father's approving smile.

Seventeen

The Tuesday morning lesson on arithmetic had been progressing smoothly until young Ethan Blackwood decided to test Sarah's authority once again. This was only his second day back after his uncle had pulled him from school during the enrollment crisis, and Sarah was disappointed to see that all the progress they'd made together seemed to have vanished. Before the trouble with the rumors, Ethan had been doing better—helping tutor the younger children and showing genuine improvement in his behavior. Now that insolence had returned, and Sarah suspected it was no accident.

"Miss Williams," Ethan drawled from the back row, his voice carrying the practiced insolence of a boy who'd been coached in defiance, "my uncle says women ain't got the mind for teaching mathematics. Says we'd learn better from a real teacher."

Several of the younger children gasped, their eyes wide as they looked between Ethan and Sarah. Emma, seated in the front row, turned around with an indignant frown.

"That's not true!" Emma declared. "Miss Williams is the best teacher we've ever had!"

"Nobody asked you, miner's brat," Ethan sneered, and Sarah saw Emma's face crumple with hurt.

Sarah felt her temper flare but forced herself to remain calm. She'd dealt with bullies before in Denver, and she recognized Ethan's behavior for what it was—a boy trying to assert power he didn't possess through cruelty toward those he perceived as weaker. It pained her to see him acting this way when she knew the kind, intelligent boy that lay beneath his uncle's poisonous influence.

"Ethan," Sarah said quietly, moving to stand beside his desk, "please step outside with me."

"I don't have to—"

"Now."

Something in Sarah's tone must have penetrated his bravado because Ethan grudgingly rose from his seat and followed her onto the schoolhouse porch. Sarah closed the door behind them, ensuring their conversation remained private.

"Ethan, you're clearly an intelligent young man," Sarah began, her voice gentle but firm. "But intelligence without kindness is like a lamp without oil—it produces no real light."

Ethan's cocky expression faltered slightly, as if he hadn't expected this approach.

"I understand you may have concerns about my teaching," Sarah continued. "But Emma is a sweet, hardworking child who deserves your respect, not your cruelty. Her father's occupation doesn't determine her worth any more than your uncle's wealth determines yours."

"My uncle says—"

"Your uncle isn't in my classroom," Sarah interrupted gently. "Here, we treat one another with the kindness Christ commanded. That means no insults, no mockery, and certainly no comments about anyone's family circumstances."

Ethan shifted uncomfortably, clearly unused to being addressed as an adult capable of making better choices.

"If you choose to remain in my classroom," Sarah said, "you'll follow the same rules as every other student. But if you find those expectations too difficult, you're welcome to discuss alternative arrangements with your uncle."

She waited, letting him process the choice she'd presented. Ethan was smart enough to recognize that leaving school would require explaining his behavior to Cyrus Blackwood—a conversation he clearly preferred to avoid.

"I'll... I'll try to do better, Miss Williams," he mumbled, not quite meeting her eyes.

"I know you will," Sarah said warmly. "And I believe you have the potential to be a real leader among the other students—the kind who protects rather than bullies."

When they returned to the classroom, Ethan's behavior was markedly improved. Sarah noticed him actually helping one of the younger boys with his sums, and she caught Emma's grateful smile when Ethan quietly apologized for his earlier comment.

The rest of the morning passed peacefully, and Sarah thought about her conversation with Jack the day before. Their reconciliation at the cemetery had lifted a weight from her heart that she hadn't fully realized she'd been carrying. It was a relief to have their friendship restored, especially given how much she'd come to value his good opinion. Of course, she reminded herself firmly, friendship was all it could ever be. The recent rumors had made it clear that anything more would be inappropriate and damaging to her reputation as an educator.

But Sarah's satisfaction was short-lived. As she dismissed the children for the day, she spotted Cyrus Blackwood approaching the schoolhouse, his expression thunderous.

"Miss Williams," he called out, his voice carrying across the schoolyard and causing several parents to turn and stare. "I need to speak with you."

Sarah's heart sank, but she maintained her composure as the children scattered to their homes for the day. "Certainly, Mr. Blackwood. How may I help you?"

"You can start by explaining why you saw fit to humiliate my nephew this morning," Blackwood said, stepping closer than was proper. "Ethan came home for the midday meal quite upset about your... discipline methods."

"I simply reminded Ethan that all students in my classroom are expected to treat one another with respect," Sarah replied calmly, though her pulse quickened at Blackwood's intimidating proximity.

"Respect?" Blackwood's voice rose. "You seem to misunderstand your place here, Miss Williams. Ethan comes from one of the founding families of this territory. He'll be a leader in this community when he's older, and the other children need to understand that. There are natural hierarchies that must be respected."

Sarah felt anger flare at his casual dismissal of the other children's worth, but she kept her voice level. "In my classroom, Mr. Blackwood, all children are equal in God's eyes and mine. Leadership is earned through character, not inherited through circumstance."

"Character." Blackwood's laugh was bitter. "How convenient that your version of character seems to ignore proper social order. Perhaps you need a reminder that you serve at the pleasure of this community's leading families."

The implied threat hung in the air like a storm cloud. Sarah straightened her spine, drawing on reserves of courage she hadn't known she possessed.

"Mr. Blackwood," she said quietly but firmly, "I was hired to educate all the children of this community to the best of my ability. That includes teaching them Christian values of kindness and respect for one another. If you find those principles objectionable, perhaps you should reconsider whether school is the right fit for Ethan."

Blackwood's face darkened at her calm defiance. "You overstep yourself, Miss Williams. Don't assume your position here is as secure as you think."

"I assume nothing, Mr. Blackwood. I simply do my job with integrity and trust that good people can recognize the difference between education and indoctrination." Sarah kept her voice steady despite her racing heart. "Now, if you'll excuse me, I have afternoon lessons to prepare."

She turned and walked toward the schoolhouse door, her hands trembling slightly but her head held high. Behind her, she heard Blackwood's angry footsteps retreating, but she didn't turn to look.

It wasn't until she heard another set of approaching footsteps that she glanced back to see Jack walking toward the school. He'd clearly witnessed the end of her confrontation with Blackwood.

"Sarah," he said, his voice filled with concern and something that might have been admiration. "Are you all right?"

"I'm fine," she replied, surprised to find that she actually was. "Mr. Blackwood and I had a difference of opinion about classroom management."

Jack studied her face carefully. "I saw him leaving. He looked... displeased."

"I imagine he was." Sarah smoothed her skirts, her composure returning. "But I handled it."

Something shifted in Jack's expression—surprise giving way to respect. "Yes," he said quietly, "you certainly did."

"Thank you," Sarah said softly.

"For what? I didn't do anything."

"Exactly." Sarah's smile was warm with gratitude. "You trusted me to handle my own difficulties. That means more than you know."

Jack's eyes warmed at her words. "I'm learning, Miss Williams. Perhaps more slowly than I should, but I'm learning."

"I had to. The children were watching." Sarah smoothed her skirts with trembling hands. "Do you think he'll cause more trouble?"

Jack's expression darkened. "Undoubtedly. But he'll find the school board less sympathetic to his complaints than he expects. You have more support in this town than you realize, Sarah."

For a moment they simply looked at each other, the afternoon sunlight creating an intimate circle around them.

"I should leave you to your day," Jack said finally, though he seemed reluctant to leave.

"Yes, of course." Sarah hesitated, then added softly, "Thank you again, Jack."

Something flickered in his eyes at her use of his given name, but he simply tipped his hat and walked away, leaving Sarah to wonder at the flutter of her heart as she watched him go.

That evening, Sarah was taking her usual after-dinner walk, enjoying the warming spring air and the lengthening daylight. The past few days had been so pleasant that she'd taken to strolling through the quieter streets of Silver Creek before settling in for the night. As she passed near the Montgomery house, she heard muffled sobs coming from the garden.

Concerned, she approached the garden gate and saw Charlotte sitting on the stone bench beneath the roses, her face buried in her hands.

"Charlotte? What's wrong?" Sarah called softly, not wanting to startle her friend.

Charlotte looked up with red-rimmed eyes. "Sarah! Oh, I didn't expect... please, come in." She gestured toward the garden gate.

Sarah entered and hurried to her friend's side, settling beside her on the bench.

"Oh, Sarah," Charlotte said through her tears, "everything is ruined. Mother found out about David, and she's forbidden me to see him anymore."

"David?" Sarah asked gently, offering Charlotte her handkerchief.

"David Miller. He came to Silver Creek a few months ago to work in the mine, and we've been... well, we've been walking out together. I didn't say anything to you because I wasn't sure where it would lead, and I knew Mother would disapprove." Charlotte's voice broke again. "Mother says he's beneath our station, that I'm throwing away my future for a mere miner."

Sarah's heart ached for her friend. She'd had no idea Charlotte was walking out with anyone - her friend had kept this completely secret.

"Do you love him?" Sarah asked quietly.

"With all my heart," Charlotte whispered. "He's kind and intelligent and hardworking. He makes me laugh, and he listens to me as if my thoughts actually matter. But Mother says that's not enough—that love doesn't put food on the table or maintain social standing."

"And what do you believe?"

Charlotte looked up with red-rimmed eyes. "I don't know anymore. Maybe Mother's right. Maybe I'm being foolish to think love could be enough."

Sarah took Charlotte's hands in hers. "May I tell you something my mother once said to me? She said that God looks upon the heart, not the bank account. That a man's worth is measured by his character, not his position in society."

"But what about practical considerations? The difference in our circumstances—"

"Are obstacles, not impossibilities," Sarah said firmly. "If David is the man you believe him to be, those differences can be overcome. Look at Ruth in the Bible—she left everything familiar to follow Naomi to a foreign land, trusting God to provide. Her faithfulness was rewarded beyond anything she could have imagined."

Charlotte's tears slowed as she listened. "You really believe that?"

"I believe God cares more about the love in our hearts than the size of our houses," Sarah said. "Money can be lost, social position can change, but character endures. If David loves you and treats you with respect, if he shares your faith and values—those are the foundations of a lasting marriage."

"Mother would never agree," Charlotte said sadly.

"Perhaps not immediately," Sarah acknowledged. "But hearts can change, especially when they see the genuine happiness love brings. Don't give up hope, Charlotte. Sometimes God's plans require patience, but they're always worth waiting for."

A rustle of movement caught Sarah's attention, and she glanced toward the house. Sarah caught only the briefest glimpse of movement in her peripheral vision, a rustle of dark fabric disappearing inside.

Had Eleanor been listening? Sarah wondered briefly, but Charlotte's renewed sobs drew her attention back to her friend's needs.

In the garden, Charlotte dried her tears and squeezed Sarah's hand gratefully. "Thank you for listening. You always know exactly what to say."

"I simply share what my mother taught me," Sarah replied humbly, though inwardly she marveled at how God seemed to use even her painful experiences to comfort others.

As they sat together under the starlit sky, both women felt the peace that comes from friendship honestly shared and burdens equally borne. Neither could know that their conversation had planted seeds that would soon bloom in ways they never expected.

EIGHTEEN

The sound of hammers echoed across the schoolyard as Jack supervised the installation of a wooden swing beneath the large oak tree. He'd noticed the children had little in the way of proper recreation during their breaks, and Charlotte had suggested that a swing would be a welcome addition.

"Rope's secure, Mr. Montgomery," August reported, testing the thick hemp lines that supported the smooth wooden seat. "Should hold even the biggest of the young ones."

"Excellent work, August. The children will be delighted." Jack examined the swing's construction, noting how the workers had carefully sanded the wooden seat to prevent splinters and secured the ropes with proper knots that wouldn't slip.

As August gathered his tools, Jack found himself pushing the empty swing gently, imagining the laughter it would soon bring to the schoolyard. The simple pleasure of providing something joyful for the children surprised him with its satisfaction.

"Mr. Montgomery?"

Jack turned to find Sarah approaching from the schoolhouse, her arms full of books and papers. She looked surprised but pleased to see him, and her gaze immediately went to the new swing.

"What a wonderful surprise!" she exclaimed, setting her books on a nearby bench. "The children will be absolutely thrilled."

"Charlotte's idea, actually," Jack said, though he was warmed by her obvious delight. "She thought they needed something more engaging than running in circles during recess."

Sarah walked over to examine the swing more closely, running her hand along the smooth wooden seat. "It's beautifully made. You're very thoughtful to provide this for them."

"It seemed a small thing," Jack replied, watching as she tested the rope's strength with gentle tugs. "Children should have some joy in their day beyond their lessons."

"Indeed they should." Sarah's smile was radiant. "May I try it? I confess I haven't been on a swing since I was quite young."

"Of course," Jack said, surprised by the request but charmed by her sudden childlike enthusiasm.

Sarah settled onto the swing, her blue dress arranged carefully around her legs. Jack gave her a gentle push, and she laughed with pure delight as she began to sway back and forth beneath the oak's spreading branches.

"It's been so long," she said, her voice filled with wonder. "I'd forgotten how it feels—like flying, almost."

Jack continued to push her gently, struck by the transformation in her demeanor. The usual careful composure had melted away, revealing a more carefree side of her nature that he found utterly captivating.

"Tell me about your childhood," he said impulsively. "Before things became difficult with your father."

Sarah's expression grew thoughtful as she swayed. "We lived in a small house with a garden where Mama grew flowers. Papa worked as a mining engineer then, evaluating sites and mineral deposits for investors back East. He would come home and tell us stories about the different mines he'd visited, the people he'd met, the beautiful landscapes he'd seen."

She paused, her voice growing wistful. "Sunday afternoons, we'd walk to the park and... I had a favorite swing there, much like this one."

"Happy memories," Jack observed gently.

"Yes. For a time." Sarah's feet touched the ground, slowing her motion. "But Papa's work required more and more travel as I grew older. He'd be gone for weeks at a time, inspecting mines throughout Colorado Territory. The work paid well when he could find it, but it was unpredictable. Then, about five years ago, he started taking longer assignments—months-long projects evaluating mining operations south of Denver."

Sarah's voice grew quieter. "Our circumstances became... more difficult. The steady income disappeared, and Mama had to take in sewing to make ends meet. Papa would send money when he could, but the letters became less frequent. Then two years ago, they stopped coming altogether."

"It's strange how something as simple as a swing can bring back so much," Sarah continued, her voice soft with memory.

Jack moved around to face her, noting how the dappled sunlight through the oak leaves created patterns across her face. "Perhaps that's why we need simple pleasures. They anchor us to joy, even when life becomes complicated."

Sarah looked up at him, her hazel eyes thoughtful. "You have an understanding heart, Jack Montgomery. More than you probably realize."

Before Jack could respond to her unexpected compliment, he noticed her glance toward the schoolhouse where her lesson plans waited. "I should let you return to your work," he said, though he was reluctant to end their conversation.

"Actually," Sarah said, rising from the swing, "would you like to see what I've been preparing for next week's lessons? I think you might find the approach interesting."

Curious despite himself, Jack followed her into the schoolhouse. The afternoon light streamed through the windows, illuminating the neat rows of desks and the carefully arranged teaching materials.

"May I?" he asked, gesturing to the papers on her desk.

"Certainly." Sarah stepped aside, though her proximity made his pulse quicken.

Jack scanned the lesson plan for the week's arithmetic. In the margins, Sarah had written small notations: "Use parable of the talents to discuss stewardship" and "Multiplication as God's blessing—remind them of loaves and fishes."

"You integrate Scripture into your mathematics lessons?" he asked, genuinely curious.

"When appropriate," Sarah replied, tucking a strand of hair behind her ear. "Children learn better when they can connect new knowledge to familiar stories. The Bible contains wonderful examples of practical wisdom."

Jack continued reading, fascinated despite himself. Her geography lesson included references to the lands Paul visited during his missionary journeys. Her literature selections featured stories that reinforced biblical principles of kindness and courage.

"This is remarkable," he said quietly. "You've created a curriculum that teaches both academic subjects and moral character."

"That's what education should do, don't you think?" Sarah moved to stand beside him, her shoulder nearly brushing his arm. "Knowledge without wisdom is like a sword without a handle—dangerous to the one who wields it."

Jack felt something stir in his chest at her words. "My father used to say something similar. He believed a man's education was worthless if it didn't make him more compassionate."

"A man with a generous heart."

"He did." Jack set the papers down carefully. "He would have appreciated your approach to teaching."

"You speak of him with such respect," Sarah observed. "He must have been a wonderful father."

"The best." Jack moved toward the window, needing distance from her perceptive gaze. "He taught me everything about running the mine, but more importantly, he taught me about responsibility to others."

"And you've honored that teaching," Sarah said softly. "The way you treat your workers, your care for the town's welfare—he would be proud."

Jack turned back to her, surprised by the conviction in her voice. "How can you be so certain?"

"Because I see his influence in everything you do," she replied simply. "A man doesn't develop your sense of honor by accident."

Jack felt something shift inside him at her words, surprised by how much her good opinion meant to him. For a moment, they stood in comfortable silence, the afternoon light creating a golden glow around them in the quiet schoolroom. He studied her face, noting the earnest sincerity in her hazel eyes, the way she spoke of his father as if she'd known him personally. The intimacy of the moment both thrilled and unsettled him, making him acutely aware of how much his feelings for this remarkable woman had deepened.

"I should gather a few things from the general store before it gets too late," Sarah said, glancing at the afternoon light slanting through the schoolhouse windows. "I'm nearly out of chalk, and I promised the children we'd have new slate pencils for tomorrow's arithmetic lesson. They seem to go through them faster than the store can keep them in stock."

"I'll walk with you," Jack offered, holding the door as they stepped outside. "I need to check on a supply order August placed yesterday."

They made their way down the dusty main street, passing the blacksmith's shop where the rhythmic ring of hammer on anvil provided a steady beat to their conversation. Sarah pointed out minor improvements she'd noticed around town—fresh paint on the church steps, new flower boxes at the bakery.

"You have an eye for detail," Jack observed, noting how she seemed to find beauty in the smallest changes.

"Mama always said that noticing the good things makes the difficult ones easier to bear," Sarah replied, stepping carefully around a puddle left from the previous day's brief shower.

As they reached the general store, Jack held the door for her, the familiar scent of coffee beans and dried goods welcoming them inside. Sarah moved efficiently through her purchases while Jack spoke quietly with Murphy about mining supplies. When she finished, they stepped back outside to find the sky had darkened considerably.

"Goodness," Sarah said, looking up at the gathering clouds. "That came on quickly."

The first rumble of thunder echoed across the valley, and Jack noticed how Sarah's shoulders tensed at the sound.

"We should get you somewhere safe before this hits," he said, noting the rapid approach of the storm. "The schoolhouse might not be the most comfortable place to weather this out. Would you consider waiting it out at our house? It's closer, and Mother and Charlotte would enjoy the company."

Sarah hesitated, glancing toward the schoolhouse, then at the increasingly ominous sky. Another low rumble of thunder decided her. "That's very kind. I confess I'd prefer not to be alone during a storm like this."

They hurried toward the Montgomery house as the first fat raindrops began to fall. By the time they reached the house, the wind had picked up considerably, sending leaves swirling across the yard.

"Come, let's wait it out in the parlor," Jack suggested as they climbed the front steps.

Inside, Charlotte was lighting oil lamps while Eleanor secured loose papers that had been scattered by the wind coming through an open window.

"Sarah, dear!" Eleanor exclaimed, looking up with a welcoming smile. "How lovely that you could join us. I was just thinking how much more pleasant it is to weather a storm with good company."

"Thank you for welcoming me," Sarah replied, setting down her parcels from the store. "I confess I'm not fond of being alone during storms like this."

"Such a sudden storm," Eleanor observed, closing the window firmly. "I hope it passes quickly."

A brilliant flash of lightning illuminated the room, followed immediately by a crack of thunder so loud it seemed to shake the house. Sarah gasped and involuntarily stepped closer to Jack, her face pale.

"Are you alright?" he asked quietly.

"I... yes, I'm fine," she said, though her trembling suggested otherwise. "Storms just make me nervous."

Another flash of lightning split the sky, and this time Sarah's reaction was unmistakable—she flinched as if the light itself caused her pain.

"Charlotte, Mother, perhaps you could check that all the upstairs windows are secure?" Jack suggested, recognizing Sarah's need for privacy.

Eleanor studied her son's face for a moment, then nodded. "Of course. Charlotte, come help me."

When they were alone, Jack guided Sarah to the sofa. "Tell me," he said gently.

Sarah wrapped her arms around herself, her eyes fixed on the rain streaming down the windows. "It's foolish, really. I'm not normally so... fragile."

"There's nothing foolish about being afraid," Jack said, settling beside her at a respectful distance. "What is it about storms that troubles you?"

For a moment, Sarah was quiet except for the sound of her rapid breathing. When she finally spoke, her voice was barely audible above the rain.

"The night Mama died, there was a storm exactly like this one. Thunder so loud it seemed to shake our little boarding house room, lightning that turned everything stark white." She paused, her hands clenched in her lap. "She was so weak by then, but the storm frightened her. She kept asking for Papa, calling his name as if he might suddenly appear."

Jack felt his heart constrict at the pain in her voice. "You were caring for her alone?"

"Yes. Papa had been gone for nearly two years by then." Another flash lit up the room, and Sarah closed her eyes tightly. "Every storm since then, I hear her voice again. I see the lightning reflecting off the tears on her face as she whispered his name."

Without thinking, Jack reached for her hand. "I'm sorry. No one should have to bear such burdens alone."

Sarah looked down at their joined hands but didn't pull away. "I keep telling myself that perhaps Papa had reasons for leaving that I couldn't understand. But watching Mama fade away, calling for someone who wasn't there..." Her voice broke slightly. "I felt so alone, Jack. So completely alone. And now, he's returned to Denver."

"He has?" Jack asked, surprised.

"Yes." Sarah's voice was thick with unshed tears. "I received a letter from my friend, Mrs. O'Grady. She says he came looking for me, that he seemed distressed to find me gone. Part of me wants to know what he has to say, but another part of me..." She trailed off, unable to finish.

"Another part of you is afraid," Jack supplied gently.

"Terrified," Sarah whispered. "What if he has some reasonable explanation that makes me feel guilty for resenting his absence? What if he doesn't? What if seeing him again only confirms that he truly didn't care enough to stay when we needed him most?"

Jack squeezed her hand gently. "I can't answer those questions, Sarah. But I can tell you that his choices don't define your worth. And whatever the truth may be, you don't have to face it alone."

"Sometimes I wonder if I'm a coward for coming to Silver Creek," she whispered. "Running away instead of confronting whatever truth awaits me in Denver."

"You didn't run away," Jack said firmly. "You chose to build something good with your life. That takes courage, not cowardice."

The storm continued to rage outside, but as they talked, Jack noticed Sarah's breathing had steadied. She no longer flinched at each lightning flash.

"You know," he said thoughtfully, "my friend Matthew used to love storms like this."

"Really?" Sarah turned to look at him, curiosity replacing some of the fear in her eyes.

"He said they were God's way of showing His power, of reminding us that we're not in control of everything." Jack smiled at the memory. "He'd stand out on his porch during storms, arms spread wide, claiming he could feel the Almighty's presence in the thunder."

"That's a beautiful way to think about it," Sarah breathed.

"Matthew believed God spoke through storms. He had this favorite passage from the book of Job—something about God answering out of the whirlwind." Jack paused, surprised by how clearly the words came back to him. "Where were you when I laid the foundations of the earth? When the morning stars sang together and all the sons of God shouted for joy?"

Sarah's eyes widened. "You remember it perfectly."

Jack stared at her, startled by his own recall. He hadn't thought about that passage in years, yet the words had flowed from his memory as if he'd read them yesterday.

"I suppose I do," he said slowly.

"Matthew sounds like a man of deep faith," Sarah observed.

"He was. He never doubted, never questioned—not even when..." Jack's voice trailed off.

"Not even when the accident happened?"

Jack nodded, his throat tight. "Even as the mine was collapsing around us, he was praying. Asking God to spare the other men, to give their families peace."

They sat in comfortable silence for a moment, listening to the rain drumming against the roof. Another flash of lightning illuminated the sky, but this time Sarah didn't flinch.

"Perhaps," she said quietly, "God is still speaking to you through storms. Through memories of a faithful friend. Through words you thought you'd forgotten."

Jack looked at her, struck by the gentleness in her voice. Six months ago, he would have dismissed such words as naïve sentimentality. But now, sitting beside this remarkable woman while reciting Scripture he'd thought erased from his memory, he considered possibilities he'd long rejected.

"You think God has been trying to reach me?" he asked.

"I think," Sarah said carefully, "that sometimes we're so focused on our pain that we miss the signs of His presence. But that doesn't mean He's given up on us."

Outside, the thunder was growing more distant, the lightning less frequent. The worst of the storm was passing, leaving behind the gentle patter of rain and the fresh scent of washed earth.

Jack studied Sarah's profile in the lamplight, marveling at her ability to find hope in the midst of her own struggles. She spoke of faith as if it were as natural as breathing, yet he sensed the questions she carried about her father's abandonment.

"Sarah," he said quietly.

"Yes?"

"Thank you. For sharing your story, for trusting me with your pain."

She turned to meet his gaze, her hazel eyes luminous in the soft light. "Thank you for listening. For reminding me that storms eventually pass."

"They do," Jack agreed, though he wasn't certain if he was speaking of weather or the tempests of the heart.

As the evening stretched on and the storm moved beyond the mountains, Jack found himself reluctant to end their conversation. For the first time in years, he felt a stirring of something he'd thought permanently lost—not quite faith, but perhaps the desire for it.

And as Sarah had suggested, maybe that desire was itself a sign that God hadn't given up on him after all.

Nineteen

A week had passed since the storm, and the warm June sunshine had finally arrived in Silver Creek, bringing with it the promise of summer. Sarah stepped out of her small quarters at the schoolhouse, breathing in the sweet scent of wildflowers that had bloomed after the recent rains. The mountains were painted in vibrant greens, and she could hear children's laughter echoing from the town as families prepared for the evening's festivities.

The monthly church supper was a cornerstone of Silver Creek's social life, bringing together families from throughout the valley to share food, conversation, and community spirit. Sarah had been looking forward to the event all week, grateful for any opportunity to strengthen her bonds with the townspeople.

She smoothed her best blue dress and gathered the apple pie she'd spent the afternoon baking, still marveling at how comfortable she'd become in her little kitchen. Living independently had its challenges, but there was something deeply satisfying about creating a home of her own.

The church grounds were already bustling with activity when Sarah arrived. Long tables covered with white cloths stretched across the grass, laden with dishes contributed by every family in town. Red, white, and blue bunting hung from the trees in anticipation of the upcoming Independence Day celebration, and children ran between the tables in games of tag.

"Sarah!" Eleanor Montgomery called out, waving from beside a table heavy with desserts. "How lovely you look! Please, bring your pie over here."

Sarah made her way through the crowd, accepting warm greetings from parents and students alike. Little Emma ran up to hug her skirts, chattering excitedly about the new swing at school, while Mrs. Patterson complimented her on the children's recent improvements in penmanship.

"Miss Williams!" Reverend Wilson approached, beaming with his characteristic enthusiasm. "What a wonderful turnout we have tonight. The entire community coming together as one family."

"It's beautiful," Sarah agreed, genuinely moved by the sight of neighbors sharing conversation and laughter. "This is what community should be."

As the evening progressed, Sarah found herself in animated discussions about everything from the children's upcoming summer activities to plans for the town's Fourth of July celebration. She was speaking with Mrs. Carter about organizing a spelling bee when she noticed two men standing apart from the festivities, their heads bent in serious conversation.

Blackwood and a man she didn't recognize were positioned near the refreshment tables, but their attention wasn't on the food. Something about their secretive manner caught Sarah's attention, and she moved closer, pretending to examine the desserts while straining to hear their words.

"—tunnel's nearly complete," Blackwood was saying quietly. "One small change to the support beams and Montgomery will have more than he bargained for."

"When?" the other man asked.

"Tomorrow night. During the shift change, when the fewest men are around." Blackwood's voice dropped even lower. "Make it look like an accident. Poor engineering, perhaps. Or faulty materials."

Sarah's blood ran cold. They were planning to sabotage Jack's mine—possibly kill innocent workers. She had to warn him immediately.

She turned to scan the crowd for Jack's familiar figure, spotting him near the church steps in conversation with the mayor. Sarah started toward him, weaving through clusters of celebrating townspeople.

"Miss Williams."

Blackwood's voice stopped her cold. She turned to find him blocking her path, his companion nowhere to be seen.

"Mr. Blackwood. Are you enjoying the supper?"

"Indeed. Such a... revealing event. One learns so much about people when they think no one is watching." His smile was cold as winter. "Tell me, my dear, how much do you actually know about your father's business ventures?"

Sarah's mouth went dry. "I beg your pardon?"

"Jonas Williams. Came down to work the silver mines south of here, didn't he? Until that unfortunate incident with the mine collapse. So many questions about faulty explosives, about who might have been responsible for cutting corners on safety."

The world seemed to tilt around Sarah. "What are you implying?"

"Nothing at all. Merely wondering if certain secrets might interest your new friends here in Silver Creek. People can be so... judgmental about family connections, especially when those connections involve mining accidents."

Sarah understood the threat perfectly. Whether true or fabricated, Blackwood could destroy her reputation with whispers about her father.

"What do you want?" she whispered.

"Simply for you to enjoy your supper without spreading idle gossip or concerning yourself with matters that don't involve you." His eyes glittered with malice. "I'm sure you understand."

Before Sarah could respond, Blackwood melted back into the crowd, leaving her standing frozen among the cheerful festivities. Her hands shook as the implications crashed over her. If she warned Jack about the sabotage plot, Blackwood would retaliate by ruining her with lies, or perhaps truths, about her father.

But she couldn't let innocent men die to protect her own reputation.

Taking a deep breath, Sarah pushed through the crowd toward Jack. She found him still speaking with Mayor Watkins about the town's expansion plans.

"Mr. Montgomery," she said, her voice steadier than she felt. "Might I have a word with you? It's rather urgent."

Jack looked up, immediately noting her pale complexion. "Of course. Mayor, if you'll excuse us?"

Sarah led him away from the crowd, toward the side of the church where they could speak privately.

"What's wrong?" Jack asked immediately. "You look as if you've seen a ghost."

"Jack, I overheard something—a conversation between Blackwood and another man. They're planning to sabotage your mine. Tomorrow night, during the shift change."

Jack's expression hardened. "Are you certain of what you heard?"

"They spoke of adjusting support beams, making it look like an accident. Jack, they could kill people."

"That—," Jack muttered, his jaw clenching. "I should have expected this. He's tried sabotage before—smaller incidents, but this..." His voice trailed off as the full implications hit him.

"I know what I heard," Sarah said firmly, though her voice trembled. "Please, you have to believe me."

Jack studied her face for a long moment. "What did Blackwood say to you afterward?"

Sarah's heart skipped. "How did you know—"

"I saw him approach you. I was making my way over when Mayor Watkins stopped me with a question about the mine contracts. By the time I looked again, Blackwood was gone and you looked terrified."

Sarah wrapped her arms around herself. "He threatened to spread rumors about my father. About some incident involving a mine collapse and faulty explosives in the southern mines."

"And you're warning me despite his threats?" Jack stepped closer, his voice soft with wonder.

"I couldn't let anyone be hurt to protect my reputation," Sarah said simply.

Something shifted in Jack's expression—surprise, admiration, and something deeper that made Sarah's pulse quicken.

"You're certain about what you overheard?"

"Positive. They mentioned tomorrow night specifically."

Jack was quiet for a moment, then nodded decisively. "I'll double the security at the mine and have August inspect all the support structures. If Blackwood is planning something, we'll be ready."

"Thank you for believing me," Sarah said, relief flooding through her.

"Thank you for risking yourself to warn me." Jack's voice was rough with emotion. "That took considerable courage."

As they stood there, the celebration continuing around them but feeling very far away, Sarah became acutely aware of Jack's proximity. His blue eyes searched her face as if he were seeing her for the first time.

"Sarah," he said quietly, then seemed to struggle with his words.

"Yes?"

Instead of speaking, Jack reached for her hand, his fingers warm and strong as they intertwined with hers. The touch sent electricity shooting up Sarah's arm, and she saw her own reaction mirrored in his eyes.

"I—" Jack began, then stopped, his gaze dropping to their joined hands. "This isn't the place for such conversations."

Sarah's heart hammered against her ribs. "What conversations?"

Jack looked up, meeting her eyes directly. "Would you... that is, would you join me for dinner tomorrow evening? To discuss the school's needs, of course. The budget for next term, supplies you might require..."

His formal words contrasted with the intensity in his voice, making it clear that school business was the last thing on his mind.

"I..." Sarah felt heat rise in her cheeks. "Yes, I would like that very much."

"Seven o'clock?"

"Seven o'clock," she agreed, her voice barely above a whisper.

They stood there for another moment, hands still joined, awareness crackling between them like lightning before a storm. Then the sound of Charlotte calling Sarah's name broke the spell.

"We should return to the celebration," Jack said reluctantly, releasing her hand.

"Yes, of course."

But as they walked back toward the crowd, Sarah felt as if everything had changed. The warmth of Jack's touch lingered on her skin, and the memory of his eyes meeting hers sent shivers through her entire body.

Tomorrow evening couldn't come soon enough—and yet she feared what it might mean for both their carefully guarded hearts.

"Sarah! There you are!" Charlotte appeared at her elbow, eyes bright with curiosity. "Whatever were you and Jack discussing so seriously? You both look rather... affected."

"School business," Sarah said quickly, but her burning cheeks betrayed her.

Charlotte's knowing smile suggested she wasn't fooled for a moment. "Of course. School business. How perfectly professional of you both."

As the evening continued around them, Sarah stole glances at Jack across the crowd. Each time their eyes met, she felt that same electric connection, that same promise of something momentous approaching.

Whatever tomorrow brought, Sarah knew there would be no going back to the safe distance they'd maintained. The fork in the road had appeared, and they were both about to choose a path that would change everything.

TWENTY

The acrid smell of smoke and dust filled Jack's nostrils as he surveyed the aftermath of the explosion. Chunks of rock lay scattered across the tunnel floor, and a section of the north wall had collapsed, blocking the passage they'd spent months carving.

Jack's jaw clenched as he realized what had happened. He'd concentrated his guards at the main tunnel after Sarah's warning, leaving only two men to patrol the smaller passages. Blackwood had been clever—hitting the north tunnel when the guards were making their rounds elsewhere.

"Anyone hurt?" Jack called out, his voice echoing in the damaged tunnel.

"No, sir," August replied, coughing as he emerged from behind a support beam. "Pure luck we were checking the equipment instead of blasting when it went off."

Jack kneeled beside the debris, running his fingers along the edge of the collapse. The sight brought back memories he'd fought to suppress: another tunnel, another collapse, Matthew's voice calling out as the ceiling came down.

"Blackwood's work," he said grimly, forcing himself to focus on the present. "Just as Sarah warned us."

"At least we were ready for it," August said, though his expression remained troubled. "Could have been much worse if we hadn't evacuated that section."

"The question now is what he'll try next," Jack replied, standing and brushing dust from his hands.

"This was just the beginning."

"Get the men out of here and post guards at all tunnel entrances," Jack ordered. "I want every inch of this mine checked for additional explosives."

As his workers scrambled to secure the area, Jack felt fury building in his chest. Sarah had risked everything to warn him, and he'd still failed to prevent this. The familiar weight of responsibility and guilt pressed down on him—the same crushing sensation he'd felt five years ago when Matthew died under his watch.

Two hours later, Jack found Blackwood in his office at the rival mine, calmly reviewing ledgers as if nothing had happened.

"Montgomery," Blackwood said without looking up. "I heard you had some trouble at the north tunnel. Structural failure, was it?"

"Cut the act, Blackwood. We both know what really happened."

Blackwood finally raised his eyes, his expression a picture of innocent surprise. "I'm afraid I don't follow. Are you suggesting I had something to do with your mining difficulties?"

"I'm stating it outright. You sabotaged my tunnel."

"That's quite an accusation." Blackwood leaned back in his chair, completely unruffled. "Do you have proof of these wild claims?"

Jack stepped closer to the desk. "I will. And when I do—"

"When you do, you'll what? Have me arrested?" Blackwood's laugh was a chilling sound, like ice cracking on a frozen lake. "Who do you think they'll believe—a respected businessman or a man whose judgment has clearly been compromised by a pretty face?"

"Leave Miss Williams out of this."

"Ah, so you admit your feelings for the schoolteacher are affecting your decisions." Blackwood's smile turned predatory. "How romantic. And how foolish. Tell me, Jack, what do you really know about sweet Sarah Williams? About why she left Denver so suddenly? About her father's questionable associations?"

"Whatever lies you're planning to spread—"

"Lies?" Blackwood tsked softly. "I never deal in lies, my dear fellow. The truth is so much more devastating. But don't worry—your Miss Williams and I have already discussed the importance of discretion."

Ice ran through Jack's veins. "What did you say to her?"

"Nothing that wasn't true. The question is whether you're prepared to face those truths, or if you'd prefer to keep living in your romantic fantasy."

Jack lunged forward, but stopped himself just short of grabbing Blackwood by the throat. "Stay away from her. And stay away from my mine."

"Or what?" Blackwood's voice was silk over steel. "Face it, Montgomery. You're distracted, emotional, making poor decisions. Your father would be ashamed."

The words hit like physical blows, but Jack forced himself to turn and leave before he did something he'd regret.

Back at his own office, Jack slammed the door and began pacing like a caged animal. Blackwood's taunts echoed in his mind—was his judgment really compromised? Was he putting his workers at risk because of his feelings for Sarah?

He moved to his desk, intending to review the security reports, when something caught his eye. While reaching for a ledger on the shelf behind his desk, his hand knocked against a small object that had been tucked between two larger volumes. A leather-bound book tumbled onto his desk with a soft thud.

Jack picked it up with trembling hands. The worn leather cover bore the initials "M.C." in faded gold lettering. Matthew's Bible. The one his friend had carried into the mines every day, claiming it brought him luck.

How long had it been sitting there, forgotten among his father's old business journals? Jack hadn't seen it since the day they'd cleared out Matthew's belongings five years ago. He must have placed it there himself and simply forgotten about it in his grief.

With growing emotion, Jack opened the cover and found an inscription in Matthew's familiar handwriting: "For my friend Jack—may you always remember that God's plans are bigger than our understanding. Matthew Carter, 1869."

Jack's throat tightened. He flipped through the pages, noting passages Matthew had underlined, verses he'd marked with careful annotations. The book fell open to a particular page in Isaiah, where Matthew had drawn a star beside verse 55:8-9.

"'For my thoughts are not your thoughts, neither are your ways my ways,' saith the Lord. 'For as the heavens are higher than the earth, so are my ways higher than your ways, and my thoughts than your thoughts.'"

The words hit Jack like a revelation. How many times had Matthew quoted this passage when Jack questioned God's plan? How many times had his friend insisted that divine wisdom exceeded human understanding?

"I don't remember putting this here," Jack said aloud, his voice hoarse with emotion.

But there it was, appearing at the exact moment he needed its message most. Another sign, just as Sarah had suggested. Jack sank into his chair, staring at the open Bible, feeling the walls he'd built around his heart beginning to crack.

An hour later, Jack stood on Henry's front porch, Matthew's Bible tucked under his arm.

"Jack?" Henry answered the door with surprise. "What brings you here?"

"I need to talk to someone," Jack said simply. "About Matthew. About other things."

Henry's weathered face softened with understanding. "Come in, son. Coffee's still warm."

They sat in Henry's modest parlor, steam rising from their cups as Jack struggled to find words for the turmoil in his chest.

"I found this today," Jack finally said, placing Matthew's Bible on the table between them. "On my desk. I don't remember putting it there."

Henry's eyes widened as he recognized the book. "I wondered what happened to this. Matthew never went anywhere without it."

"He gave it to me before he died. I mean, not directly—it was in his belongings with a note saying I should have it. I put it away because it hurt too much to look at."

"And now?"

Jack ran his fingers along the worn cover. "Now I'm wondering if Matthew somehow wanted me to find it today. After everything that's happened with Sarah, with these signs she keeps talking about."

"Ah." Henry leaned back in his chair. "So, we're talking about Miss Williams."

"Am I losing my mind, Henry? These coincidences, these moments that seem too perfectly timed to be random—am I seeing things that aren't there?"

"What does your heart tell you?"

Jack laughed bitterly. "My heart is the problem. I think I'm falling in love with her, and it's clouding my judgment. Blackwood said—"

"Blackwood said what he needed to say to shake your confidence. That man's been trying to undermine you for years." Henry leaned forward. "Tell me about Sarah. What do you see when you look at her?"

"I see..." Jack paused, surprised by the emotion that welled up. "I see kindness. Strength. Faith that never wavers, even when she's afraid. She makes me want to be the man my father raised me to be."

"And that troubles you?"

"It terrifies me. What if I'm wrong about her? What if caring for her puts others at risk? What if God isn't really speaking through these signs, and I'm just a fool grasping at hope?"

Henry was quiet for a long moment, studying Jack's face. "You know, my daughter asked me a similar question once, years ago when Joseph was courting her."

"She did?"

"She said, 'Papa, how do I know if this is God's will or just my own desire?' You know what I told her?"

Jack shook his head.

"I said, 'When God puts the right woman in a man's path, He changes that man's heart to reflect His own love. If Sarah makes you want to be more compassionate, more faithful, more like Christ—then maybe that's your answer.'"

"And if I'm wrong? If I'm seeing signs that aren't there?"

Henry smiled gently. "Then at least you'll have tried to listen for God's voice again. That's more than you've done in five years."

That evening, Jack stood before his mirror, adjusting his collar for the third time. His hands were unsteady—ridiculous for a man of thirty-three facing a simple dinner with a lady. But there was nothing simple about Sarah, and nothing simple about what he was feeling.

When Jack arrived at the schoolhouse at precisely seven o'clock, Sarah answered the door wearing a dress of dark green that brought out the green flecks in her eyes. She'd arranged her hair in a loose braid, and Jack felt his breath catch.

"Good evening, Jack," she said, her cheeks pink with what might have been nervousness.

"Sarah. You look beautiful."

She ducked her head at the compliment. "Thank you. Shall we go?"

They walked together through the quiet evening streets toward the Montgomery house, making polite conversation about the day's events. When they arrived, Eleanor and Charlotte greeted Sarah warmly.

"We've already eaten," Eleanor explained graciously. "We thought you might prefer to discuss school business without our chatter. We'll be in the parlor if you need anything."

"We hope you don't mind," Charlotte added with a barely suppressed smile, though her eyes sparkled with mischief. "Mrs. Finch has prepared a lovely dinner for you both."

As Eleanor and Charlotte settled in the adjacent parlor—close enough to serve as proper chaperones but far enough to allow private conversation—Jack and Sarah took their places at the dining table. Mrs. Finch had outdone herself with roasted chicken, fresh vegetables, and warm bread.

"This is much more elegant than anything I could have managed," Sarah said, suddenly anxious.

"Mrs. Finch enjoys having someone special to cook for," Jack assured her, though he doubted he'd be able to taste anything with his nerves so tangled.

As they ate, conversation initially focused on safe topics—the school's progress, the town's growth, the weather. But as the evening progressed and they grew more comfortable, their words grew more personal.

"What did you dream of being when you were young?" Sarah asked, her chin propped on her hand as she watched him across the table.

"A preacher, actually," Jack said, surprising himself by admitting it. "I wanted to travel as a missionary, to see the world while serving God."

"What changed your mind?"

Jack was quiet for a moment. "My father died, and suddenly I had responsibilities I couldn't abandon. The mine, the town, my family—they all needed me here."

"Do you regret it? Staying, I mean?"

"I thought I did, for a while. After Matthew's accident, I convinced myself that God was punishing me for choosing duty over calling." Jack met her eyes. "But lately, I've been wondering if maybe this was always my calling. Maybe home was where I meant to serve."

"And what's changed your mind?"

Jack's gaze grew intense. "You have."

Sarah's breath caught, and color flooded her cheeks. "Jack..."

"I'm sorry. I didn't mean to make you uncomfortable."

"You haven't. It's just... I never expected..." She trailed off, looking down at her hands.

"Expected what?"

"To matter to someone like you. To feel..." She looked up, meeting his gaze bravely. "To feel as if my heart might belong to someone again."

The words hung between them, heavy with meaning. Jack glanced toward the parlor where Charlotte's soft laughter could be heard, then reached across the table, covering Sarah's hand with his.

"Sarah, there's something I need to tell you. About today, about the mine—"

"Was anyone hurt?" she asked immediately, fear flickering in her eyes.

"No, thank God. But there was an explosion in the north tunnel this morning—just as you warned."

Sarah's face went pale. "Oh, Jack. Even with the warning, he still managed to—I'm so sorry. I should have been able to give you more details, more time to prepare—"

"You gave me exactly what I needed. Because of your warning, I had extra security in place, and no one was in that tunnel when it happened." Jack's voice was firm. "You saved lives, Sarah."

"But he still damaged the mine. And now Blackwood will retaliate for my interference. The things he threatened to say about my father—"

"Let him try." Jack's voice was fierce, though he kept it low. "I won't let him hurt you, Sarah. I promise you that."

Their eyes met across the table, and Jack felt the last of his defenses crumble. Whatever Blackwood threatened, whatever complications lay ahead, he couldn't deny what was happening between them.

The mantle clock chimed half past eight, and Sarah glanced toward the parlor where Eleanor and Charlotte were quietly conversing over their needlework.

"I should return to the schoolhouse," Sarah said softly, though she made no move to withdraw her hand from his. "It's getting late."

"Yes," Jack agreed, though the last thing he wanted was for this evening to end. "I'll walk you home."

After bidding goodnight to Eleanor and Charlotte, who both looked pleased with how the evening had progressed, Jack and Sarah stepped out into the warm night air. They strolled through the quiet streets toward the schoolhouse, neither speaking but both acutely aware of the other's presence.

When they reached the schoolhouse gate, Sarah turned to face him.

"Thank you for tonight," she said. "For trusting me about the mine, for believing in me when others might not."

"Thank you for warning me. For seeing something in me worth saving."

They stood there in the moonlight, the space between them charged with unspoken longing. Jack reached up to touch her face, his thumb tracing the line of her cheek.

"Sarah," he whispered.

She stepped closer, her eyes fluttering closed as his head bent toward hers. Their lips were mere inches apart when the church bell tolled nine o'clock, the sound reverberating through the still night air.

Sarah startled, stepping back with her hand pressed to her chest. "I should... that is, I need to..."

"Of course," Jack said, though his voice was rough with barely contained emotion. "Good night, Sarah."

"Good night, Jack."

As he watched her disappear into her quarters, Jack turned and began the walk back to the Montgomery house, his heart pounding with the intensity of what had almost happened between them.

His feelings for Sarah ran deeper than he'd ever allowed himself to acknowledge. The way she'd looked at him tonight, the trust and something more shining in her hazel eyes—it had shaken him to his core.

All his attempts to guard his heart, all his carefully constructed walls—they were crumbling piece by piece. The question now was whether he had the courage to let them fall completely, and whether he could trust in the signs that seemed to point him toward a future he'd never dared to imagine.

TWENTY-ONE

The letter arrived on a crisp Wednesday morning, delivered by the same postal clerk who had brought Mrs. O'Grady's first message weeks ago. Sarah's hands trembled as she recognized the familiar handwriting—bolder than her mother's elegant script, but bearing the same slant she remembered from her childhood.

My dearest Sarah, Mrs. O'Grady informed me that you have secured a position in Silver Creek. I am relieved to know you are well and established. I have urgent matters to discuss with you regarding debts that have come to light and certain obligations that require immediate attention. I will arrive in Silver Creek within the fortnight. Your loving father, Jonas Williams

Sarah read the letter twice, her heart sinking with each word. Not once did he mention her mother's death or express sorrow for his absence during her illness. The phrase "urgent matters" and "debts" made her stomach clench with familiar dread.

What debts could there be? She had paid her mother's medical bills and settled their modest accounts before leaving Denver. The only explanation was that her father had somehow incurred obligations using their family name—a thought that made her feel sick.

"Miss Williams?" Emma's voice from the classroom doorway interrupted her troubled thoughts. "Are you all right? You look pale."

Sarah quickly folded the letter, forcing a smile. "I'm fine, Emma. Just some news from Denver that I wasn't expecting."

"Good news or bad news?" Emma asked with the directness of childhood.

"I'm not certain yet," Sarah replied honestly. "Now, shall we work on those arithmetic problems we discussed yesterday?"

But as the morning progressed, Sarah found it increasingly difficult to concentrate on her lessons. Her father's letter had awakened all the old fears—the uncertainty, the feeling of having no control over circumstances that could destroy everything she'd worked to build.

At midday, while the children were outside for their lunch break, Sarah noticed Emma hadn't joined the others in their usual games. Through the window, she saw the girl standing by the schoolyard gate, speaking earnestly with her grandfather Walter Henley, whose weathered face was creased with worry.

Moments later, Emma came running toward the school building, her face streaked with tears.

"Miss Williams!" Emma burst through the classroom door. "Please, you have to come! Papa collapsed at the mine, and they brought him home, but he won't wake up properly!"

Sarah immediately set aside her personal troubles. "Emma, slow down. Tell me exactly what happened."

"Grandpa came to get me," Emma said between sobs. "He said Papa was coughing real bad this morning, worse than usual. Mr. Montgomery said he shouldn't work today, but Papa insisted. Then he just... fell down. They carried him home, but Grandpa doesn't know what to do!"

Mr. Henley appeared in the doorway, his hat in his hands. "Miss Williams, I hate to ask, but Dr. Martinez is in Denver for the week. Joseph's breathing something awful, and I don't know how to help him. Emma said you cared for your mother when she was ill."

"Of course," Sarah said without hesitation, grabbing her shawl. "Let me dismiss the children early, and I'll come immediately."

After sending the students home with instructions to tell their parents school would resume the next day, Sarah hurried to the modest Reynolds cottage. Inside, she found Joseph lying unconscious on his narrow bed, his breathing shallow and labored. His skin had a grayish pallor that reminded her painfully of her mother's last days.

"He's been poorly for weeks," Mr. Henley explained quietly, "but he insisted on working. Said he couldn't afford to miss days with Emma to feed and clothe."

Sarah approached the bed, her heart breaking at the sight of the man whose family had been so kind to her since her arrival in Silver Creek. "Has he been coughing blood?"

"Some," Mr. Henley admitted reluctantly. "But he made me promise not to tell Emma."

Sarah nodded, understanding. She had watched her mother hide similar symptoms to avoid frightening her. "I'll do what I can until Dr. Martinez returns."

For the next two days, Sarah divided her time between teaching and nursing Joseph Reynolds. She prepared herbal teas her mother had taught her to make, kept watch during fever spells, and helped Mr. Henley manage Emma's care. The work was exhausting but necessary—the Reynolds family had no one else to turn to.

It was during her second evening at the cottage that Jack appeared at the door, his expression tense with concern.

"How is he?" Jack asked quietly, removing his hat as he entered.

"Stable, but weak," Sarah replied, stepping onto the small porch to speak privately. "His lungs are badly damaged. I suspect from years of mine dust."

Jack's jaw tightened. "I should have insisted he stop working when the coughing started. I knew he was pushing himself too hard."

"You couldn't have forced him to rest," Sarah said gently. "He's a proud man trying to provide for his daughter."

"Like his father-in-law," Jack observed, glancing toward where Mr. Henley sat beside Emma near the fireplace. "Both too stubborn for their own good."

They stood in comfortable silence for a moment, watching the evening shadows lengthen across the small yard.

"Sarah," Jack said finally, his voice heavy with concern, "there's something else you should know. There's a stranger in town asking questions about the mine. Claims to be investigating mining safety for the territorial government."

Sarah's stomach clenched, though she tried to keep her expression neutral. "Questions?"

"He's particularly interested in the recent explosion and our safety procedures. But August says something about him doesn't sit right—too interested in me personally." Jack ran a hand through his hair, looking suddenly weary. "The description fits a tall, well-dressed man with graying hair. Has official-looking papers."

Sarah felt ice form in her stomach but forced herself to remain calm. Could this stranger be her father? The timing would align with his letter, but why would he be investigating mines under false pretenses?

Jack was quiet for a moment, and Sarah could see the weight of multiple problems settling on his shoulders. The mine sabotage, now this investigation—it was one burden after another.

"Jack, my mother used to quote a verse when troubles seemed to pile up like storm clouds. 'Come unto me, all ye that labor and are heavy laden, and I will give you rest.' She believed that no burden was too heavy when shared with God—and with those who care for us." Sarah's voice was gentle but firm. "Whatever's coming, we'll face it together. You're not alone in this."

Jack's eyes met hers, and some of the tension in his face eased. "I needed to hear that today."

As Jack prepared to leave, he paused at the garden gate. "Sarah? Thank you. For the reminder, and for... everything."

Watching him disappear into the gathering dusk, Sarah felt a mixture of gratitude and growing dread. If the stranger was indeed her father, his presence could complicate everything she'd built in Silver Creek. But why hadn't she told Jack about the letter? Something held her back—perhaps shame about her father's abandonment, or fear that revealing her family's troubles would damage Jack's growing regard for her.

Whatever her father's true purpose in Silver Creek, Sarah sensed difficult choices lay ahead. And she wasn't certain she was prepared for what those choices might cost her.

Twenty-Two

The territorial land office clerk spread the surveyor's maps across his desk, his finger tracing property lines with practiced efficiency. Jack studied the documents with growing alarm, seeing his worst suspicions confirmed in black ink.

"When did Blackwood acquire the Harrison claim?" Jack asked, pointing to the property directly north of Montgomery land.

"Two weeks ago. Paid cash, well above market value." The clerk shuffled through additional papers. "Same with the Peterson plot to the east, and the old Murphy site down by the creek."

Jack felt his jaw tightened as the pattern became clear. Blackwood was systematically purchasing every piece of land surrounding the Montgomery mine, creating a strategic stranglehold that would control all access routes and potential expansion.

"What about the financial arrangements? Did he secure loans for these purchases?"

The clerk consulted another ledger. "That's the odd thing, Mr. Montgomery. Mr. Blackwood paid in full for each property, despite rumors that his Denver investments haven't been performing well lately."

Jack thanked the man and left the office with his mind racing. If Blackwood was struggling financially, where had he found the capital for such aggressive land acquisition? The purchases represented a massive investment—one that suggested his endgame was worth considerable risk.

That evening, Jack spread the survey maps across his study desk, marking the newly acquired properties in red ink. The pattern was unmistakable: Blackwood was creating a noose around Montgomery Mining, positioning himself to control everything that came in or went out.

A knock interrupted his analysis. "Come in."

August Hart entered with Sheriff Taylor close behind, both men wearing grim expressions that immediately put Jack on alert.

"Gentlemen," Jack said, rising. "This looks serious."

"It is," Sheriff Taylor replied, settling his considerable bulk into a chair. "That territorial inspector who's been asking questions around town? Got a telegram back from Denver yesterday. There's no Jonas Williams on the territorial payroll, and no authorized mining safety investigation in this district."

Jack felt ice form in his stomach. "Jonas Williams?"

"Same last name as our schoolteacher," August confirmed. "Could be coincidence, but the man's been asking very specific questions about the accident five years ago, about equipment failures that caused the collapse."

"And about Miss Williams," Sheriff Taylor added, his voice heavy with concern. "Whether she has access to mine information, whether you've discussed business matters with her, how close you two have become."

Jack's jaw tightened. "You think he's building some kind of case?"

"In my experience, when someone starts asking those kinds of questions while posing as a government official, they're either planning blackmail, fraud, or something worse." Taylor leaned forward. "Jack, I've been sheriff here for twelve years. This has all the markings of a setup."

August nodded grimly. "Man's been staying at the boarding house for three days, talking to anyone who'll listen. But it's not random conversation—he's methodical, like he's gathering specific intelligence."

Jack moved to the window, staring out at the lights of Silver Creek below. Sarah had mentioned her father's letter, his talk of debts and obligations. Now the man had appeared under false pretenses, investigating Jack's business while asking pointed questions about his own daughter.

"Where does this leave us?" Jack asked, turning back to the two men.

"Carefully watching our backs," Sheriff Taylor replied. "And maybe keeping some distance from potential complications until we know what we're dealing with."

The implication about Sarah sent anger flaring through Jack's chest. "Sheriff, Miss Williams has done nothing but serve this community with distinction. I won't have her character questioned based on her father's actions."

"Easy, Jack," Taylor raised his hands. "I'm not accusing the lady of anything. But family connections can be complicated, especially when money and deception are involved."

August crossed his arms. "What do you want us to do, Jack? Confront him directly?"

"No. Keep monitoring his activities, but don't let him know we're onto him." Jack moved back to his desk, studying the survey maps. "I need to understand what he's really after before we make any moves."

"And Miss Williams?" Sheriff Taylor asked. "Are you going to warn her that her father's in town?"

Jack was quiet for a long moment, weighing his options. "Not yet. If she's innocent in whatever this is, knowing might put her in danger. If she's not..." He left the sentence unfinished.

After the two men left, Jack remained standing over the survey maps, his mind working through possibilities. Blackwood's land purchases, the fake investigation, Sarah's father's mysterious agenda—the pieces were forming a pattern, but one he couldn't quite decipher.

Whatever was coming, Jack sensed they were building toward a confrontation that would test everything he'd built in Silver Creek. His mine, his reputation, his growing feelings for Sarah—all of it hung in the balance.

The walls of his study seemed to close in around him. Jack needed air, needed space to think. He grabbed his hat and stepped out into the cool evening, intending to walk the perimeter of his property to clear his head. Instead, his feet carried him down the hill toward town, past the general store and the hotel, until he stood before the white clapboard church.

The building looked peaceful in the moonlight, its simple steeple reaching toward the star-filled sky. Jack remembered the Sundays of his youth, sitting in the front pew with his parents while Reverend Wilson's predecessor spoke of God's providence and protection. How certain everything had seemed then, how clear the lines between right and wrong.

Now, with doubt gnawing at his chest and suspicion poisoning his thoughts about the woman he'd begun to love, that certainty felt like a luxury he could no longer afford.

"Beautiful evening for contemplation."

Jack turned to find Reverend Wilson stepping out of the church, a small oil lamp in his hand. The older man's kind eyes crinkled with gentle humor as he approached.

"Reverend," Jack said, touching the brim of his hat. "I didn't mean to disturb you."

"Not disturbing at all. I often find myself here late in the evening, preparing sermons or simply enjoying the quiet." Wilson gestured toward the church steps. "Care to sit for a moment? You look like a man with something weighing on his mind."

Jack hesitated, then settled beside the reverend on the worn wooden steps. "I suppose I am."

"Would you like to talk about it? Sometimes speaking our troubles aloud helps us see them more clearly."

For a moment, Jack considered deflecting with pleasantries about mine business or town affairs. Instead, he spoke honestly. "Reverend, how does a man know when he's being tested by God versus when he's simply facing the consequences of poor judgment?"

Wilson set his lamp down between them, the soft light creating a circle of warmth in the darkness. "That's a profound question, Jack. What makes you ask?"

"It feels like everything I've built, everything I care about, is under attack. My mine, my family's reputation, my..." Jack paused, searching for the right words. "My growing feelings for someone whose circumstances are becoming increasingly complicated."

"Ah." Wilson nodded with understanding. "Miss Williams."

"Among other things, yes." Jack ran his hands through his hair. "I thought I was hearing God's voice again, Reverend. After years of silence, I started seeing signs, feeling guided toward something good. But now I'm wondering if I was just seeing what I wanted to see."

"Tell me about these signs."

Jack felt foolish, but something in Wilson's patient manner encouraged honesty. "Sarah's arrival in Silver Creek when we desperately needed a teacher. The way she challenged my cynicism without condemning it. Finding Matthew's Bible when I needed to remember his faith." He shook his head. "But now there are complications that make me question everything."

"What complications?"

"Blackwood is systematically buying up land around my mine, positioning himself to strangle our operations. He's spreading rumors about Sarah's character and qualifications. And now..." Jack stopped, unable to share the details about Jonas Williams without betraying Sarah's privacy.

"And now you're facing opposition that makes you doubt whether your path is truly God's will," Wilson finished gently.

"Exactly. How do I know if this is a test of faith or a warning that I've been deceiving myself?"

Wilson was quiet for a long moment, his gaze fixed on the stars overhead. "Jack, may I share something from my own experience?"

"Please."

"When I was called to minister here in Silver Creek twenty years ago, I had doubts. The previous minister had left under difficult circumstances, the congregation was divided, and I was young and inexperienced. Every challenge that arose made me question whether I'd misunderstood God's calling."

"What changed your mind?"

"A wise mentor told me something I've never forgotten: 'God's will isn't revealed by the absence of obstacles, but by the presence of grace to overcome them.'" Wilson turned to face Jack directly. "The question isn't whether you'll face trials, but whether you have the strength and wisdom to navigate them faithfully."

Jack considered this. "But how do I distinguish between God's testing and my own poor judgment?"

"Look at the fruits of your choices," Wilson suggested. "Has your growing faith brought you closer to God's character—more compassion, more courage, more love for others? Has it made you want to serve rather than be served?"

"Yes," Jack said without hesitation. "Sarah has changed me in ways I didn't think possible. She's made me want to be better, to trust again, to hope again."

"Then perhaps that's your answer. God often works through the people He places in our lives, even when—especially when—the circumstances seem challenging."

"And if Blackwood succeeds in destroying what I'm trying to build?"

Wilson smiled, the expression visible in the lamplight. "Then you'll face that trial with the same faith that's brought you this far. Remember, Jack, God's plans aren't always about avoiding suffering, but about finding purpose within it."

They sat in comfortable silence for several minutes, listening to the night sounds of Silver Creek settling into sleep. Jack felt some of the tension in his chest easing, replaced by a quiet resolve.

"Thank you, Reverend," he said finally. "You've given me a great deal to think about."

"Sometimes we all need reminding that we're not walking this path alone." Wilson stood, gathering his lamp. "I'll be praying for wisdom for you, Jack. And for Miss Williams too. Whatever challenges lie ahead, you'll face them better together than apart."

As Wilson disappeared back into the church, Jack remained on the steps for a few more minutes, looking up at the star-filled sky. His circumstances hadn't changed—Blackwood was still circling like a predator, Jonas Williams was conducting his mysterious investigation, and Sarah's future in Silver Creek remained uncertain.

But something in Jack's heart had shifted. Instead of feeling overwhelmed by forces beyond his control, he felt a familiar stirring of the faith that had once sustained him. Whatever tests lay ahead, he wouldn't face them alone.

Standing, Jack made his way back up the hill toward home, his steps lighter than they'd been in days. Tomorrow would bring new challenges, but tonight he chose to trust in the God who worked through both trials and blessings to accomplish His purposes.

And if Sarah Williams was part of that purpose—as every instinct in his heart insisted she was—then no amount of opposition from Blackwood or complications from her father would ultimately prevail against them.

The question now was whether he'd have the courage to act on that faith when the testing truly began.

Twenty-Three

S arah stepped out of the schoolhouse into the warm afternoon sunshine, grateful for a brief respite from her students' energy. She needed to visit the general store for thread to repair a torn seam in her green dress—the one she'd worn to dinner at the Montgomery house. The memory of that evening brought a flutter to her stomach that she quickly suppressed.

"Sarah!" Charlotte's voice called from across the street. Her friend hurried over, but something in her expression immediately put Sarah on alert.

"Charlotte, what's wrong? You look upset."

Charlotte glanced around nervously, then moved closer. "I've been hoping to catch you alone. It's about David—Mother has forbidden me to see him at all now. She's even enlisted Jack to help enforce her decision."

Sarah's heart ached at the pain in Charlotte's voice. "I'm so sorry. Has there been any change in her position?"

"None. She's more determined than ever that I marry someone of 'appropriate standing.'" Charlotte's voice grew bitter. "She's even mentioned that the Hendersons' eldest son will visit next month. She seems to think exposure to 'suitable young men' will cure me of my foolish attachment."

"And how do you feel about that?"

"Miserable. David and I have managed a few stolen moments—brief conversations after church, a chance meeting at the post office—but it's not enough. I'm wondering if Mother's right, if love really isn't sufficient for a practical marriage."

Sarah took Charlotte's hands gently. "Don't let despair make that decision for you. Sometimes the obstacles that seem insurmountable are simply tests of how much something truly means to us."

"Do you really believe that?"

"I have to," Sarah said. "The alternative is to give up hope entirely, and I'm not ready to do that yet."

Charlotte squeezed her hands gratefully. "Thank you. It's good to hear that from someone who understands."

After promising to visit soon, Sarah continued toward the general store, her mind still on Charlotte's troubles. Perhaps there was a way to help her friend, though she wasn't sure what that might be.

The bell above the door chimed as Sarah entered Patterson's store, and she was immediately greeted by Mrs. Parker's eager smile.

"Miss Williams! How lovely to see you, dear. What brings you in today?"

"I need some thread to mend a dress," Sarah replied, moving toward the notions counter. "Dark green, if you have it."

"Of course, of course." Mrs. Parker bustled around the counter, her eyes bright with the anticipation of someone bursting with news. "You know, my dear, the most extraordinary thing has happened. We have a visitor in town—a territorial inspector investigating mining safety."

Sarah kept her expression neutral as she examined the available thread. "How interesting."

"Yes, and here's the remarkable part—his name is Williams! The same as yours!" Mrs. Parker leaned closer conspiratorially. "Jonas Williams, a distinguished gentleman with graying hair. Surely it can't be a coincidence?" She paused, her eyes narrowing slightly as she studied Sarah's face. "You know, now that I think about it, he has your same eyes. The same shape to his features. That's what was nagging at me when we first met—you reminded me of someone, and now I know who!"

Sarah's hands stilled on the spool of thread. "Jonas Williams?"

"You know him then? Oh, I knew it!" Mrs. Parker clapped her hands together triumphantly. "I told my husband there was something familiar about you the moment I saw you. Is he a relation? A cousin perhaps? Or—" Mrs. Parker's eyes widened with sudden understanding. "My goodness, could he be your father? The one who went to work the southern mines?"

Sarah felt the blood drain from her face. Her father was here, in Silver Creek, posing as a territorial inspector? The implications crashed over her like a cold wave.

"Miss Williams? Are you quite all right? You've gone terribly pale."

"I'm... yes, I'm fine." Sarah forced herself to focus. "Where is this Mr. Williams staying?"

"At the boarding house on Elm Street. He's been there three days now, asking very thorough questions about mine operations. Such a dedicated public servant!" Mrs. Parker beamed with civic pride. "Though I must say, he seems interested in the Montgomery mine. I suppose it being the largest operation in the area, that makes perfect sense."

Sarah's stomach churned. Her father, investigating Jack's mine under false pretenses—what could he possibly be planning?

"Did he... did he mention having family in the area?" Sarah asked carefully.

"Not specifically, but when I mentioned our wonderful new schoolteacher was also named Williams, he seemed quite interested. I do hope you'll have a chance to meet! It would be such a lovely coincidence if you're related."

Sarah paid for her thread with trembling hands, Mrs. Parker's chatter becoming a distant buzzing in her ears. As soon as she could politely escape, she hurried from the store and made her way toward Elm Street, her mind racing with questions and dread.

The boarding house was a modest two-story building with a front porch where a few guests sat enjoying the afternoon air. Sarah approached the proprietor, Mrs. Henderson, who was tending to flower boxes.

"Excuse me, I'm looking for Mr. Jonas Williams. I understand he's staying here?"

"Oh yes, the territorial inspector. Room seven, second floor. Though I believe he's out at the moment—had business at the mines this afternoon."

At the mines. Sarah's heart hammered against her ribs. "Thank you."

She climbed the stairs on unsteady legs and knocked softly on the door of room seven. No answer. Sarah tried the handle and found it unlocked—a carelessness that would have appalled her careful mother.

The room was spartanly furnished but showed signs of extended occupancy. Clothes hung in the wardrobe, papers scattered across the small desk. Sarah moved closer to examine the documents, her breath catching as she recognized technical drawings and survey maps.

Maps of the Montgomery mine.

"Sarah?"

She spun around to find her father standing in the doorway, his face a mixture of surprise and something that might have been guilt. He looked older than she remembered, his clothes well-made but showing wear, his eyes holding shadows that hadn't been there before.

"Papa." The word came out as barely a whisper.

Jonas stepped into the room and closed the door behind him. "I was wondering when you'd find me."

"Why are you here? And why are you pretending to be a territorial inspector?"

Jonas moved to the window, gazing out at the town below. "It's complicated, Sarah."

"Then uncomplicate it. I received your letter about debts and obligations. Now I find you here under false pretenses, investigating the mine owned by people who have been kind to me. What kind of trouble have you brought to Silver Creek?"

Jonas turned back to her, his expression weary. "The kind that could destroy us both if we're not careful."

"What does that mean?"

"It means that some mistakes follow a man wherever he goes. And sometimes the only way to make things right is to risk making them worse." He gestured toward the papers on the desk. "I'm trying to prevent a catastrophe, Sarah. But I need you to trust me."

"Trust you?" Sarah's voice rose with two years of suppressed anger and hurt. "You left us when Mama was dying. You disappeared without a word, leaving us to struggle alone. Now you appear with false credentials and mysterious papers, asking for trust? What possible reason could I have to trust you?"

Jonas flinched as if she'd struck him. "Because despite everything, I'm still your father. And because the alternative to trusting me might be watching innocent people die."

Sarah stared at him, seeing a stranger wearing her father's face. "What have you done, Papa?"

"What I had to do to survive. And now I'm trying to undo some of the damage." He moved toward her, his expression earnest. "Sarah, I can't explain everything yet—it's too dangerous. But I need you to stay away from Jack Montgomery until this is resolved."

"Absolutely not."

"You don't understand the forces at work here—"

"Then explain them!"

Jonas was quiet for a long moment, his internal struggle visible on his weathered face. "There are people who profit from mining disasters, Sarah. People who create accidents for financial gain. I've been... associated with them in the past."

"Associated how?"

"In ways I'm not proud of. But I'm trying to make amends now. I'm gathering evidence to stop them."

Sarah felt her legs grow weak. "Are you saying you've been involved in causing mining accidents?"

"I'm saying I've made mistakes that cost lives. And now I'm trying to prevent more deaths, even if it costs me my own life."

The room seemed to spin around Sarah. Her father, involved in mining disasters? People dead because of his choices? She gripped the back of a chair to steady herself.

"Who are these people?"

"I can't tell you that yet. But Sarah, I need you to promise me you'll be careful around Montgomery. I don't know how deep his involvement goes."

"Jack isn't involved in anything corrupt!"

"How can you be certain? You've known him for a few months. I've known men like this for years—men who present themselves as pillars of the community while profiting from others' misfortune."

Sarah straightened, finding her voice again. "Because I know his character. Because I've seen how he treats his workers, how he cares for this town. Because when someone tried to sabotage his mine, he put his men's safety above everything else."

Jonas's eyes sharpened. "Someone tried to sabotage his mine?"

"Cyrus Blackwood. I overheard him planning it and warned Jack in time."

"Blackwood." Jonas's face went pale. "Sarah, you need to stay as far away from Cyrus Blackwood as possible."

"Why? What is your connection to him?"

Before Jonas could answer, the sound of heavy footsteps on the stairs made them both freeze. Jonas quickly gathered the papers from his desk, shoving them into a leather satchel.

"You need to leave," he whispered urgently. "Now. Through the back stairs."

"Papa, I need answers—"

"Tonight, after dark, meet me at the chapel behind the church. It's quiet there, and we can talk privately without being seen. Come alone, and don't tell anyone where you're going."

"I can't just—"

"Sarah." Jonas gripped her shoulders, his eyes intense. "If you've ever trusted me, trust me now. Lives depend on it—possibly including yours."

The footsteps had reached the second floor landing. Sarah looked at her father one last time, seeing desperation and something that might have been genuine love in his weathered face.

"Tonight," she whispered, then slipped out the back door just as someone knocked on the front door of room seven.

As Sarah made her way back toward the schoolhouse through side streets and alleys, her mind reeled with everything she'd learned. Her father was involved with people who caused mining disasters for profit. He claimed to be trying to stop them now, but could she believe him? And his warnings about Jack—were they motivated by genuine concern or by his own guilt and paranoia?

One thing was certain: the careful life she'd built in Silver Creek was about to become infinitely more complicated. And tonight's meeting might determine whether she could salvage any of it, or whether her father's past would destroy everything she'd come to love about her new home.

Including the man she was realizing she loved more than she'd ever admitted to herself.

TWENTY-FOUR

J ack stood outside the boarding house on Elm Street, his jaw set with grim determination. The revelation that the mysterious territorial inspector was named Jonas Williams had kept him awake all night. The man claimed to be conducting official business, but his questions were too specific, his interest in the Montgomery mine too focused.

And then there was Sarah's reaction when he'd mentioned the mysterious investigator. The way her face had gone pale, the careful neutrality in her voice—she knew something she wasn't telling him.

Jack climbed the stairs to the second floor, each step adding weight to the dread in his chest. Whatever Jonas Williams was really doing in Silver Creek, it wasn't official government business. The question was whether he was working with Blackwood or against him—and how much Sarah knew about her father's true purpose.

Jack knocked firmly on the door of room seven. "Mr. Williams? Jack Montgomery. I'd like a word."

The door opened to reveal a man who bore an unmistakable resemblance to Sarah—the same thoughtful hazel eyes, the same determined set to his jaw. But Jonas Williams looked like a man who had fallen far from better circumstances. His clothes, while clean, were worn thin and carefully mended. His once-dignified bearing had been worn down by years of difficult work and harder choices, and his eyes held shadows that spoke of burdens heavier than physical labor. He was still a distinguished man beneath the weathering, but life had clearly taken its toll.

"Mr. Montgomery." Jonas stepped back, gesturing him inside. "I wondered when you'd come calling.

The room was spartanly furnished but showed signs of extended occupancy. Papers scattered across the small desk caught Jack's attention—technical drawings and what appeared to be survey maps.

"I know you," Jack said, studying the man's face. "But you're not Jonas Williams. You're Jonas Fletcher. You were here five years ago."

Jonas's shoulders sagged in defeat. "I am Jonas Williams. But yes, when I was here before, I went by Jonas Fletcher. I used that name for all of Blackwood's... business arrangements."

"So you lied about your identity then, and you're lying about your purpose now?"

"I lied then to protect my real identity from being connected to what I was doing. I'm using my real name now because..." Jonas's voice grew heavy. "Because I'm trying to make amends for what Jonas Fletcher did."

"We need to talk," Jack said, closing the door behind him. "About your real reason for being in Silver Creek."

Jonas moved to the window, gazing out at the town below. "Straight to the point. I respect that in a man."

"I know you're not a territorial inspector. The sheriff confirmed it with Denver yesterday."

"Did he now?" Jonas's tone remained conversational, but Jack noticed his shoulders tense slightly.

"So I'll ask again—what are you really doing here? And what's your connection to Cyrus Blackwood?"

This time Jonas's reaction was unmistakable—a sharp intake of breath, a momentary tightening around his eyes. "What makes you think I have any connection to Blackwood?"

Jack studied the older man's face, noting the careful way he'd phrased his response. "Because men like you don't just happen to show up in towns like Silver Creek asking detailed questions about mine operations. Someone sent you, or someone's paying you."

Jonas was quiet for a long moment, his internal struggle visible. When he finally spoke, his voice was heavy with something that sounded like regret.

"You're right. I do have a connection to Blackwood. But it's not what you think."

"Then enlighten me."

Jonas moved to the desk, his hand hovering over the scattered papers. "I've worked for him before. Done things I'm not proud of. But I'm here now to stop him."

"Stop him from what?"

"From doing to your mine what he's done to others." Jonas picked up one of the technical drawings, and Jack could see his hands trembling slightly. "He's planning another accident. One that will make his previous sabotage attempts look like minor inconveniences."

Jack felt ice form in his stomach. "You have proof of this?"

"Some. Not enough yet, which is why I need more time." Jonas met Jack's gaze directly. "But I know his methods, his patterns. I know because I've helped him implement them before."

The confession hung between them like a physical weight. Jack felt rage building in his chest, but also a cold calculation. If Jonas was telling the truth, he might be their only chance to stop Blackwood permanently.

"How many people have died because of what you've done for him?"

Jonas closed his eyes. "Too many. Good men with families who trusted their employers to keep them safe."

"And now you expect me to trust you?"

"I expect you to let me try to prevent more deaths." Jonas's voice grew urgent. "Blackwood is planning something for soon. During a shift change, when the maximum number of workers will be in the tunnels."

Jack's blood ran cold. "When? How soon?"

"I don't know exactly. That's what I'm trying to find out." Jonas hesitated, then seemed to steel himself. "But Jack—Mr. Montgomery—there's something else you need to know about your mine. About why Blackwood wants it so badly."

"What?"

Jonas's voice dropped to barely above a whisper. "Your mine has been targeted before. More than once. The recent sabotage attempts aren't Blackwood's first tries at destroying your operation."

The room seemed to spin around Jack. "What are you saying?"

"I'm saying Blackwood has been after your operation for longer than you know. And I'm saying I know because..." Jonas's voice broke. "Because I was involved. In the past."

Jack lunged forward, grabbing Jonas by the shirtfront. "You've sabotaged my mine before?"

"Not recently," Jonas said quickly, not struggling against Jack's grip. "But years ago. Before I understood the full cost of what I was doing."

"How many years ago?" Jack's voice was deadly quiet.

Jonas met his gaze with obvious difficulty. "Five years."

The words hit Jack like a physical blow. Five years ago. The accident that killed Matthew.

"You killed my friend," Jack said, his voice barely a whisper.

"I provided information that led to deaths, yes." Jonas's voice was steady despite the fear in his eyes. "I told Blackwood's men where the supports were weakest, which sections would cause the most damage if compromised. I've carried that guilt every day since. It's part of why I left my family—I couldn't face them knowing what I'd become."

Jack released him and stepped back, his whole body trembling with rage. "Matthew Carter. That was his name. He had parents who adored him, friends who would have died for him." His voice rose with each word. "He trusted me to keep him safe, and you—you gave them the information they needed to murder him for money."

"Mr. Montgomery—"

"Don't!" Jack's roar filled the small room. He grabbed the nearest chair and hurled it against the wall, the wood splintering with a crash that echoed his shattered heart. "Don't you dare speak his name or try to justify what you did!"

Jonas pressed himself against the wall, but he didn't try to flee. "You have every right to your anger—"

"My anger?" Jack laughed bitterly, the sound harsh and broken. "My anger doesn't begin to cover what I feel. Do you know what your 'information' cost me? Do you know what it's like to hold your best friend's hand while he dies, calling for his mother, because some stranger decided his knowledge was worth more than Matthew's life?"

Jonas's face crumpled. "I'm sorry. I know it means nothing, but I'm—"

"You're right. It means nothing." Jack stood there, chest heaving, fists clenched so tight his knuckles were white. For a long moment, the only sound was his ragged breathing as he fought for control.

When he spoke again, his voice was deadly calm. "Why tell me this? Why not just disappear again?"

"Because running didn't bring anyone back. Because hiding didn't ease the guilt. And because if I don't act now, Blackwood will kill more innocent men." Jonas straightened his clothing with shaking hands. "I can't undo what I've done, Mr. Montgomery. But I can try to prevent future tragedies."Jack stared at Jonas, seeing not just the man who'd destroyed his life but potentially the key to preventing future tragedies. "What kind of proof do you have against Blackwood?"

"Some documentation. Records of payments. But I need more evidence to ensure his conviction. Real evidence that even his influence can't overcome."

"This could all be an elaborate lie. A way to get close to my operation for Blackwood."

"It could be," Jonas agreed. "But ask yourself this—if I were still working for him, would I be telling you about past incidents? Would I be admitting to my part in your friend's death?"

Jack took the papers Jonas offered, scanning technical drawings that showed detailed knowledge of Montgomery mine operations. The scope of planning was staggering, but the intent wasn't entirely clear.

"If this is real, why haven't you gone to the authorities?"

"Because I'm implicated in past crimes. Because Blackwood has connections everywhere. Because without ironclad evidence, he'll walk free and find ways to silence anyone who testified against him."

"Including your daughter?" Jonas's face went ashen. "Sarah knows nothing about my past crimes. I've kept her out of it deliberately."

"But Blackwood already knows she's your daughter. He's threatened to spread rumors about your family's... circumstances."

"I know." Jonas's voice was heavy with despair. "That's part of why I had to act quickly. He's been holding that threat over me, using Sarah as leverage to ensure my cooperation. But if he realizes I'm actively working against him now..."

"Then he'll follow through on his threats against her," Jack finished grimly.

"Exactly. She doesn't know what kind of business brought me here, or what I've done in the past. But if Blackwood decides to destroy her reputation out of spite..."

Jonas moved to the window, peering out cautiously. "A schoolteacher's reputation is everything. He could ruin her life just to punish me."

Jack felt the weight of impossible choices settling on his shoulders. Trust the man who'd killed his best friend? Risk Sarah's safety on the word of someone who'd already proven capable of terrible betrayal? Or let Blackwood proceed with his plan because the only witness was compromised?

"I need time to think about this," Jack said finally. "Time is what we don't have. Blackwood's getting suspicious. I've been pushing for more details about his plans, and he's starting to ask questions."

"What kind of questions?" "About my loyalty. About whether I can still be trusted." Jonas's voice grew desperate. "If he decides I'm a liability, Sarah becomes his primary target for revenge."

The answer to that prayer might determine whether Silver Creek faced salvation or destruction in the days ahead.

Twenty-Five

Sarah arrived at the chapel fifteen minutes early, her heart hammering with nervous anticipation. The small building sat quietly in the evening shadows, its simple wooden cross silhouetted against the darkening sky. She clutched her mother's Bible against her chest, seeking comfort from its familiar weight as she prepared for what might be the most important conversation of her life.

She pushed open the heavy wooden door and stepped inside, breathing in the familiar scents of beeswax and old wood. The chapel was smaller than the main church, used primarily for private prayer and small gatherings. Tonight, it felt like a sanctuary where she might finally learn the truth about her father's mysterious return.

Sarah settled into a pew near the front and opened her mother's Bible, seeking comfort in the familiar ritual. She turned to Psalm 27, her mother's favorite passage during difficult times: "The Lord is my light and my salvation; whom shall I fear?"

But as the minutes ticked by, fear began to creep into her heart despite the comforting words. By seven-thirty, her father was half an hour late. By eight o'clock, Sarah felt the familiar chill of abandonment settling over her like a shroud.

"He's not coming," she whispered to the empty chapel, her voice echoing off the plain walls.

The realization hit her with devastating force. Once again, her father had made a promise he couldn't keep. Once again, she was left waiting alone, hoping for a man who had already disappeared from her life.

Sarah closed her Bible with trembling hands, fighting back tears that threatened to spill over. She'd been a fool to believe he'd changed, that his return to Silver Creek meant anything more than another scheme or business opportunity that would ultimately lead to his departure.

"Mama, what should I do?" she asked the empty air, wishing desperately for her mother's gentle wisdom. "How many times am I supposed to forgive someone who keeps breaking my heart?"

The silence that answered felt like judgment. Her mother would have counseled patience, forgiveness, faith in God's plan. But sitting alone in the chapel where her father had promised to meet her, Sarah felt her mother's unwavering faith wavering.

She rose to leave, anger replacing hurt in her chest. No—she wouldn't simply accept this abandonment as she had two years ago. She was no longer the helpless girl who waited passively for others to make decisions about her life. If her father thought he could simply disappear again without explanation, he was wrong.

Sarah strode out of the chapel with purpose, her steps quickening as she made her way toward the boarding house on Elm Street. She would confront him directly about his broken promise, demand the truth about why he'd really come to Silver Creek, and make it clear that she was done being treated like a child who could be dismissed at will.

The boarding house sat quiet in the evening shadows, warm light spilling from the windows of the first floor. Sarah climbed the stairs to the second floor, her determination growing with each step. He was in room seven—and she wouldn't let him hide behind excuses this time.

She knocked firmly on the door. "Papa? It's Sarah. We need to talk."

Silence.

Sarah knocked again, harder this time. "Papa, I know you're in there. You promised to meet me tonight, and when you didn't come—"

The door swung open under her knocking, revealing that it hadn't been properly latched. Sarah stepped inside, calling out, "Papa?"

The room was empty.

Not just empty of people, but empty of belongings. The wardrobe stood open, showing bare hooks where clothes had hung. The desk was cleared of papers. Even the washbasin had been emptied and dried.

Sarah's heart sank as the truth became clear. He hadn't simply been late to their meeting—he was gone. Again.

She moved through the small space like someone in a dream, looking for any sign that he'd been there at all. It was then that she noticed the piece of paper on the desk, folded and marked with her name in her father's familiar handwriting.

With shaking hands, Sarah unfolded the note:

My dearest Sarah,

I cannot meet you tonight as planned. Circumstances have arisen that require my immediate departure from Silver Creek. Please do not try to follow me or contact me—it would only put you in danger.

I know this seems like another abandonment, but I swear to you it is not. Everything I do now is to protect you from consequences of my past mistakes.

Trust no one completely—even those who seem to care for you may have their own reasons for kindness. Be especially wary of getting too close to anyone connected to the mining business.

I love you more than you will ever know.

Your father

Sarah read the letter twice, her heart breaking with each word. The vague warnings, the mysterious departure, the familiar pattern of promises broken and explanations that explained nothing—it was exactly like his disappearance two years ago.

She sank into the chair by the desk, staring at the letter until the words blurred through her tears. The familiar feelings of abandonment washed over her—the helpless anger, the crushing disappointment, the terrible fear that she wasn't worth staying for.

But alongside those old wounds, new questions began to surface. Her father's warnings about trusting people in the mining business seemed oddly specific. And his mention of "consequences of past mistakes" suggested there was more to his departure than simple cowardice.

Sarah thought about Jack's reaction when he'd mentioned the territorial inspector. The way his expression had grown guarded, almost suspicious. Had he known something about her father that he hadn't shared?

A sound in the hallway made her freeze—footsteps approaching, then stopping outside the door. Sarah quickly folded the letter and tucked it into her reticule, her heart racing. Had her father returned? Or was it someone else—perhaps the "rough men" Mrs. Parker had mentioned seeing around town?

The footsteps moved on, and Sarah released a breath she hadn't realized she'd been holding. She needed to leave before someone discovered her in the empty room. But as she rose to go, something on the floor beside the bed caught her eye.

A small piece of torn paper, as if something had been ripped up hastily. Sarah picked it up, recognizing what appeared to be part of a map with markings that looked like mine locations. Her father's work, perhaps—evidence of whatever business had really brought him to Silver Creek.

She pocketed the fragment and made her way quietly from the room, closing the door behind her. As she descended the stairs, she could hear Mrs. Henderson's voice from the kitchen, speaking with another guest about the weather. No one had seen her come or go.

Outside, the evening air felt cold against her tear-stained cheeks. Sarah looked up at the window of room seven, now dark and empty, and felt something fundamental shift inside her. The girl who had once waited passively for others to make decisions about her life was truly gone now.

Her father's warnings echoed in her mind as she walked back toward the schoolhouse. Trust no one completely. Be wary of those connected to the mining business. But those warnings raised more questions than they answered.

People in Silver Creek had been acting strange lately. Jack's increased security at the mine. Sheriff Taylor's frequent visits to various businesses. Even Charlotte had mentioned that her mother seemed more worried than usual about town affairs.

Perhaps her father's departure wasn't another selfish abandonment. Perhaps he'd left to protect her from something genuinely dangerous—something connected to his mysterious business in Silver Creek.

Sarah made a decision that would have horrified her mother but felt absolutely right in her heart. Instead of waiting passively for answers that might never come, she was going to find out the truth herself.

Her father had warned her to trust no one completely, but he hadn't forbidden her from asking questions. And if there was one thing Sarah Williams had learned from her years of teaching children, it was that the right questions, asked persistently enough, usually revealed the truth.

As she reached her quarters at the schoolhouse, Sarah looked back toward the boarding house, then up at the mountains silhouetted against the star-filled sky. Somewhere out there, her father was running from something—or someone. And somewhere in Silver Creek were the answers to questions that had been plaguing her since his arrival.

Tomorrow morning, she would begin looking for those answers. And she would start with the one person who might know more than he was telling her—Jack Montgomery.

TWENTY-SIX

J ack had barely slept after his confrontation with Jonas Williams. The man's
admission of involvement in Matthew's death had shaken him to his core,
but the immediate threat to his workers demanded action over revenge. He'd
stationed extra guards around the mine and sent word to Sheriff Taylor, but the
feeling that events were spiraling beyond his control gnawed at him constantly.

The morning brought disturbing news. August appeared at Jack's office
before dawn, his weathered face grim with concern.

"Jack, we've got problems. Big problems."

"What now?"

"Found evidence of tampering near the north tunnel entrance. Someone's
been there overnight—fresh tool marks on the support beams, and this." August held up a small piece of metal. "Looks like part of a detonation device."

Jack's blood ran cold. "How much damage?"

"Hard to say without a full inspection, but whoever did this knew what they
were doing. Professional work." August's voice dropped. "And there's more.
One of the night guards saw lights moving around the old mining camp north
of town around midnight. Could be nothing, but..."

"But it could be where they're planning their final move," Jack finished
grimly. "Double the day guards and start a complete inspection of every tunnel.
I want to know exactly what we're dealing with."

As August departed to implement the security measures, Jack found himself
pacing his office like a caged animal. Jonas had warned him that Blackwood

was planning something, but the vague timeline had left him guessing. Now it seemed the attack was imminent.

A commotion outside drew his attention to the window. Sarah was walking rapidly up the hill toward the mine office, her face flushed with exertion and something that looked like determination mixed with distress. Even from a distance, Jack could see the tension in her posture.

He met her at the door before she could knock. "Sarah? What's wrong?"

"Jack, I need to speak with you. It's about my father." Her voice was steady, but he could see her hands trembling slightly. "He's here in Silver Creek, isn't he? You've known all along."

"Come in," he said, ushering her into his office and closing the door. "Yes, I know he's here. How did you find out?"

"I went to confront him last night when he didn't show up for our meeting. Found his room at the boarding house empty except for this." Sarah pulled out a folded piece of paper with shaking hands. "He's gone, Jack. Left without explanation, just like before."

Jack read the note, his expression darkening with each line. Jonas's warnings about trusting people in the mining business struck him as particularly ominous, given what he now knew about the man's past.

"Sarah, there's something I need to tell you about your father. Something difficult."

She looked up at him with eyes that seemed suddenly older, more weary. "I thought there might be. You've been acting differently since you learned about the territorial inspector named Williams. What do you know about him?"

Jack struggled with how much to reveal. Jonas had begged him to keep Sarah out of danger, but her father's sudden departure had clearly left her in the dark about very real threats.

"Your father isn't who he claims to be. He's not a territorial inspector."

"I suspected as much when he couldn't give me straight answers about his work," Sarah said quietly. "But what is he really doing here?"

"He has a connection to Cyrus Blackwood. A business relationship that goes back several years."

Sarah's face went pale. "What kind of business relationship?"

Before Jack could answer, the sound of rapid hoofbeats outside drew their attention. Through the window, they could see a rider approaching at dangerous speed—one of Jack's mine workers, his face streaked with dust and panic.

Jack stepped outside with Sarah close behind. "What is it, Peterson?"

"Mr. Montgomery!" the man gasped, barely able to speak from exertion. "Found something terrible at the old mining camp. You need to come quick!"

"What did you find?"

"A man, sir. Beaten something awful. Says his name is Williams. Says he needs to speak with you and Miss Williams right away before they come back for him."

Sarah's gasp was audible. "Papa!"

"How badly is he hurt?" Jack demanded.

"Bad enough. Conscious, but barely. And Mr. Montgomery..." Peterson's voice dropped. "He keeps saying they're going to blow the mine today. Says we need to evacuate everyone immediately."

Jack felt ice form in his stomach. "Mount up, Peterson. Lead the way."

"Jack, I'm coming with you," Sarah said firmly.

"Sarah, if this is a trap—"

"That's my father out there, possibly dying. I'm coming." Her voice carried a finality that brooked no argument.

The ride to the old mining camp took twenty minutes over rough terrain. Jack's mind raced with possibilities—was this Jonas's way of finally revealing the full truth, or had Blackwood's men discovered his double cross and beaten the information out of him?

They found Jonas Williams lying in the ruins of an old equipment shed, his face swollen and bloodied, his clothes torn. But his eyes were alert, and he struggled to sit up when he saw them approaching.

"Sarah," he whispered through split lips. "Thank God you're safe."

Sarah dropped to her knees beside him, her anger at his abandonment temporarily forgotten in the face of his obvious suffering. "Papa, what happened? Who did this to you?"

"Blackwood's men. Found out I was gathering evidence against him." Jonas gripped her hand weakly. "Had to make them think I was running away, but they caught me before I could get clear of town."

"Why didn't you just come to me?" Jack asked, kneeling on Jonas's other side. "I could have protected you."

Jonas laughed bitterly, then winced at the pain it caused. "You would have protected the man who killed your best friend? I don't think so."

Sarah's eyes widened in shock. "What does he mean, Papa?"

Jonas met her gaze with obvious difficulty. "I was involved in the mining accident that killed Jack's friend Matthew five years ago. I helped cause that collapse."

The confession hit Sarah like a physical blow. "No. Papa, you couldn't have—"

"I did. I falsified safety reports, used substandard materials, ignored warning signs. All because Blackwood paid me well to look the other way." Jonas's voice grew weaker. "Three good men died because of my greed."

Jack watched Sarah's face crumple as the full weight of her father's crimes settled over her. But even as she struggled with this revelation, Jonas continued speaking with desperate urgency.

"But that's not why they beat me. They beat me because I've been gathering evidence to stop Blackwood from doing it again. Today."

"Today?" Jack's attention snapped back to the immediate threat. "What's planned for today?"

"The afternoon shift change. Three o'clock. He's got men positioned to trigger a massive collapse that will kill dozens of workers." Jonas struggled to pull something from his torn coat. "The charges are already in place. Have been for weeks. They're just waiting for maximum casualties."

Jack took the blood-stained papers Jonas offered—detailed maps showing explosive placements throughout the Montgomery mine, timed to detonate during the busiest part of the afternoon shift.

"My God," Jack breathed. "This would destroy half the tunnels."

"And everyone in them," Jonas confirmed. "Jack, you have to evacuate the mine. Now. Before three o'clock."

Sarah looked between her father and Jack, her face a mask of conflicting emotions. "How do we know this isn't another lie? Another scheme?"

"Because, daughter," Jonas said softly, "I'm probably going to die from what they did to me, and I want my last act to be saving lives instead of taking them."

Jack studied the maps, his mind racing. The placement of the charges was sophisticated, designed to create a cascade failure that would be impossible to stop once it began. Whether or not Jonas could be trusted, the threat was too specific and detailed to ignore.

"We need to get you to a doctor," Jack said, starting to lift Jonas.

"No time. Take Sarah somewhere safe and evacuate your workers. Blackwood's men will be back soon—they think they killed me, but they want to make sure."

"I'm not leaving you here to die," Sarah said fiercely.

"You're not leaving me here to die," Jonas replied with a weak smile. "You're giving me the chance to do something right for once in my miserable life."

The sound of approaching horses in the distance made them all freeze. Multiple riders, moving fast.

"That'll be them," Jonas said grimly. "Jack, get Sarah out of here. Use the back trail toward Miller's Creek. They won't expect you to go that way."

"Papa—" Sarah began.

"I love you, daughter. More than I ever showed you. Now go, before it's too late for all of us."

Jack made a split-second decision. He scooped up the explosive placement maps and grabbed Sarah's arm. "We have to leave. Now."

As they reached their horses, Sarah turned back one last time to see her father struggling to his feet, preparing to face his captors with whatever courage he had left. Despite everything he'd done, despite all the pain he'd caused, she felt her heart breaking for the broken man who was finally trying to choose sacrifice over self-preservation.

"Will he survive this?" she asked Jack as they rode hard toward Miller's Creek.

Jack's face was grim as he considered the question. "I don't know. But if these maps are accurate, we need to focus on saving the men who are definitely going to die if we don't warn them in time."

Behind them, the sound of gunshots echoed across the valley, but they didn't look back. Whatever was happening at the old mining camp, their priority now was preventing a catastrophe that would make Matthew's death look like a minor accident.

As they rode toward what might be the most important hour of their lives, Jack found himself praying for the first time in years—not just for the safety of his workers, but for the soul of a man who had finally found the courage to choose redemption over survival.

Even if it cost him everything.

TWENTY-SEVEN

The ride back to Silver Creek had been a desperate race against time. After hearing the gunshots echo across the valley behind them, Jack had made the decision to circle back toward town via the Miller's Creek trail, avoiding the main roads where Blackwood's men might be watching.

Every minute that passed brought them closer to three o'clock—closer to catastrophe.

Now Sarah's hands shook as she helped Jack spread the blood-stained maps across Sheriff Taylor's desk. The technical drawings showing explosive placements throughout the Montgomery mine made the full scope of Blackwood's murderous plan terrifyingly clear.

"Three o'clock," Sheriff Taylor said grimly, checking his pocket watch. "That gives us less than two hours to evacuate the mine and find these charges."

"Can it be done?" Sarah asked, studying the complex diagram that might as well have been written in a foreign language.

"If we're lucky and Blackwood doesn't realize we're onto him," Jack replied, already moving toward the door. "I need to get to the mine immediately and start the evacuation."

"What about my father? We can't just leave him—"

"Sarah," Jack turned back, his eyes filled with compassion but also steely determination. "Your father knew the risks when he chose to face Blackwood's men. The best way to honor his sacrifice is to save the lives he died trying to protect."

Sheriff Taylor was already gathering his gun belt and deputies. "Miss Williams, I need you to go to the church and ring the emergency bell. Get Reverend Wilson to spread the word—we need every able-bodied man in town to help with the evacuation and search."

Sarah felt a moment of panic at being given such responsibility, then drew strength from her mother's memory. This was no time for uncertainty. "What should I tell them?"

"The truth. That lives are at stake and we need immediate help." Jack paused at the door, his gaze meeting hers. "Sarah, can you handle organizing the towns-people while we handle the mine?"

The question carried weight beyond its simple words. Was she strong enough to take charge in a crisis? Could she be counted on when lives hung in the balance?

"Yes," she said firmly. "I can handle it."

The next hour passed in a whirlwind of activity that would remain etched in Sarah's memory forever. The emergency bell's frantic tolling brought people running from every corner of Silver Creek—miners' wives clutching frightened children, shopkeepers abandoning their stores, even elderly Henry Carter hobbling as fast as his legs could carry him.

"Listen to me!" Sarah called out from the church steps, her voice carrying over the worried murmur of the crowd. "There's been a threat against the mine. All workers need to be evacuated immediately, and we need volunteers to help search for explosive devices."

A gasp ran through the assembled townspeople. Mrs. Patterson stepped forward, her face pale with fear. "My husband's working the afternoon shift. Is he safe?"

"We're making sure everyone gets out safely," Sarah assured her, though her own heart was racing with fear for Jack, who had disappeared into the dangerous tunnels. "But I need all of you to help. Mrs. Patterson, can you organize the other wives to set up a medical station at Dr. Martinez's office? We may have injured people to care for."

As Sarah delegated tasks and coordinated the town's response, she felt a strange sense of clarity descending over her. This was what her mother had tried to teach her about faith—not passive waiting for God to solve problems, but active trust that He would provide strength for whatever tasks lay ahead.

v2·Latest

Copy

Publish

"Miss Williams!" Emma came running up the church steps, her young face bright with excitement rather than fear. "I saw men with guns heading toward the mine! Three of them on horseback, riding real fast!"

Sarah's blood ran cold. Armed men heading directly to the mine—where Jack was underground searching for explosive charges.

"Emma, I need you to stay here and help Mrs. Patterson with the medical station. Can you do that for me?"

"Yes, ma'am!" Emma darted away with the fearless energy of childhood.

Sarah's mind raced. She had to warn Jack and Sheriff Taylor herself—there was no time to send someone else, and she wouldn't put anyone in danger. As the evacuation continued around her, Sarah felt the weight of terrible urgency pressing down on her chest. Every second that passed brought them closer to three o'clock, closer to catastrophe.

She was moving between the church and Dr. Martinez's clinic when she saw them clearly—three men on horseback cresting the hill above town, riding hard toward the mine with deadly purpose. Even from a distance, she recognized the cold elegance of Cyrus Blackwood leading the group, his dark coat streaming behind him like the wings of some predatory bird.

Sarah's heart hammered against her ribs. If Blackwood was coming to the mine personally, it meant the situation had escalated beyond his original plan. Perhaps he'd discovered that Jonas had betrayed him, or maybe Jack's evacuation efforts had forced his hand. Either way, Jack and Sheriff Taylor were walking into a trap.

Without stopping to consider the wisdom of her actions, Sarah abandoned her coordination duties and ran toward the mine. Her skirts whipped around her legs as she pushed herself harder than she'd ever run before, her breath coming in sharp gasps that burned her lungs. Behind her, the emergency bell continued its frantic tolling, but the sound seemed to fade as her world narrowed to a single desperate purpose.

She had to reach Jack before Blackwood did.

The mine office came into view just as August Hart emerged, his face black with coal dust and etched with grim urgency. Sweat streaked the grime on his forehead despite the cool mountain air.

"Miss Williams! What are you doing here? It's not safe—"

"Blackwood's coming!" she gasped, her chest heaving as she pointed toward the approaching riders who were now less than a mile away. "Three men, armed, heading straight for the mine!"

August's weathered face went hard as granite. "Jack's still down in tunnel four with the sheriff, trying to locate those charges. If Blackwood's coming here personally..."

"It's a trap," Sarah finished, the terrible understanding flooding through her like ice water. "He wants Jack underground when the explosions happen. He's going to trigger them manually."

"We need to warn them." August started toward the mine entrance, then stopped as the sound of thundering hooves grew louder. "But if we go down there now, we'll all be trapped."

Sarah could see Blackwood's group clearly now—close enough to make out the weapons they carried, close enough to see the cold determination on their faces. In minutes, they would reach the mine entrance.

"I'll go warn them," August said desperately, then caught Sarah's arm as she moved toward the mine entrance. "Miss Williams, get back to town. Whatever happens here, you don't want to be caught in it."

But Sarah was already running toward the mine entrance, her teacher's instincts overriding her personal safety. She'd spent months caring for these children whose fathers worked underground. She'd grown to love this community that had welcomed her. And somewhere in those dark tunnels was the man she was beginning to realize she loved more than her own life.

She would not stand by helplessly while others risked everything.

The mine entrance loomed before her like a mouth opening into the earth itself. Sarah had never been underground before, and the darkness that swallowed the wooden support beams filled her with primitive terror. But she forced herself forward, moving as quietly as possible into the echoing depths.

Behind her, she heard the clatter of hooves as Blackwood and his men reached the mine entrance. Their voices carried clearly in the still air—harsh commands and the metallic sound of weapons being readied.

"Seal the main entrance. No one gets out until this is finished."

The words sent ice through Sarah's veins. She pressed herself against the tunnel wall, her heart hammering as she realized she was now trapped inside with Jack and Sheriff Taylor—but also that Blackwood's men were sealing their tomb.

Moving deeper into the mine, she called out in the softest whisper she dared, "Jack... Jack..."

Her voice seemed to disappear into the darkness ahead, swallowed by the weight of stone and timber. She moved deeper into the tunnel, following the main shaft toward distant sounds, praying her voice would carry to the man she desperately needed to warn.

Even as fear threatened to overwhelm her, she thought of her mother's unwavering faith, of her father's final attempt at redemption, of Jack's courage in facing danger to protect his workers.

"Be strong and courageous," she whispered, reciting the verse her mother had taught her as a child. "Do not be afraid or terrified, for the Lord your God goes with you."

Armed with that promise, Sarah Williams moved deeper into the darkness, determined to find Jack and warn him of the trap closing around them all. Behind her, the sound of Blackwood's boots echoed in the tunnel entrance, and ahead lay the uncertain fate of the man she loved and the community she'd sworn to protect.

But for the first time since her father's abandonment two years ago, Sarah felt no doubt about her purpose. God had brought her to Silver Creek for this moment, and she would not fail Him or the people counting on her courage.

TWENTY-EIGHT

The sound of Sarah's whispers echoing through the mine tunnels hit Jack like a physical blow. She was down here, in the most dangerous place possible, just as Blackwood's final gambit was about to unfold.

"Sarah!" he shouted back, his voice carrying a mixture of relief and terror. "Stay where you are! Don't come any deeper!"

But even as he called out the warning, Jack could hear the sound of multiple sets of boots entering the mine behind her. Blackwood had arrived, and Sarah was trapped between them.

"Jack," Sheriff Taylor whispered urgently from beside him in tunnel four, "we've got problems. Found three of the charges, but there's at least six more according to Jonas's map, and now we've got hostiles in the mine."

Jack's mind raced with impossible calculations. They were deep in the mine, with explosive charges hidden throughout the tunnels and armed men blocking their escape route. Sarah was somewhere in the darkness between them and Blackwood, probably terrified and certainly in mortal danger.

"Sheriff, can you work your way back toward the main tunnel and try to protect Sarah?"

"What about the remaining charges?"

"I'll keep searching. Someone has to find them before three o'clock, and I know this mine better than anyone."

Taylor nodded grimly and began moving carefully back toward the mine entrance, his gun drawn and ready. Jack turned deeper into tunnel four, his lantern casting eerie shadows on the support beams as he searched for signs of tampering.

The next fifteen minutes felt like hours. Jack found two more charges hidden behind false support beams, their timing mechanisms already counting down toward the three o'clock deadline. With shaking hands, he managed to disconnect the detonation wires, thanking God for the basic engineering knowledge his father had insisted he learn.

But as he worked, the sounds of conflict echoed through the mine—shouted commands, the sharp crack of gunfire, and worst of all, Sarah's voice calling his name with desperate urgency.

"God," Jack prayed aloud as he searched for the remaining charges, "I don't know if You're listening to me anymore. I know I turned away from You when Matthew died. But Sarah doesn't deserve to pay for my failures. Please, if You're there, help me save her."

The prayer felt rusty on his lips, like a language he'd forgotten how to speak. For five years, he'd convinced himself that God had abandoned him to face life's cruelties alone. But here in the darkness, with death closing in from multiple directions, he found himself reaching out to the only source of help that might be enough.

A new sound made him freeze—Jonas Williams's voice, weak but unmistakably alive, calling out from somewhere in the tunnel system.

"Jack! The charges in tunnel two are on a separate timer! They're set to go off in ten minutes, not at three o'clock!"

Jack's blood turned to ice. Jonas was alive, but more importantly, he was revealing that Blackwood's plan was even more diabolical than they'd realized. The afternoon shift workers had been evacuated, but if charges were set to detonate in ten minutes, there were still people in the mine who would be killed.

Jack ran toward the sound of Jonas's voice, his lantern swinging wildly as he navigated the maze of tunnels. He found the older man propped against a support beam in tunnel three, his face a mask of blood and pain but his eyes alert with desperate purpose.

"Jonas! How did you get here?"

"Escaped when Blackwood's men came back to finish me off. Been following them through the old mining trails." Jonas struggled to pull a paper from his torn coat. "Jack, there's something else. The charges in tunnel two—they're positioned to cause a complete collapse. Not just that section, but a chain reaction that will bring down the whole mine."

Jack stared at the blood-stained diagram Jonas handed him. The placement was diabolical in its precision—charges positioned to create a cascade failure that would turn the entire Montgomery mine into a tomb.

"How much time?"

"Less than ten minutes now." Jonas gripped Jack's arm with surprising strength. "But there's something you need to know. Blackwood's not just trying to destroy your mine—he's trying to kill you personally. This whole thing is revenge for rejecting his offers."

"Then we stop him."

"We?" Jonas's eyes widened. "Jack, I'm the man who helped kill your best friend. Why would you trust me to help?"

Jack looked at the broken man who had caused him so much pain, and felt something shift inside his chest. The wall of anger and resentment he'd carried for five years was cracking, not from weakness but from a strength he'd forgotten he possessed.

"Because right now, you're the only person who knows where all the charges are planted. And because..." Jack paused, the words coming from somewhere deeper than conscious thought. "Because Matthew would want me to choose saving lives over seeking revenge."

Jonas's eyes filled with tears. "Matthew would be proud of the man you've become. And this will give me a chance at redemption, to try to make up for my sins."

"Then help me honor his memory by saving lives instead of taking them."

Jonas gripped Jack's arm more tightly. "Jack, there's something else I need to say. If we don't make it out of here... Sarah deserves a man who will love her the way she deserves to be loved. A man of faith and honor." His voice grew urgent despite his weakness. "Promise me you'll take care of her. Promise me you won't let my mistakes define her future."

Jack met the older man's desperate gaze. "Jonas, we're both getting out of here. You can take care of her yourself."

"Promise me," Jonas insisted. "She's the only good thing I ever had a hand in creating. Don't let that be lost because of what I've done."

"I promise," Jack said quietly. "But you're going to have the chance to tell her yourself how much you love her."

Together, they made their way toward tunnel two, Jonas leaning heavily on Jack's shoulder as they navigated the dangerous terrain. Behind them, the sounds of conflict continued—Sheriff Taylor's voice shouting warnings, the echo of gunfire, and Sarah's voice calling out updates on Blackwood's position.

They found tunnel two in chaos. Blackwood himself was there, working frantically to manually trigger the charges that would bring down the entire mine. When he saw Jack and Jonas approaching, his face twisted with rage.

"Montgomery! You should have stayed out of my business!"

Blackwood raised a gun, but his hands were shaking with either rage or desperation. The shot went wide, sparking off the stone wall near Jack's head.

"It's over, Blackwood," Jack called out, advancing slowly with his own weapon drawn. "The mine's been evacuated. Your plan failed."

"Failed?" Blackwood laughed bitterly. "I still have enough explosives to bury you alive. And your precious schoolteacher is trapped in tunnel one with my men. Even if I die, you'll lose everything that matters to you."

The words hit Jack like a physical blow. Sarah was trapped with armed men, and he was here dealing with charges that could explode at any moment. He couldn't save both the mine and the woman he loved.

In that moment of impossible choice, Jack felt something he hadn't experienced in five years—absolute trust in a power greater than himself.

"God," he prayed silently, "I can't do this alone. I need You. Please show me what to do."

The answer came not as a voice or vision, but as a memory—Matthew's favorite verse about God speaking through the storm. And suddenly Jack understood. God wasn't absent from this crisis. He was present in Jonas's decision to help despite his guilt, in Sarah's courage to enter the mine despite her fear, in the townspeople's willingness to risk their lives for strangers.

"Jonas," Jack said quietly, "can you handle the detonation device while I deal with Blackwood?"

"Are you sure you trust me with that responsibility?"

Jack met the older man's gaze directly. "I'm sure."

As Jonas moved toward the explosive charges, his hands steady despite his injuries, Jack advanced on Blackwood with a calm he hadn't felt in years. Not the calm of resignation, but the peace that came from knowing he wasn't facing this alone.

"Cyrus, you can still walk away from this. No one else has to die."

"Like Matthew didn't have to die?" Blackwood snarled. "Your friend was going to expose my operations. He had to be stopped."

The casual admission of premeditated murder sent rage coursing through Jack's veins, but underneath the anger was something stronger—grief for his friend, yes, but also gratitude for the years of friendship they'd shared, and determination to prevent others from suffering the same loss.

"Matthew died because you chose greed over human life," Jack said steadily. "But his death won't be meaningless if it prevents other families from losing their fathers, their sons, their friends."

Blackwood raised his gun again, but this time his hands were steadier. "Touching sentiment, Montgomery. Too bad you won't live to—"

The gunshot echoed through the tunnel, but it wasn't Blackwood who fired. Sheriff Taylor appeared from the shadows, his smoking revolver pointed at the spot where Blackwood had been standing. The mine owner lay motionless on the tunnel floor, his schemes finally ended.

"Sorry I'm late," Taylor said grimly. "Had to make sure Miss Williams was safe first."

"Sarah—is she—?"

"Scared but unharmed. She's helping coordinate the final evacuation from outside." Taylor surveyed the explosive devices Jonas was carefully dismantling. "Looks like we got here just in time."

As Jonas completed his work on the last detonator, Jack felt a profound sense of completion settling over him. The charges were disarmed, Blackwood was dead, and Sarah was safe. But more than that, somewhere in the darkness of the mine he'd nearly lost everything, Jack had found something he'd thought was gone forever—his faith.

Not the simple, unquestioned faith of his youth, but something deeper and more tested. Faith that had been refined by suffering, strengthened by doubt, and ultimately proven in the crucible of impossible choices.

"It's done," Jonas said quietly, stepping back from the dismantled charges. "The mine is safe."

Jack looked at the man who had helped kill his best friend, and felt the last vestiges of hatred dissolve from his heart. "Thank you, Jonas. Matthew would have forgiven you too, you know."

"I hope so," Jonas replied. "I truly hope so."

As they made their way back toward the surface, toward Sarah's waiting arms and the community that had rallied to save them all, Jack offered a silent prayer of gratitude for the God who worked through broken people to accomplish His perfect purposes.

The signs had been there all along—in Jonas's decision to seek redemption, in Sarah's courage to enter the mine, in the townspeople's willingness to risk everything for their neighbors. God hadn't been absent during Jack's years of anger and doubt. He'd been patiently waiting for Jack to recognize His presence in the love and sacrifice of the people around him.

Now, emerging from the darkness into the brilliant Colorado sunshine, Jack Montgomery knew with absolute certainty that he would never walk alone again.

TWENTY-NINE

S arah's heart hammered as she watched the mine entrance, surrounded by what seemed like half of Silver Creek. The entire community had rallied in response to the emergency bell, and now they waited in tense silence for word from the men who had risked their lives underground.

"There!" Emma Reynolds pointed excitedly. "I see them!"

Three figures emerged from the darkness of the mine entrance—Sheriff Taylor supporting a limping Jonas Williams, and behind them, Jack Montgomery, his face blackened with rock dust but his eyes bright with something that looked like peace.

"Jack!" Sarah ran toward him without thought for propriety or dignity, throwing herself into his arms with relief that made her sob. He was solid and warm and wonderfully alive, his arms closing around her with fierce gratitude.

"It's over," he murmured against her hair. "Blackwood's dead. The charges are disarmed. It's over."

Eleanor rushed forward and embraced her son with tears streaming down her face, while Charlotte fussed over Jonas's injuries with the efficiency of someone who had found her calling in caring for others.

"Papa," Sarah said, stepping back from Jack to look at her father properly. The beating he'd taken was evident in every line of his face, but his eyes held a clarity she hadn't seen since childhood. "Are you—?"

"I'm alive, daughter. More alive than I've been in years." Jonas reached for her hand with fingers that shook from exhaustion and pain. "Sarah, there are things I need to tell you. About Matthew's death, about why I really left Denver. Things you deserve to know."

Dr. Martinez intervened before Sarah could respond. "Mr. Williams, you need medical attention immediately. The confessions can wait until you're not bleeding."

As the doctor led Jonas toward his clinic, Jack took Sarah's hands in his, his grip warm and steady. "Sarah, your father saved my life down there. And more than that—he saved the entire mine. Without his knowledge of where the charges were placed..."

"I saw you choose to trust him," Sarah said softly, though her voice was still shaky from the terror of the past hours. "Even knowing what he'd done. Jack, how were you able to forgive him?"

Jack was quiet for a moment, his eyes distant as he considered the question. "I think I finally understood what Matthew always tried to tell me about grace. That forgiveness isn't about what people deserve—it's about choosing mercy over justice because that's what God does for us every day."

Sarah felt something shift in her chest at his words. This was the man she'd fallen in love with—not the angry, bitter mine owner who'd lost his faith, but the compassionate leader who could see past his own pain to offer redemption to others.

"Jack," she said carefully, "you sound different. Like something's changed."

"Something has changed." Jack's voice carried a wonder that made her heart skip. "Down in that tunnel, facing what might have been my last moments, I finally stopped running from God. And you know what I discovered?"

"What?"

"He was never chasing me. He was just waiting for me to come home."

Before Sarah could respond, they were surrounded by townspeople wanting to hear the story, to celebrate the end of the threat, to thank Jack for his courage. But even in the midst of the crowd, Sarah felt the intimacy of the moment they'd shared. Jack Montgomery had found his way back to faith, and somehow, she'd been part of that journey.

August appeared at Jack's elbow, his weathered face creased with concern and curiosity. "Jack, what happened down there? All we heard was gunshots, then nothing."

"Blackwood tried to trigger the charges manually when he realized his plan had failed," Jack explained, his arm still around Sarah's waist. "Sheriff Taylor had to shoot him to stop him. Jonas helped me locate and disarm the remaining explosives."

A murmur of amazement rippled through the crowd. Mrs. Patterson stepped forward, her earlier suspicions of the Williams family clearly transformed. "Mr. Williams risked his life to save our mine? After everything..."

"After everything, he chose to do what was right," Jack said firmly. "That's what matters now."

Sarah watched her father being helped toward Dr. Martinez's clinic, surrounded by townspeople who had gone from viewing him with suspicion to treating him like a hero. The transformation was remarkable, but she wondered if Jonas himself understood the magnitude of what had changed.

Two hours later, Sarah sat beside her father's bed in Dr. Martinez's clinic, watching him sleep fitfully as the doctor's ministrations took effect. The full extent of his injuries had been shocking—broken ribs, a concussion, cuts and bruises that spoke of systematic brutality. But he was alive, and more importantly, he was at peace in a way she hadn't seen since her childhood.

Jack appeared in the doorway, cleaned up now but still showing the effects of his underground ordeal. "How is he?"

"Resting. Dr. Martinez says he'll recover fully, given time." Sarah looked up at Jack, noting the exhaustion in his face. "You should be resting too."

"Can't sleep yet. Too much to process." Jack pulled up a chair beside her. "Sarah, about what happened down there—your father told me something I think you should know."

Sarah waited, her heart racing at the intensity in Jack's voice.

"When I asked him why he was helping me, he said he wanted to prove to you that redemption was possible. That even someone who had failed as badly as he had could still choose to do the right thing in the end." Jack's voice grew soft.

"Sarah, your father faced almost certain death to save people he'd never met, just to prove himself worthy of your love."

Tears spilled down Sarah's cheeks. "I never asked him to prove anything."

"He knows that. But he needed to prove it to himself." Jack squeezed her hand gently. "He also said something else as we were walking out of the tunnel. He said watching you become the woman you are despite his failures showed him that grace was real. That if God could work through his mistakes to create something beautiful like you, then maybe there was hope for him too."

Sarah looked down at her father's sleeping face, seeing past the bruises to the man who had once taught her to read, who had told her bedtime stories, who had left to protect her from the consequences of his choices even when it broke both their hearts.

"He's going to wake up a different man," she said quietly. "I can see it already."

"As am I," Jack replied. "Sarah, what happened in that mine changed me. Not just my faith, but my understanding of what really matters. Of who really matters."

Before Sarah could ask what he meant, Dr. Martinez entered the room with Sheriff Taylor close behind. The sheriff looked grim but satisfied, the expression of a man who had finally seen justice done.

"How's our patient, Doc?" Taylor asked.

"He'll live. Probably be on his feet in a week or so." Dr. Martinez checked Jonas's pulse with professional efficiency. "Though he's going to need considerable rest and care."

"Good, because we're going to need his testimony." Taylor turned to Jack and Sarah. "Found Blackwood's body and enough evidence in his office to convict a dozen men. Looks like your father's been keeping detailed records of everything, Miss Williams. Names, dates, payments—it's all there."

Sarah felt a chill of apprehension. "What does that mean for Papa?"

"Well, that's complicated. He's certainly guilty of past crimes, but his cooperation in stopping Blackwood, his willingness to risk his life to save innocent people..." Taylor shrugged. "I suspect any judge will take that into consideration. Especially with half the town ready to testify on his behalf."

"The town?" Sarah looked confused.

"Sarah," Jack said gently, "you should see what's been happening while we were dealing with the crisis. The entire community has rallied around your father. People who barely knew his name are organizing to help with his recovery."

"They started calling him a hero," Taylor added. "Can't say I've ever seen anything like it. A man's past being wiped clean by one act of courage."

As if summoned by their conversation, a gentle knock came at the clinic door. Charlotte appeared, carrying a basket covered with a checkered cloth.

"I hope I'm not disturbing," she said softly. "Mrs. Henderson sent soup for Mr. Williams, and several other ladies wanted me to bring flowers." She gestured to the bouquet in her other hand. "Half the town has stopped by the house asking for news."

Sarah felt overwhelmed by the outpouring of support. "I don't understand. Yesterday, people were suspicious of Papa. Now..."

"Now they've seen what real courage looks like," Jack said simply. "Your father didn't just risk his life—he did it for people who had every reason to distrust him. That kind of sacrifice changes how people see a man."

As the evening wore on, a steady stream of visitors appeared at the clinic. Henry Carter came to thank Jonas personally for preventing what could have been a massacre in the mines. Mrs. Patterson brought fresh bread and an apology for her earlier harsh words. Even some of the miners who might have been killed by the explosives stopped by to pay their respects to the man they now called their savior.

Each visitor brought the same message: Jonas Williams had redeemed himself in the eyes of Silver Creek through his final act of courage. The community had chosen to focus on his sacrifice rather than his sins, and in doing so, they had offered him something he'd never dared hope for—a second chance at belonging somewhere.

"It's like watching grace in action," Sarah murmured to Jack as they stepped outside for fresh air. "Not just the theological concept, but real, practical love."

"Your father isn't the only one experiencing grace," Jack replied, his voice thoughtful. "I think the whole town is learning what it means to forgive, to see people as more than their worst mistakes."

As they stood together in the gathering dusk, Sarah felt a profound sense of completion. The crisis that had threatened to destroy everything she'd built in Silver Creek had instead become the catalyst for healing—not just for her father, but for Jack's faith, for the community's unity, and for her own understanding of what love really meant.

"Sarah," Jack said quietly, "I need to tell you something else your father said down in the mine."

She looked up at him, noting the intensity in his expression.

"He asked me to take care of you. Said you deserved a man who would love you the way you deserve to be loved." Jack's voice grew husky with emotion. "And I realized that's exactly what I want to do. Not because he asked me to, but because I can't imagine my life without you in it."

Sarah's breath caught. "Jack..."

"I know this isn't the time or place for such declarations. We've both been through too much today to think clearly about the future. But I needed you to know—you've become the most important thing in my life. More important than the mine, than my pride, than anything else in this world."

Sarah reached up to touch his face, noting how the lines of exhaustion couldn't hide the peace in his eyes. "You've become that for me too. When I came to Silver Creek, I was just trying to survive. You taught me that I could do more than survive—I could thrive. I could love and be loved in return."

They stood there in the gathering darkness, hands joined, hearts full of gratitude for the day's deliverance and hope for whatever future God had planned for them.

"There's going to be a lot to work through," Jack said quietly. "Your father's recovery, the investigation into Blackwood's activities, rebuilding the mine's reputation."

"We'll face it together," Sarah replied with quiet certainty. "Whatever comes next, we'll face it together."

Just then, Jonas's voice called weakly from inside the clinic. "Sarah? Are you there?"

They hurried back inside to find Jonas awake, his eyes clearer than they'd been in hours. "Papa! How are you feeling?"

"Like I've been trampled by a herd of cattle," Jonas said with a weak smile. "But alive. More alive than I've felt in years." His gaze moved to Jack. "Did we stop him? Are the miners safe?"

"We stopped him," Jack confirmed. "And the whole town knows what you did to save them."

Jonas's eyes filled with tears. "I can never undo what I did to Matthew and those other men. But maybe... maybe I can live the rest of my life trying to make amends."

"Papa," Sarah said softly, taking his hand, "you already have. Today you chose courage over cowardice, sacrifice over selfishness. That's the man I always believed you could be."

"The man your mother always believed I could be," Jonas whispered. "God rest her soul."

As the night deepened over Silver Creek, the three of them sat together in the quiet clinic—father and daughter reconciled at last, and the man who had chosen forgiveness over vengeance. Outside, the town settled into peaceful rest, its people secure in the knowledge that the threat had passed and justice had been served.

Tomorrow would bring new challenges and new opportunities to serve their community. But tonight, Sarah Williams felt the deep satisfaction that comes from witnessing redemption in action. Her father had found his way back to the man he was meant to be, Jack had found his way back to God, and she had found her place in a community that had chosen love over fear.

The signs had been there all along, she realized—in the kindness of strangers who became family, in the love that grew from friendship, in the faith that survived even the darkest trials. God's plan had been bigger than any of them could have imagined, weaving their separate stories into something beautiful and strong and lasting.

As she held her father's hand and felt Jack's presence beside her, Sarah offered a silent prayer of thanksgiving for the God who worked all things together for good, even when the path seemed impossible to understand.

THIRTY

J ack woke to sunlight streaming through his bedroom window and the sound of voices drifting up from the kitchen below. For a moment, he lay still, marveling at the simple pleasure of being alive to see another morning. The events in the mine felt like something from another lifetime, yet the peace that had settled over his heart remained as real as the dawn breaking over Silver Creek.

He dressed quickly and made his way downstairs, following the scent of coffee and the murmur of conversation. In the kitchen, he found his mother and Charlotte preparing what appeared to be enough food to feed half the town.

"Good morning," he said, kissing his mother's cheek. "Planning to open a restaurant?"

"The whole town will be here this afternoon for the celebration," Eleanor replied, her voice warmer than Jack had heard it in years. "After what happened yesterday, people need to come together, to give thanks, to heal."

Jack poured himself coffee and studied his mother's face. Something fundamental had changed in Eleanor Montgomery. The rigid propriety that had defined her for so long had been replaced by something softer, more genuine.

"Mother, are you feeling unwell? You seem different."

Eleanor paused in her kneading of bread dough, a small smile playing at her lips. "Yesterday I watched my son risk his life to save others, and I saw a young woman I'd initially judged harshly display more courage than many men possess. It has a way of clarifying what truly matters in life."

Charlotte looked up from the vegetables she was chopping, her eyes bright with excitement. "Jack, Mother has something wonderful to tell you. About David and me."

Eleanor wiped her hands on her apron and turned to face her son directly. "I've been a fool. I've spent so much time worrying about social position and proper matches that I nearly prevented your sister from finding genuine happiness."

"Mother?" Jack set down his coffee cup, intrigued by this unexpected development.

"David Miller is a good man. Yesterday, when the crisis began, he was one of the first to volunteer for the rescue efforts. He organized the younger men, coordinated with the sheriff's deputies, and never once thought of his own safety." Eleanor's voice grew firm with conviction. "A man's character is revealed in times of crisis, and David's character is beyond reproach."

Charlotte's face was radiant with joy. "She's given us her blessing, Jack. David and I can be married!"

Jack felt a surge of happiness for his sister, mixed with admiration for his mother's transformation. "I'm glad, Charlotte. David's a good man, and he loves you deeply."

"There's more," Eleanor continued. "I've realized that my objections to David were based on the same prejudices that made me doubt Sarah's worth when she first arrived. I judged people by their circumstances rather than their character, and I was wrong."

The mention of Sarah made Jack's pulse quicken. "Speaking of Sarah, how is she this morning? And her father?"

"I stopped by Dr. Martinez's clinic an hour ago," Charlotte said. "Mr. Williams is much improved, and Sarah looks like she actually slept a few hours. Dr. Martinez says he can be moved to more comfortable quarters this afternoon."

"Good. I want to make sure he has everything he needs for his recovery." Jack paused, then added, "I'm thinking of offering him a permanent position at the mine. Chief Safety Inspector, with full authority to implement whatever measures he deems necessary."

Eleanor's eyebrows rose. "The man who was involved in Matthew's death? Jack, are you certain that's wise?"

"I'm certain it's right," Jack replied firmly. "Yesterday, Jonas Williams proved that people can change, that redemption is possible. And his knowledge of mine safety could prevent other tragedies. Matthew would approve."

Before Eleanor could respond, a knock at the front door interrupted their conversation. Charlotte hurried to answer it, returning moments later with David Miller at her side, his usually confident demeanor replaced by nervous anticipation.

"Mr. Montgomery," David said formally, "I hope I'm not intruding. I wanted to speak with you about... well, about Charlotte."

Jack studied the young man who had captured his sister's heart. David's clothes were clean but worn, his hands calloused from mine work, his manner respectful but not servile. Yesterday's crisis had indeed revealed his character—and it was good.

"What about Charlotte?" Jack asked, though his tone was not unkind.

"I'd like to ask for her hand in marriage, sir. I know I'm not what you might have hoped for your sister, but I love her more than life itself, and I'll work every day to be worthy of her."

Eleanor stepped forward before Jack could respond. "David, you've already proven yourself worthy. Yesterday's events showed us all what kind of man you are—brave, selfless, dedicated to protecting others. I couldn't ask for a better husband for my daughter."

David's eyes widened in surprise. "Mrs. Montgomery, I... thank you. I promise you won't regret this decision."

"I know I won't," Eleanor said warmly. "Now, Jack, I believe David is waiting for your blessing as well."

Jack extended his hand to David. "Welcome to the family. But I have one condition."

David's face tensed. "Yes, sir?"

"You'll continue working at the Montgomery mine. We need good men, and Charlotte deserves a husband who's near enough to come home every night."

"Yes, sir!" David's relief was palpable as he gripped Jack's hand. "Thank you, Mr. Montgomery. Both of you. I'll make you proud."

As Charlotte threw herself into David's arms with joyful tears, Jack felt a deep satisfaction. His family was healing, growing, becoming something stronger than it had been before the crisis. Love was triumphing over fear, grace over judgment.

"When will the wedding be?" Eleanor asked practically.

"As soon as possible," Charlotte said, beaming up at David. "We've waited long enough."

"Next month," David suggested. "That will give us time to prepare properly, and for Mr. Williams to recover enough to attend."

The mention of Jonas reminded Jack of the day's responsibilities. "I should check on the mine, make sure yesterday's evacuation didn't cause any lasting problems. And I want to speak with some of the men who were forced to work for Blackwood."

"Forced?" Eleanor asked.

"Sheriff Taylor discovered that several men who left Montgomery Mining over the past months were actually coerced into working for Blackwood. Threats against their families, false debts—the man was more vicious than we realized."

David nodded grimly. "I heard talk about that. John Davidson and Bill Hudson both disappeared suddenly, said they'd found better work elsewhere. But their wives seemed scared whenever anyone mentioned it."

"I want to invite them back," Jack said. "Clean slate, no questions asked. They were victims as much as anyone."

As the morning progressed, Jack made his way through Silver Creek, checking on his workers and their families, assessing the aftermath of yesterday's crisis. What he found filled him with pride for his community.

The townspeople had rallied together with remarkable unity. Those who had evacuated were helping to inspect and secure the mine workings. Families were sharing resources with those who had been affected by Blackwood's schemes. Most remarkably, several men who had been forced to work for Blackwood had already approached August Hart about returning to Montgomery Mining.

"They're ashamed of what they were forced to do," August explained as they walked through the mine office. "But they're good men, Jack. They just got caught in Blackwood's web of threats and coercion."

"Bring them to see me this afternoon," Jack decided. "I want them to know they're welcome back without any stigma attached."

"That's generous of you."

"It's what my father would have done. And it's what's right."

By afternoon, the Montgomery house was filled with what seemed like half of Silver Creek. The "small celebration" Eleanor had planned had grown into a full community gathering, with tables of food stretching across the front lawn and children playing games while their parents shared stories of yesterday's dramatic events.

Jack found himself moving through the crowd, accepting thanks and congratulations that felt both humbling and overwhelming. But his eyes kept searching for Sarah, and when he finally spotted her near the dessert table, his heart lifted with relief.

She wore her green dress—the one that brought out the color of her eyes—and though she looked tired, there was a glow about her that spoke of inner peace. She was deep in conversation with Mrs. Patterson and several other ladies, clearly discussing her father's condition.

"Mr. Montgomery!" Sheriff Taylor appeared at Jack's elbow, his expression satisfied. "Good to see you looking rested. I've got news about the investigation."

"What did you find?"

"More than we expected. Blackwood kept meticulous records of every illegal scheme he'd been running. We've identified victims across three territories, and we've recovered enough evidence to prosecute his remaining associates."

Jack felt a grim satisfaction. "And the men he forced to work for him?"

"Cleared of any wrongdoing. The evidence shows they were coerced through threats and blackmail." Taylor's expression grew troubled. "But there's something that doesn't add up, Jack. Blackwood's been operating on borrowed money for months—heavily in debt according to his ledgers. Yet somehow he had enough cash to buy out smaller claims and fund this elaborate sabotage operation."

"What are you suggesting?"

"Someone was backing him. Someone with deep pockets and their own reasons for wanting Montgomery Mining destroyed." Taylor lowered his voice. "The problem is, his records about this mysterious investor are coded. Names replaced with numbers, meetings referenced only by dates and locations."

Jack felt a chill run down his spine. "So we might not have seen the end of this."

"That's my concern. Blackwood was vicious, but he was also desperate. Men like that usually have someone pulling their strings—someone who stays in the shadows and doesn't get their hands dirty."

Jack absorbed this troubling news, then forced himself to focus on what he could control. Whatever shadow threat might still exist, his immediate responsibility was to his community and the men who had suffered under Blackwood's schemes.

"I want the men forced to work for Blackwood to know they're welcome at Montgomery Mining. No questions asked, no recriminations."

"I already told them. They'll be here this afternoon to speak with you personally."

As if summoned by their conversation, John Davidson approached, his hat in his hands and his face creased with shame and anxiety.

"Mr. Montgomery," he said quietly, "I need to apologize for leaving your employ so suddenly. I want you to know it wasn't by choice."

"Tom, you don't need to apologize for being victimized by a criminal," Jack said firmly. "Sheriff Taylor has explained the situation. The question is: do you want your job back?"

John's eyes widened with surprise and relief. "Yes, sir. More than anything. Working for you was the best job I ever had."

"Then consider yourself rehired. Same position, same pay, and we'll forget the past few months ever happened."

As word spread through the crowd about Jack's generous policy toward Blackwood's former victims, several other men approached with similar stories of coercion and forced compliance. Each time, Jack's response was the same: welcome back, no questions asked, fresh start for everyone.

"You're doing a good thing," Sarah said, appearing at his side as the latest conversation concluded. "Those men need to know they can trust you."

"Trust has to be rebuilt after what Blackwood did to this community," Jack replied, acutely aware of her presence beside him. "But it starts with forgiveness and second chances."

"Speaking of second chances," Sarah said softly, "Papa wants to speak with you. He's feeling much better, and Dr. Martinez says he can attend the celebration for a few hours."

Jack followed Sarah toward the house, where they found Jonas sitting in a chair on the front porch, still bandaged and bruised but alert and peaceful. A steady stream of townspeople had been approaching him throughout the afternoon, offering thanks and sharing stories.

"Jack," Jonas said, struggling to rise.

"Stay seated," Jack insisted, pulling up a chair beside him. "How are you feeling?"

"Like I've been given a gift I don't deserve," Jonas replied honestly. "The way this community has welcomed me, after everything I've done... it's more grace than I ever dared hope for."

"You earned it yesterday. You risked everything to save innocent lives."

Jonas shook his head. "No, Jack. What I did yesterday was simply choose to be the man I should have been all along. The grace came from watching people choose to see that potential rather than dwelling on my failures."

"About your future," Jack said, "I have a proposition for you. I'd like to offer you a permanent position at Montgomery Mining. Chief Safety Inspector, with full authority to implement whatever protocols you think necessary."

Jonas's eyes filled with tears. "You would trust me with that responsibility?"

"I would. Your knowledge could prevent other families from suffering what Matthew's family suffered. What you suffered yesterday, knowing what your past choices had cost."

"I accept," Jonas said simply. "And I promise you, no worker will ever be endangered on my watch. Not again."

As the afternoon wore on, Jack found himself observing the celebration with a deep sense of satisfaction. Charlotte and David were glowing with happiness as they shared their engagement news. Eleanor was bustling around with more energy and joy than he'd seen from her in years. The community had come together in a way that felt both healing and transformative.

But most of all, he was aware of Sarah—the way she moved through the crowd, offering comfort to those who needed it, sharing in others' joy, serving as a bridge between different groups of people. She had become the heart of this community in ways that went far beyond her role as schoolteacher.

As the sun began to set over Silver Creek, painting the mountains in shades of gold and crimson, Jack found himself standing with Sarah on the edge of the crowd, watching the celebration continue around them.

"It's beautiful," Sarah said softly. "To see everyone come together like this, to see healing happening in real time."

"It wouldn't have happened without you," Jack replied. "You've been the catalyst for so much of this transformation."

"I think you give me too much credit."

"I don't think I give you nearly enough." Jack turned to face her fully, his heart racing with the decision he'd been contemplating all day. "Sarah, there's something I need to ask you."

"What is it?"

"Will you walk with me? There's something I want to show you."

Curious, Sarah allowed him to guide her away from the celebration, toward the path that led to the church. As they walked, Jack felt his nervousness growing, but also his certainty. Yesterday had shown him what truly mattered, and he was done waiting for the perfect moment.

Sometimes, he'd learned, the perfect moment was simply the one where you finally found the courage to speak your heart.

THIRTY-ONE

The evening air was cool and sweet as Jack guided Sarah along the familiar path toward the church, his heart hammering against his ribs with each step. Behind them, the sounds of celebration continued to drift from his family's house—laughter, conversation, the contented murmur of a community at peace. But Jack's attention was focused entirely on the woman walking beside him, her hand resting lightly on his arm as they navigated the worn trail in the gathering dusk.

"It's beautiful tonight," Sarah said softly, her gaze drifting over the mountains that surrounded Silver Creek like protective guardians. "After everything that's happened, it feels almost miraculous to see such peace."

"Miraculous," Jack repeated, testing the word on his tongue. Six months ago, he would have scoffed at such language. Now, after everything they'd weathered together, it seemed like the only appropriate description. "Yes, I think that's exactly what it is."

They reached the white clapboard church, its simple steeple silhouetted against the star-filled sky. Jack paused, his nerves nearly getting the better of him as he contemplated what lay ahead. In his pocket, Matthew's mother had given him her son's ring years ago—a simple gold band that Matthew had planned to give to the girl he'd been courting before the accident. Mrs. Carter had pressed it into Jack's hands at Matthew's funeral, saying her son would have wanted his best friend to have it when the time came.

Jack had never imagined that time would come. For five years, the ring had sat in his desk drawer, a painful reminder of dreams cut short. But yesterday, when he'd returned home from the mine and found it sitting on top of the papers where he'd left Matthew's Bible, he'd understood. This was meant to be Sarah's ring. Matthew would have loved her generous spirit, her unwavering faith, her courage in the face of adversity.

"Jack?" Sarah's voice broke through his reverie. "You seem nervous. Is everything all right?"

"Everything is perfect," he said, and meant it. "There's just something I want to show you first. Something important."

He led her around the side of the church, toward the small cemetery that lay beyond the building. The moon was bright enough to illuminate their path, casting everything in silver light that made the familiar landscape look almost ethereal. Sarah followed without question, though he could sense her curiosity growing with each step.

"I used to come here as a form of punishment," Jack said as they approached the cemetery gate. "After Matthew died, I would visit his grave to remind myself of my failures, to feed the anger and guilt I carried. It felt like the only honest thing I could do—torment myself with what I'd lost."

Sarah's hand tightened on his arm. "And now?"

"Now I understand that avoiding this place was avoiding part of myself. The part that loved my friend, that treasured his memory, that needed to grieve properly in order to heal." Jack opened the gate with steady hands. "Come. There's someone I want you to meet."

They walked among the weathered headstones, past the graves of Silver Creek's founding families, the miners who had died in earlier accidents, the children who had succumbed to illness or injury in a harsh frontier environment. Each marker told a story of lives lived and lost, of dreams fulfilled and cut short. But tonight, instead of feeling overwhelmed by the weight of all that sorrow, Jack felt a strange peace settling over him.

"Here," he said, stopping before a simple granite headstone marked with Matthew's name and dates. "Matthew Carter. My best friend since we were boys."

Sarah read the inscription aloud: "Beloved son and friend. 'God works all things for good.'" She looked up at Jack with understanding in her eyes. "This is where your faith was broken."

"And where it's been restored," Jack replied, kneeling to brush away some fallen leaves from the base of the stone. "Sarah, I need to tell you about Matthew. About the kind of man he was, and why I think he would have loved you as much as I do."

Sarah's breath caught at his words, but she said nothing, simply kneeling beside him in the soft grass.

"Matthew believed in signs," Jack began, his voice growing stronger as he spoke. "He saw God's hand in everything—the way birds migrated, the patterns of weather, the people who came into our lives at exactly the right moments. I used to tease him about it, call him superstitious. But Matthew would just smile and say, 'Jack, God speaks to those who know how to listen.'"

Jack reached into his pocket, his fingers closing around the small velvet box he'd placed there earlier. "After the accident, I stopped listening. I convinced myself that if God existed at all, He was either powerless to prevent tragedy or simply didn't care about the suffering of good people. I closed my heart to any possibility of divine guidance."

"What changed?" Sarah asked softly.

"You did." Jack turned to face her fully, the moonlight illuminating the love and wonder in her hazel eyes. "From the moment you arrived in Silver Creek, you've been a walking testament to Matthew's faith. The way you trust in God's plan even when you can't understand it. The way you see His hand in the smallest kindnesses. The way you believe in redemption even for people like your father, like me."

Sarah's eyes filled with tears. "Jack..."

"Let me finish," he said gently. "Yesterday, in that mine, facing what I thought might be my last moments, I finally understood what Matthew had been trying to tell me all those years. God doesn't prevent every tragedy, but He walks with us through them. He doesn't spare us from suffering, but He redeems it, uses it to shape us into the people He means us to be."

Jack stood, drawing Sarah to her feet with him. "And sometimes, if we're very blessed, He sends us signs so clear that even the most stubborn, faithless men can't ignore them."

"What kind of signs?" Sarah whispered.

"Like a schoolteacher arriving in Silver Creek at the exact moment we needed her most. Like finding Matthew's Bible on my desk just when I needed to remember his faith. Like your father choosing redemption over self-preservation, proving that grace is real and powerful." Jack's voice grew husky with emotion. "Like falling in love with a woman who makes me want to be the man God always intended me to be."

Sarah's tears were flowing freely now. "Oh, Jack."

"Sarah Elizabeth Williams," Jack said, dropping to one knee before Matthew's grave, "I believe God brought you into my life for a purpose greater than either of us could have imagined. You've restored my faith, healed my heart, and shown me what real love looks like."

He pulled out the velvet box, opening it to reveal Matthew's ring gleaming in the moonlight. "This ring belonged to Matthew. His mother gave it to me, saying he would have wanted his best friend to have it when the right woman came along. I think Matthew would have loved your courage, your compassion, your unwavering faith in God's goodness."

Sarah gasped, her hands flying to her mouth as she stared at the simple gold band.

"Will you marry me, Sarah? Will you be my wife, my partner in faith, my companion for whatever joys and sorrows God has planned for us?" Jack's voice broke slightly. "Will you help me honor Matthew's memory by building a life filled with the kind of love and faith he always believed in?"

For a moment, Sarah seemed unable to speak, overwhelmed by the emotion of the moment. Then she sank to her knees beside him, her hands cupping his face as tears streamed down her cheeks.

"Yes," she whispered. "Yes, Jack Montgomery, I will marry you. I will love you and walk beside you and trust in God's plan for our lives together."

Jack slipped the ring onto her finger with trembling hands, marveling at how perfectly it fit, as if it had been made for her. Then he drew her into his arms, kissing her with all the love and gratitude that filled his heart to overflowing.

When they finally broke apart, Sarah was laughing through her tears. "Matthew would have approved of this proposal, I think. Having his grave as witness to our promises."

"I think he would have," Jack agreed. "And I think he would have loved watching you transform our entire community with your faith and kindness."

They sat together in the grass beside Matthew's grave, Sarah's head resting on Jack's shoulder as they watched the stars wheel overhead. The peace that had settled over Silver Creek seemed to encompass them like a blessing, and Jack felt the last vestiges of the anger and bitterness he'd carried for five years finally dissolve completely.

"Jack," Sarah said quietly, "there's something I need to tell you about my father."

"What is it?"

"This afternoon, while you were dealing with the men returning to work, Papa told me something. About why he really left Denver two years ago." Sarah's voice grew thoughtful. "He said he'd discovered that some of his mining associates were planning to expand their operations to Colorado Territory. He was afraid that if he stayed, they would force him to participate in sabotaging mines here."

Jack felt a chill of understanding. "So he left to protect the mining communities here, including Silver Creek."

"Yes. But he also left because he was ashamed of what he'd already done, and he didn't want Mama and me to know the truth about his involvement in those earlier accidents." Sarah lifted her head to look at Jack. "He said letting Mama die while he was away was his punishment for choosing cowardice over courage."

"And now?"

"Now he says God gave him a second chance to choose correctly. To protect innocent people instead of harming them." Sarah's voice filled with wonder.

"He told me that seeing you forgive him showed him what grace really means. That if the man whose best friend he'd helped kill could offer him redemption, then maybe God's forgiveness was real too."

Jack felt tears sting his eyes. "Matthew would have forgiven him. Matthew forgave everyone."

"Papa wants to visit Matthew's grave to ask his forgiveness directly. Is that... would that be all right with you?"

"More than all right. I think it would be exactly what Matthew would have wanted." Jack squeezed her hand gently. "Your father has been carrying that guilt for five years, just like I've been carrying my anger. Maybe it's time for both of us to lay those burdens down."

They sat in comfortable silence for several minutes, each lost in their own thoughts about redemption, forgiveness, and the mysterious ways God worked to heal broken hearts. The night air was filled with the scent of wildflowers and the distant sound of music from the celebration still continuing at the Montgomery house.

"Sarah," Jack said finally, "I have something else I want to tell you. About the future, about what I hope our marriage will be."

"Tell me."

"I want us to build something together that honors both our gifts. You've shown me how education can transform lives, and I've learned how industry can support and strengthen a community. I'm thinking of expanding the school, maybe adding programs for adult education, technical training for the miners."

Sarah's eyes lit up with excitement. "Oh, Jack, that would be wonderful! So many of the miners can barely read or write. And their wives could benefit from classes in household management, child care, basic medicine..."

"We could build a real educational center, something that serves the entire community. And we could fund scholarships for exceptional students to attend college back East." Jack's voice grew animated as he warmed to the subject. "Your father could develop safety training programs that could be shared with mines throughout the territory."

"It sounds like a dream come true," Sarah said softly. "But Jack, are you sure you want to take on such an ambitious project? It would require enormous amounts of time and money."

"I'm sure. Because I've learned something important from watching you teach. The greatest legacy a person can leave isn't wealth or property—it's the lives they've touched, the minds they've opened, the hope they've inspired." Jack brought her hand to his lips, kissing her ring finger where Matthew's ring now gleamed. "I want our marriage to be a partnership in service, Sarah. I want us to use whatever gifts God has given us to make Silver Creek a place where everyone can thrive."

"Then that's exactly what we'll do," Sarah replied with quiet conviction. "Together."

As if summoned by their conversation about the future, a soft rustling in the oak tree above Matthew's grave drew their attention upward. A small bird was working industriously on a nest, weaving twigs and bits of grass together with patient determination.

"Look," Sarah whispered, pointing to the busy creature. "Even in the darkness, she's building something beautiful."

Jack watched the bird's careful work, remembering Matthew's love for these small creatures and his belief that they carried messages of hope. "Matthew always said birds were God's reminder that no matter how dark things seem, new life is always coming."

"Your friend was wise."

"He was. And I think he would have loved you, Sarah Williams soon-to-be Montgomery." Jack stood, helping her to her feet. "Shall we go back and share our news with the family?"

"In a moment." Sarah placed her hand on Matthew's headstone, her touch gentle and reverent. "Thank you, Matthew Carter, for being the kind of friend who helped shape Jack into the man I love. Thank you for believing in signs and grace and second chances. I promise I'll love him well."

The words hung in the night air like a blessing, and Jack felt a profound sense of completion wash over him. The past had been redeemed, the present was filled with joy, and the future stretched ahead bright with promise. Whatever challenges lay ahead—and there would be challenges—he and Sarah would face them together, anchored by faith and strengthened by love.

As they walked back toward the lights of home, hand in hand, Jack offered a silent prayer of gratitude for the God who worked all things together for good, even the deepest sorrows and most devastating losses. Matthew's death had brought him to his knees, but it had also prepared his heart to recognize the gift when Sarah Williams walked into his life.

The signs had been there all along, just as she'd always insisted. God had been speaking through every kindness, every challenge, every moment of grace. Jack had simply needed to learn how to listen with the heart of faith rather than the cynicism of loss.

Now, with Sarah's hand in his and her ring on her finger, Jack Montgomery finally understood what Matthew had tried to tell him all those years ago. God's plans were bigger than human understanding, but they were always, always good. And sometimes, if you were very blessed indeed, those plans included love that redeemed the past and illuminated the future with hope.

Behind them, the bird continued its patient work in the oak tree, building something beautiful in the darkness. Ahead of them, the lights of Silver Creek beckoned like a promise of home, family, and all the joys that awaited hearts brave enough to trust in grace.

THIRTY-TWO

S arah stood before the mirror in Charlotte's bedroom, her hands trembling as she attempted to fasten the tiny pearl buttons that ran up the back of her wedding dress. The gown was made of pale green silk that Charlotte had special-ordered from Denver, and together they had spent weeks sewing the delicate details—tiny tucks at the bodice, lace trim at the sleeves, and a skirt that fell in graceful folds to the floor. The soft green color brought out the emerald flecks in Sarah's hazel eyes and complemented her chestnut hair beautifully.

"Let me help you with that," Charlotte said, bustling into the room with Eleanor close behind. Both women's faces were radiant with joy, their excitement infectious as they fussed over the final details of Sarah's wedding preparation.

"You look absolutely beautiful, dear," Eleanor said softly, her voice thick with emotion. "Your mother would be so proud."

Sarah felt tears threaten to spill over at the mention of her mother. "I wish she could be here to see this day."

"She is here," Charlotte said firmly, securing the last button with gentle fingers. "Love like that doesn't disappear just because someone is no longer with us physically. She's watching over you today, I'm certain of it."

A soft knock at the door interrupted them. "Sarah?" her father's voice called through the wood. "May I speak with you for a moment?"

Eleanor and Charlotte exchanged meaningful glances. "We'll give you some privacy," Eleanor said. "We need to check on the flowers anyway."

Sarah opened the door to find her father standing in the hallway, looking more distinguished than she'd seen him in years. Dr. Martinez had worked wonders over the past month, and while Jonas still bore some faint bruises from his ordeal with Blackwood's men, his eyes held a peace and clarity that spoke of complete healing—both physical and spiritual.

"Papa," she breathed, stepping back to let him enter. "You look wonderful."

"And you look radiant," Jonas replied, his voice rough with emotion as he took in the sight of his daughter in the beautiful green dress that made her hazel eyes sparkle like jewels. "That color suits you perfectly, and Charlotte did wonderful work on the dress."

They stood looking at each other for a moment, both overwhelmed by the magnitude of this day. A month ago, Sarah had been resigned to the possibility that she might never see her father again. Now he was here, healthy and whole, preparing to walk her down the aisle to marry the man she loved with all her heart.

"Sarah, there's something I need to give you," Jonas said finally, reaching into his coat pocket. "Something that should have been yours long ago, but I... I couldn't bear to part with it after your mother died."

He pulled out a small velvet pouch, his hands shaking slightly as he opened it. Inside lay a delicate gold locket, its surface engraved with tiny roses that had worn smooth with age and loving handling.

"Your grandmother's locket," Sarah whispered, her eyes filling with tears. "The one that belonged to Grandmother Williams, and then to Mama."

"I couldn't let it go," Jonas confessed, his voice barely audible. "It's been in our family for three generations. Your grandmother gave it to your mother on her wedding day, and your mother wore it every day we were married. But it belongs to you now, on your wedding day."

With reverent hands, Sarah took the locket, feeling its familiar weight in her palm. She opened it carefully, gasping at what she found inside—a tiny lock of her mother's dark hair, carefully braided and tied with a faded blue ribbon.

"Mama's hair," she breathed, unable to speak through her tears.

"Let me," Jonas said gently, taking the locket and moving behind her to fasten it around her neck. "There. Now she'll be with you as you walk down that aisle."

Sarah touched the locket where it rested against her heart, feeling a warmth that seemed to emanate from more than just the metal. "Thank you, Papa. For keeping this safe, for coming back to me, for choosing to be the man I always knew you could be."

Jonas placed his hands on her shoulders, meeting her gaze in the mirror. "Sarah, I know I failed you and your mother in ways that can never be fully forgiven. I abandoned you when you needed me most, let my own shame and fear override my duty as a husband and father."

"Papa—"

"Let me finish," he said gently. "I can't change the past, but I can promise you this: I will spend every day of the rest of my life trying to be worthy of the grace you and this community have shown me. And I will never, ever abandon you again."

Sarah turned in his arms, embracing him tightly. "I love you, Papa. Despite everything, I have always loved you."

"And I love you, my darling girl. More than my own life." Jonas pulled back to look at her, his eyes bright with unshed tears. "Now then, shall we get you married to that fine young man who's waiting for you at the altar?"

The church was packed to overflowing when Sarah and her father arrived. It seemed as though the entire population of Silver Creek had turned out for the wedding, their faces beaming with joy and affection. Sarah felt overwhelmed by the outpouring of love from the community that had become her true home.

Reverend Wilson stood at the altar in his finest robes, his kind face radiant with happiness. Beside him waited Jack, resplendent in a dark suit that emphasized his tall, strong frame. When he saw Sarah appear in the doorway, his face transformed with such joy and love that she felt her heart skip a beat.

Charlotte had preceded her down the aisle as maid of honor, looking beautiful in rose-colored silk. David Miller stood as Jack's best man, his face glowing with happiness at his own recent engagement to Charlotte. The entire scene was suffused with such joy and hope that Sarah felt as though she were living in a dream.

But as the organ began to play and she took her father's arm, everything felt perfectly, wonderfully real. This was her life, her choice, her future walking toward her in the form of the man who had captured her heart so completely.

The congregation rose as Sarah began her walk down the aisle, and she was struck by the faces turned toward her—Mrs. Parker dabbing at her eyes with a handkerchief, Henry Carter beaming with grandfatherly pride, Emma Reynolds practically bouncing with excitement in her front-row seat. These people had become her family in every way that mattered, and their love and support surrounded her like a blessing.

"Who gives this woman to be married to this man?" Reverend Wilson asked when they reached the altar.

"I do, with all my love and blessing," Jonas replied, his voice strong and clear. He placed Sarah's hand in Jack's, then leaned forward to kiss her cheek. "Be happy, my darling daughter," he whispered.

As her father took his seat in the front pew, Sarah turned to face Jack fully. The love in his eyes took her breath away, and she felt a profound sense of rightness settle over her. This was exactly where she was meant to be, with this man, in this moment, surrounded by this community of people who had become family.

"Dearly beloved," Reverend Wilson began, his voice carrying clearly through the packed church, "we are gathered together today in the sight of God to join together this man and this woman in holy matrimony..."

The familiar words washed over Sarah like a blessing, but her attention was focused entirely on Jack's face, on the way he was looking at her as though she were the most precious thing in the world. When it came time for them to exchange vows, his voice was steady and strong.

"Sarah Elizabeth Williams, I take you as my wife, to love and to cherish, in sickness and in health, for richer or poorer, for better or worse, as long as we both shall live. I promise to be your faithful husband, your partner in all things, and to love you with the same unconditional love that God has shown us both."

Sarah's voice trembled slightly as she repeated the sacred words, but her conviction was absolute. "Jackson Thomas Montgomery, I take you as my husband, to love and to cherish, in sickness and in health, for richer or poorer, for better or worse, as long as we both shall live. I promise to be your faithful wife, your companion in faith and service, and to love you with all my heart for all of my days."

When Jack slipped the wedding band onto her finger, nestling it against Matthew's ring that had become her engagement ring, Sarah felt a sense of completion that went beyond mere ceremony. This wasn't just a union between two people—it was the culmination of God's plan that had brought them together through trial and triumph, loss and redemption.

"You may kiss your bride," Reverend Wilson announced with a broad smile.

Jack's kiss was tender and reverent, filled with all the love and promise of their future together. When they broke apart, the church erupted in joyful applause and cheers that seemed to shake the rafters.

As they walked back down the aisle as husband and wife, Sarah caught glimpses of beaming faces—Eleanor dabbing at her tears with a delicate handkerchief, August Hart grinning broadly, Dr. Martinez nodding with satisfaction at how well Jonas looked. But it was the sight of her father, standing in the front pew with tears streaming down his face and pure joy radiating from his expression, that made her own tears spill over.

The reception was held on the grounds of the Montgomery house, with tables stretching across the lawn and enough food to feed twice the number of guests. Mrs. Finch had outdone herself with the wedding cake, a three-tier confection decorated with sugar roses that looked almost too beautiful to eat.

Sarah found herself swept from group to group, accepting congratulations and well-wishes from what felt like every person in Silver Creek. The children from her school had prepared a special song, and their sweet voices singing "Amazing Grace" brought tears to nearly every eye present.

"Mrs. Montgomery," Emma said importantly, tugging on Sarah's dress, "I made you something special!"

She thrust a carefully wrapped package into Sarah's hands, beaming with pride as Sarah opened it to reveal a pressed flower collection, each bloom carefully labeled in Emma's careful handwriting.

"These are all the flowers from our schoolyard," Emma explained. "I thought you might like to remember your first year teaching here."

"Oh, Emma, it's beautiful," Sarah said, kneeling to embrace the little girl. "I'll treasure it always."

As the afternoon wore on, Sarah felt surrounded by love in its purest form. She danced with Jack to a fiddle tune played by one of the miners, laughed at Charlotte's excited chatter about her own upcoming wedding to David, and marveled at the transformation in her father as he moved through the crowd, accepted and welcomed by people who had chosen to see his redemption rather than dwell on his past mistakes.

"Are you happy, my love?" Jack asked during a quiet moment as they stood together watching the celebration.

"Happier than I ever dreamed possible," Sarah replied, leaning into his strong embrace. "When I came to Silver Creek, I thought I was simply trying to survive, to build some kind of life from the pieces of what I'd lost. I never imagined I would find such joy, such love, such a perfect sense of belonging."

"God had plans for you here that were bigger than you could have imagined," Jack said, echoing the words she'd spoken to him so many times during their courtship.

"For both of us," Sarah corrected. "He used every trial, every challenge, every moment of doubt to bring us to this point. Even the difficulties with Papa, even Blackwood's schemes—it all worked together for good, just like the Bible promises."

As the sun began to set over Silver Creek, painting the mountains in shades of gold and pink, Sarah felt a profound sense of gratitude wash over her. She thought of her mother, and somehow she knew that somewhere in the eternal realm, Elizabeth Williams was watching with joy as her daughter began this new chapter of her life.

The locket at her throat seemed to warm against her skin, a tangible reminder of the love that had shaped her and the faith that had sustained her through every trial. She was exactly where God had always intended her to be—in the arms of the man He had chosen for her, surrounded by the community He had led her to serve, embarking on a future bright with promise and purpose.

"What are you thinking about, Mrs. Montgomery?" Jack asked, using her new name with obvious pleasure.

"I'm thinking about signs," Sarah replied with a smile. "About how God has been speaking to us all along, weaving our stories together in ways we never could have imagined. About how love really can redeem anything, heal any wound, bridge any gap."

"Even the gap between a faithless mine owner and a trusting schoolteacher?"

"Especially that one," Sarah said, standing on her tiptoes to kiss her husband's cheek. "After all, some of God's greatest miracles happen when two imperfect people choose to love each other perfectly."

As the stars began to appear in the darkening sky, Sarah Williams Montgomery looked out over her new life with a heart full of gratitude and eyes bright with hope. The future stretched ahead unknown but not uncertain, for she faced it hand in hand with the man God had chosen for her, supported by a community that had become family, and sustained by a faith that had been tested and proven true.

Whatever tomorrow might bring, she was ready to meet it with joy.

Epilogue

S arah Montgomery stood at the window of the newly completed Silver Creek Educational Center, watching the last rays of fall sunlight paint the mountains in shades of gold and crimson. In her arms, three-month-old Grace slept peacefully, her tiny fist curled around a lock of her mother's hair. The baby had been born with her father's dark hair and what the town's new doctor, Dr. Daniel Harrison, proclaimed were the most alert hazel eyes he'd ever seen on an infant.

"She's going to be a handful, that one," Dr. Harrison had said with a knowing smile when Grace was born. "I can already tell she has her mother's intelligence and her father's determination."

The thought made Sarah smile as she gazed down at her daughter's perfect features. Grace Elizabeth Montgomery—named for the grace that had brought her parents together and for Sarah's beloved mother whose memory lived on in the family locket Sarah now wore every day.

"There you are," Jack's voice came from behind her, warm with the contentment that had characterized their marriage from its very beginning. "I was wondering where my two favorite ladies had disappeared to."

Sarah turned to find her husband approaching, his sleeves rolled up and his hair slightly mussed from the afternoon's work. Even after two years of marriage, the sight of him still made her heart skip a beat. The lines of grief and anger that had once marked his face had been replaced by laugh lines and the peaceful expression of a man who had found his place in God's plan.

"Grace wanted to see the new building," Sarah said, settling into Jack's embrace. "I think she approves of what we've accomplished."

Jack looked around the spacious classroom with obvious pride. The Silver Creek Educational Center had exceeded even their most ambitious dreams. What had begun as plans for an expanded school had grown into a comprehensive learning facility that served the entire community. The main building housed classrooms for children of all ages, while the attached wings contained workshops for technical training, a library that rivaled some in Denver, and meeting rooms where adults could attend evening classes in reading, writing, and arithmetic.

"Your father's safety training program graduated twelve men yesterday," Jack reported, settling into the chair beside Sarah's. "Two of them have already been hired by mines in neighboring towns specifically because of their Montgomery certification."

Sarah felt a surge of pride for her father's transformation. Jonas had thrown himself into his work as Chief Safety Inspector with the passion of a man seeking redemption, and his comprehensive training programs were becoming the standard throughout the Colorado Territory. More importantly, not a single serious accident had occurred at Montgomery Mining since he'd taken charge of safety protocols.

"And the women's domestic science classes?" Sarah asked.

"Mrs. Patterson says they're booked solid through Christmas. Apparently, your lessons on household budgeting and basic medicine are in high demand." Jack reached over to stroke Grace's soft cheek with one gentle finger. "Our daughter is going to grow up in a town where education is valued by everyone, not just the wealthy."

The sound of children's laughter from the playground outside drew their attention to the window. Through the glass, they could see Emma Reynolds—now thirteen and one of Sarah's most promising students—leading a group of younger children in a game of tag. The sight never failed to warm

Sarah's heart. Emma had blossomed under the individualized attention the expanded school could provide, and she was already talking about becoming a teacher herself someday.

"Emma's been asking about helping with the younger children's reading classes," Sarah mentioned. "I think she has a natural gift for teaching."

"Like her teacher," Jack said, pressing a kiss to Sarah's temple. "Though I suspect our Miss Reynolds will have ambitions beyond Silver Creek when she's older."

Before Sarah could respond, a knock at the classroom door interrupted their peaceful moment. Dr. Harrison appeared in the doorway, his medical bag in one hand and his two-year-old son Colin balanced on his hip.

"I hope I'm not disturbing," the doctor said with his characteristic gentle smile. "Elizabeth is visiting with Mrs. Miller, and this young man insisted on coming to see the baby."

"Not disturbing at all," Sarah said warmly. "Please, come in."

Dr. Daniel Harrison had arrived in Silver Creek six months ago, bringing with him impeccable credentials from medical colleges back East and a gentle bedside manner that had quickly won over the entire community. His wife Elizabeth was a refined woman from Boston who had adapted to frontier life with surprising grace, and their son Colin was the pride and joy of every woman in town.

"Baby!" Colin declared with toddler enthusiasm, reaching toward Grace with chubby hands.

"Gentle touches," Dr. Harrison reminded his son, guiding the little boy's hand to softly pat Grace's arm. "She's very small still."

Sarah watched the interaction with amusement, noting how carefully Dr. Harrison monitored his son's every movement. The man was clearly devoted to his family, and his love for his wife and child was evident in everything he did.

"How are you feeling, Sarah?" Dr. Harrison asked, settling Colin more securely on his hip. "Any concerns about your recovery?"

"None at all. I feel stronger every day." Sarah adjusted Grace's blanket as the baby stirred slightly. "You were right about nursing becoming easier. I'm sure the next time, it will be as easy as apple pie."

"Next time?" Jack raised an eyebrow with mock surprise. "Are you planning something I should know about, Mrs. Montgomery?"

Sarah laughed, feeling heat rise in her cheeks. "I was speaking hypothetically, Mr. Montgomery."

"Ah, but hypothetically, you wouldn't be opposed to the idea?"

"I think Grace should at least learn to walk before we start discussing siblings," Sarah replied, though the warmth in her voice suggested the topic wasn't entirely unwelcome.

Dr. Harrison chuckled at their gentle banter. "In my professional opinion, you're both young and healthy enough to have a houseful of children if you choose. Though I'd recommend spacing them at least two years apart for Sarah's health."

As if summoned by the mention of children, Charlotte appeared in the doorway with David close behind her. Sarah's sister-in-law was glowing with her own news—she and David had announced just last week that they were expecting their first child.

"There you are!" Charlotte exclaimed, hurrying over to peer at Grace. "Mother is looking everywhere for you. She says it's time for Grace's evening feeding, and she won't be denied her grandmother privilege of tucking her in and saying evening prayers."

"Eleanor has certainly taken to grandmotherhood with enthusiasm," Jack observed with amusement. "I think she spoils Grace more in a day than we do in a week."

"It's wonderful to see her so happy," Sarah said. "She's like a completely different person than when I first arrived in Silver Creek."

Indeed, Eleanor Montgomery had been transformed by her granddaughter's arrival. The rigid, judgmental woman who had once worried about social propriety had been replaced by a doting grandmother who spent hours singing lullabies and reading fairy tales to baby Grace. Her acceptance of David as a son-in-law had been complete and enthusiastic, and she frequently declared that love matches were far superior to arranged marriages.

"Speaking of transformations," Charlotte said, settling into a nearby chair, "have you seen Papa Williams lately? He's been positively beaming ever since Mrs. Henderson agreed to let him court her."

Sarah felt a surge of happiness for her father. Jonas had been hesitant to pursue any romantic attachment, feeling that his past made him unsuitable for a good woman's affections. But Mrs. Henderson, the boarding house proprietor who had witnessed his transformation firsthand, had gradually drawn him out of his shell with her quiet kindness and practical nature.

"They make a lovely couple," Sarah agreed. "And Mrs. Henderson says she's never felt safer or more cared for in her life."

"Your father has become quite the gentleman," Dr. Harrison observed. "I've enjoyed our conversations about mining safety. The man has an encyclopedic knowledge of every technique and innovation in the field."

As the afternoon faded into evening, their small gathering was joined by other members of Silver Creek's extended family. August Hart stopped by to report on the day's mining operations, his weathered face creasing with smiles as he played peek-a-boo with Grace. Henry Carter arrived with a handmade wooden rattle he'd carved for the baby, and even Sheriff Taylor made an appearance to share news from the territorial capital.

The conversation flowed easily from mining operations to crop yields, from the excitement of Colorado's new statehood just last month to plans for the upcoming harvest festival. "Hard to believe we're no longer territorial citizens," August mused. "Colorado statehood opens up all kinds of opportunities for expansion and growth."

"The new state laws on mining regulations will help standardize safety practices across all operations," Jonas added with satisfaction. "What we've implemented here at Montgomery Mining could become the model for the entire state."

"Sarah, dear," Eleanor said, appearing in the doorway with her arms outstretched for Grace, "I really must insist on taking this precious child so you can finish your conversation without worrying about her. She's been far too patient with all this adult talk."

"Of course," Sarah said, reluctantly transferring her daughter to Eleanor's eager arms. "Though I think she enjoys listening to everyone talk. She seems fascinated by different voices."

"Well, of course she does! She's a Montgomery woman already—naturally curious about everything happening around her," Eleanor said with obvious pride, settling Grace more comfortably in her arms. "I'll just take her to the nursery where she can have some quiet time."

"Intelligent babies often enjoy listening," Dr. Harrison agreed. "Early exposure to conversation and music can enhance cognitive development significantly."

As Eleanor carried Grace away for her evening routine, cooing softly to her granddaughter, the others began to disperse to their own families and evening responsibilities. Soon, only Jack and Sarah remained in the quiet classroom, watching the last light fade from the mountains.

"Do you ever wonder what would have happened if you hadn't come to Silver Creek?" Jack asked, pulling Sarah closer to his side.

"Every day," Sarah replied honestly. "But then I remember what my mother used to say about God's plans being bigger than our understanding. I think everything that brought me here—Papa's leaving, Mama's death, even the storm that damaged the schoolhouse—was part of a design we couldn't see at the time."

"Even Blackwood's schemes?"

"Even those. If he hadn't forced the crisis, you might never have found your way back to faith. Papa might never have found the courage to seek redemption. The community might never have come together the way it has."

Jack was quiet for a moment, contemplating her words. "It's humbling to think that our worst trials were actually part of God's best plans for us."

"That's what faith is, isn't it? Trusting that even when we can't see the purpose, there is one. And that even our mistakes and failures can be redeemed for good."

They sat in comfortable silence, watching the first stars appear in the darkening sky. The sounds of Silver Creek settling into evening drifted through the open window—children being called in for supper, the distant sound of a fiddle from the saloon, the gentle murmur of families gathering around their dinner tables.

"Jack," Sarah said softly, "do you think we'll always be this happy?"

"I think we'll face challenges," Jack replied honestly. "Life has a way of testing us when we least expect it. But I also think that whatever comes, we'll face it together, with faith and the support of this community we've helped build."

"And with Grace to remind us what really matters."

"And with Grace to remind us what really matters," Jack agreed.

As they finally rose to head home to their own dinner table and their waiting daughter, Sarah felt a profound sense of gratitude wash over her. The girl who had arrived in Silver Creek two years ago, frightened and alone, had been transformed into a woman surrounded by love and purpose. She had found not just a husband and a home, but a calling that used every gift God had given her.

The educational center stood as a testament to what could be accomplished when people worked together with shared vision and common purpose. The mine operated with safety standards that were becoming the envy of the territory. The town thrived with the kind of prosperity that came from genuine community rather than mere commercial success.

But more than any external achievement, Sarah treasured the internal transformation she had witnessed—in Jack's restored faith, in her father's redemption, in her own growth from dependence to strength. God had indeed worked all things together for good, weaving their separate stories into a tapestry of grace that was more beautiful than any of them could have imagined.

As they walked home through the quiet streets of Silver Creek, past the church where they had been married and the schoolhouse where Sarah had first found her calling, she offered a silent prayer of thanksgiving for the God who specialized in taking broken things and making them beautiful again.

The future stretched ahead unknown but not uncertain, for it would be shaped by the same faithful love that had brought them this far. And whatever tomorrow might bring to the growing town of Silver Creek, Sarah Montgomery knew that she would meet it with joy, surrounded by the family God had given her and sustained by the faith that had carried her through every storm.

Behind them, the lights of the educational center glowed warmly in the darkness, a beacon of hope and learning that would serve Silver Creek for generations to come. And in the distance, the mountains stood sentinel over the valley, eternal and unchanging, as if blessing all the human dreams and endeavors sheltered in their shadow.

Grace would grow up in this place of beauty and purpose, surrounded by love and rooted in faith. And someday, God willing, she would add her own chapter to the ongoing story of Silver Creek—a story of redemption, community, and the endless possibility that existed when people chose to trust in something greater than themselves.

The signs had been there all along, Sarah reflected as they reached their front door. In every challenge overcome, every heart changed, every life touched by grace. God had been writing a love story not just between two people, but between a community and its Creator, and the best chapters were yet to come.